THE INVISIBLE BODY

Jenny Cutts

STOPPED CLOCK PRESS

STOPPED CLOCK PRESS

First published in 2021 by Stopped Clock Press
Copyright © Jenny Cutts 2021

The moral right of the author has been asserted.

ISBN 978-1-914001-02-4
Stopped Clock Press Ltd.
Company Number 12829670

www.jennycutts.com

THE INVISIBLE BODY

CHAPTER 1

That's the sound of glass smashing. Someone is breaking into the house.

Waking with a fearful jolt, she sits up in the double bed, eyes wide in the darkness, focussing on the sound. Heart thudding, she strains her ears to scan the dark, now-silent, house.

Glancing at the unruffled side of the mattress, she tells herself, *Sarah, this is down to you. Don't. Be. Scared.*

Moonlight is creeping through the curtains, casting wispy shadows over the thick carpet. She folds back the covers; cool sheets gliding over the half-empty bed. She slips her legs out of the sleep-warmed softness and plants her feet silently on the floor.

Crossing to the dresser, she eases out the top drawer as quietly as she can. The runner makes a faint groan. She rummages through neatly folded clothing, moving aside the cold, leathery, neglected Bible, her fingers rifling through the tangle of fabrics until she finds it – a thick and heavy torch.

She creeps to the bedroom door, pausing and listening, trying to control her speeding breath. She turns the door handle with a trembling hand and slinks out onto the landing. *Don't be scared.*

She advances down the hallway, slowly, pausing at a bedroom door. The rainbow array of stickers that flock around the name plate have had the life sucked out of them; bleached blandly grey by the moonlight falling through the window at the top of the stairs.

She stops to listen at the door. All is quiet. She adjusts her grip on the torch and tiptoes down the stairs. Senses heightened, adrenaline pumping, she notices the scent of the colour-leeched flowers on the sill and the slight squeak of the bannister under her clammy palm.

She can't hear any noises coming from downstairs and hopes she has imagined it in a dream. She presses on, stepping stealthily along the hallway, making her way to the kitchen at the rear of the house. She stops at the closed door, listening and summoning the courage to find out what is on the other side.

She holds her breath and the silence settles around her. Slowly, she raises the torch and, brandishing it like a weapon, bursts through the door.

Nobody is there.

She can see the muted moonlight through the kitchen windows, the scalloped edges of the blinds casting waves of shadow across the linoleum floor. The room is empty. She exhales with relief.

Grasses, leaves and branches dance percussively in the back garden, a multitude of grey fingers pointing in the whispering darkness. She hears the ghostly sigh of a lone gust of wind; the small cool breath of night air blowing through a jagged tear in the door pane. The gash is leaking earthy garden smells into the room.

She switches on the torch and peers at the back door. She was right about the smashed glass.

Swinging around her spotlight, she catches a glimpse of something surprising on the kitchen counter and steadies the pool of light for a closer look.

There on the work surface is some kind of sculpture: a pyramid of pans, dishes, mugs and cutlery all arranged in an impossible pile. It looks skeletal in its tentative, pre-carious arrangement and has no business being there. The chunky torch thuds, brick-heavy, onto the lino by her feet and Sarah darts into the hall.

She turns on the telephone-desk lamp and flicks through an address book. Her shaky fingers turn the dial to make a call.

'It's me. Something really strange is happening, can you come here? Now? Okay, tomorrow morning then. We need you.'

***

And in a dark hiding place, blood is coagulating, pulled by gravity to the parts of the body resting on the dusty floor. It reddens the flesh with blotches and leaves her face an unnatural pallor – the ghoulish complexion of the re-cently dead.

CHAPTER 2

In another house, in another town, a youngish man wears a child-sized wizard hat and cape covered in constellations. He is waiting for a kettle to boil and watching the dawn seep across the sky.

The boiling kettle breaks his reverie, and he pours the bubbling water into a waiting mug of instant coffee. He wanders through the downstairs rooms of the house, stopping to consider the odd painting or family photograph as he goes.

A shelf of toys catches his attention, and he rolls a miniature van along on its tiny wheels. It's the mystery machine from *Scooby Doo*. Then he puts it back in place and heads towards the front door. Just before reaching it, he remembers to remove the starry hat and cape and leaves them on a toy box where he found them.

He ambles across the road to a similar house and pushes open the front door.

Inside, casually sipping the freshly made coffee, he paces around the ground floor, quite aimlessly, before discovering the living room.

Spying a bookshelf, the man glides across to take a closer look. He finds a showy library of familiar titles – books that everyone has heard of, but few have read:

The I Ching, A Brief History of Time, A Room of One's Own...

He picks out a thick copy of *Hamlet* and pauses, sitting on his haunches, lost in thought. After considering the volume for several minutes, he finally decides to put it back on the shelf. He pulls out a copy of *How to Win Friends and Influence People*, tucks it under his arm and retraces his steps to the suburban street outside.

The rising sun is colouring everything pink.

Drifting approximately down the middle of the quiet avenue, the man strolls along to the end of the row, reading the book jacket as he goes. At the end of the terrace, he rounds a low wall and starts walking up the path. Seeing a child's bike propped by the wall, he pauses and sets down the things. Then he kneels to lift the small bicycle pump from the frame. After inflating the front tyre, he stands and smiles. He props the bike back against the wall and collects the mug and book.

He continues to the building, ascends a set of exterior steps and enters a small apartment on the third floor. The neat kitchen-living room connects with a well-appointed balcony. He sets the book down on the coffee table and slides open the balcony door.

A shimmer of sunlight carves itself along the thick metal ribbon that fences the decking. A spectacular view of the bay unfurls to the south-east, beyond a stretch of willowy grasses and shore-side reeds that flutter on the morning air. The dawn's infant rays shimmer, mesmerically, in peaky troughs on the distant waves and angle a warm glow into the living room. After a moment, the man goes back inside and starts running the bath.

As it fills, he investigates a stylish record player that nestles among a decent collection of vinyl in the living room. He sips the coffee and flips through the collection before selecting *Idle Moments* by Grant Green.

He takes the record from its sleeve carefully, holding its sharp, thin edges between his fingertips, and places it gently on the turntable, easing the stylus into the groove. The silver arm rides along the disc in a perfect spiral, rising and falling in millimetre waves.

The sudden, soft crackle of the speakers coming to life is followed by a laconic piano and brush snare rhythm, guitar and vibraphone soon falling in. The perfect notes fill the space and spill out into the morning. The sunrise thickens over rippling water in the bay.

He checks on the bath, which is filling nicely, agitating the foaming water with his fingers. Then he retraces his steps to the front door and opens it fully, propping it ajar with a ceramic plant pot. He ambles back through the flat and steps out onto the balcony, taking a seat on the small, cushioned bench and resting his crossed legs on the railing. Salt-tinged eddies carry the scent of fresh-cut grass and the sickly-sweet buds of late summer. Soft morning breezes tickle his toes.

A couple of coffee bubbles break gently against the inside rim of his mug. After a few minutes of tranquil sipping, he places the drink on the decking and steps up onto the balcony rail. He wobbles a little before reaching a point of equilibrium and closes his eyes.

Then the youngish man jumps off – feet-first, like a child tombstoning into water from a cliff.

***

Zoya is freewheeling on her bicycle down a very steep hill.

The bike chain whirs. Fresh, cool air slides past her face invigoratingly, sculpting her mass of soft curls into shifting shapes that flame behind her as she accelerates, beaming.

High above the town fly fast-darting speckles – swallows yet to leave for Africa. The expansive glow of dawn glints from windows with a golden pulse, outlining tiles and gutters with shadow.

Further down the hill, where the incline flattens, Zoya peels off into a formidable yet familiar street of grand old Victorian town houses and decelerates to a safer, more acceptable, speed. Faded white lines track the centre of the road in broken Morse code dashes and the residences line the route like cardboard cut-outs.

She pedals and glides around the smooth streets, enjoying the clear air, the warming morning and the peace.

She passes Carl Ridgeway as he's opening his garage, no doubt starting the day with some early-morning do-gooding. He waves.

'Morning, Zoya!'

'Morning, Carl!'

She arcs around the small park, its wrought-iron fencing casting rhythmic shadows that strobe-pattern the road.

As she whizzes along the quiet streets, the regular pacing of the Victorian houses soon gives way to a jazzy percussion of architectural styles.

She freewheels.

The chain of streetlamps blink out as the sunrise bathes the town in natural light. Tiny songbirds flit from bush to bush.

Zoya cuts through a mews row in an even older part of town, just because she likes the street. She spots windows pinging to life with warm, yellow light and hears car doors thudding shut as early risers get on their way. The town is waking up.

She cycles on. In the valley of straight, formal streets by the old parish church, she encounters another cyclist coming her way – the unmistakeable outline of Quentin Tosca on his magic trike. As they draw closer, she smiles to see that the white-haired eccentric is accompanied by a large, white rabbit sitting serenely in the front basket.

'Morning, Quentin. Morning, Mrs Miggles. Lovely morning for a ride, isn't it?'

'Good morning, Zoya. She won't answer you, my dear; she's a lagomorph. Pass my warmest regards to your father!' he replies, his voice fading into the distance as the trike passes.

Cutting through an alleyway, she emerges at the corner shop, dismounts and leans her bike casually against the wall. She goes into the shop and hears the bright, familiar chime of the old-fashioned bell on the door.

Inside, Doris Pugh is behind the counter, looking at an attractively designed poster that the Audobon brothers have brought in. They all welcome Zoya with warm smiles. She heads to the refrigerator to collect a cold milk carton, clammy with condensation, and then joins them at the till.

Felix Audobon, sporting his habitual cravat and neat white beard, hands her a flyer.

'Zoya, my dear! Are you coming to the fair?'

'I hope so. I've told Tom and Rhoda I'd love to "woman" the stall there… This looks really good!'

'Will your father be able to make it down for the fair, do you think?' Caspar Audobon asks, thumbing his braces absent-mindedly. 'Do invite him, won't you?'

'Of course. How's it all coming along?'

'Wonderfully. Can't think why it has taken Shilly-on-Sea so long to come up with it.'

'Well, let me know if there's anything I can do to help…' Zoya says brightly.

'Thank you my dear, you *are* a sweetheart!' Caspar exclaims, 'but I'm sure you have plenty to keep you busy.'

'We just hope to see you there, darling,' Felix adds, 'enjoying yourself.'

'Okay, well, I have to get back with this milk – breakfasts are depending on it. See you soon.'

Zoya leaves the shop, stows the milk carton in the basket and mounts her bicycle. Pedalling off, this time, in the direction of the steep road that leads straight to the distinctive house on the hill.

CHAPTER 3

In the Stevens' suburban semi, a flurry of police activity is taking place.

Officers are busy taping off the kitchen door and back garden, taking photographs, sketching plans, dusting for prints and generally making a mess of Sarah's linoleum. A couple of constables can be seen through the open doorway, checking for footprints in the back garden beyond.

Sarah watches the changing choreography of uniformed figures with a worried frown as Chief Inspector Frank Barrow stands with her at the countertop. They are at the side with the cooker and the utensils arranged like flowers in a vase, not the other side… with the thing.

The Formica slab presses its angular corners into her palm as she leans anxiously on the edge, gripping a little too hard. Sarah's eight-year-old son, Matthew, clings shyly to her other hand, his slim matchstick fingers warm in her palm. She catches the chemical scent of the fingerprint dust being brushed all over her kitchen door and windows. The smell is mingling with the whiff of the earthy soil being trekked across her recently bleached floor. She wrinkles her nose.

'Thanks for coming over,' she says, again.

'We take all reported crimes seriously. And you're still our sister-in-law, Sarah. At least as far as Vanessa and I are concerned. We know you've had a rough–'

'Thanks anyway,' she interjects, cutting him off. 'Will you find the burglar?'

'About that... It doesn't look like anyone actually entered the house, and nothing's taken, you say? So, it's just the broken pane and...' – he nods towards the awkwardly balanced kitchen sculpture – '*that*.'

'Don't move anything!' Sarah pleads.

A constable stops before handling one of the mugs.

Then, calming down, she adds: 'Please, can you just leave it where it is, please. I've got someone coming to look at that.'

***

Piping coffee pours into the stripey mug and Zoya nods at the customer who is thanking her for his refill.

She carries the jug back to its place behind the long, shiny counter and watches a small, fluffy cloud traverse the sky.

A friendly voice cuts through the moment.

'Thanks, see you later.'

'Bye, Cara, see you later!' she replies, before her friend slips out through the glassy porch at the corner nearest the beach.

Zoya collects a warm plate of full English breakfast from the kitchen hatch. The smell of fried meats and eggs and toasting bread is even stronger there. She serves the meal to the customer, placing it on the table with a smile. On her way back to the counter, she notices Rhoda Sorrel crouched by a high chair, entertaining a small child. She is dancing a small plastic elephant along the tabletop towards the girl and doing a funny little voice. The toddler giggles as the elephant 'jumps' onto her shoulder.

The child's mother emerges from the café toilet and thanks Rhoda for watching her.

'It's my absolute pleasure,' Rhoda replies, standing up. 'She's a dream.'

Her husband, Tom, emerges through the staff door next to the kitchen and hands Rhoda a jacket. They are on their way out.

'So, you'll be alright until Lee is in at 11?' Tom checks as they move toward the door.

'Yes, that's the breakfast rush over with now. Alan and I can manage perfectly well, don't worry. We've only run the café several million times before,' Zoya answers playfully. Then her features fall into a more serious expression and she lowers her voice. 'Good luck with... everything today,' she says, holding the gaze of Rhoda who smiles weakly back.

'Thanks, Zoya,' she almost whispers, a touch of emotion moistening her eye.

Tom strokes his wife's long silky hair protectively and they turn to leave. Through the windows that curl from corner to corner, Zoya watches as they walk along the high street to their car. She sees Tom putting his arm around Rhoda protectively, the sea breeze catching their hair as they go.

The door swings open again, almost immediately, and the swell of seaside sounds flash suddenly into the café before receding again to the ambient window-muffled soundtrack of distant bird calls, seagull shrieks and gentle waves that accompany life in the small coastal town.

A young lad in baggy jeans and check shirt bounces in, swinging a bundled stack of magazines.

'Where'd'you want them?' he asks her, running his words together.

'What's that?'

'*Porden Chronicle*. Hot off the press. Shall I leave them over here by your noticeboard?'

'Oh yes, sure, thanks.'

Using his handy pocketknife to cut the bundle cord, Evan deposits the stack alongside other local flyers and ad-verts on the small table.

'Actually, you're in it this week. Not you personally, but Shilly. Page 17. Creepy!'

He grins, flicking his curtained hair off his face.

Zoya shifts behind the counter, looking slightly puz-zled, so the delivery lad hands her the top copy before turn-ing to head back to his van.

'Thanks. Er… Don't believe everything you read…?'

'See you next time,' Evan calls, chuckling, then leaves the café, hopping back into his van, which he had left run-ning, radio blaring, at the kerbside.

Sunshine is pouring through the glass, causing the thin mullions to shadow-slice the airy space into segments like a cake.

Finding the café at a quiet lull, Zoya flicks through the local magazine to page 17 to find a small article headed POLTERGEIST SPOTTED IN SHILLY-ON-SEA.

Together with a black-and-white photograph showing some dining chairs stacked up in a weird arrangement, she finds an odd little story.

Spooky happenings have been observed in a suburban house in Shilly-on-Sea that the resident, a 35-year-old housewife, is at a loss to explain. A disturbance in the middle of the night led to the discovery of the ghostly sculpture made of kitchen utensils but no sighting of the spectre itself. Paranormal experts stated that this is the typical behaviour of a poltergeist, which is a type of ghost that moves physical objects around, often creating balancing sculptures out of dining chairs (pictured) or other household items, and stress there is no reason to be scared.

Zoya rolls her eyes and guffaws a little.

'So, what's the creepy story?' Ray asks, between glugs of hot black coffee, his eyes twinkling.

'Oh, some nonsense about a poltergeist stacking stuff up. Just some ridiculous story. I don't know how they get away with putting stuff like that in.'

'The *Chronicle*? Well known for it. I don't know who runs that paper, but they seem to be frustrated ghost hunters. Always slipping in crazy stories and supernatural stuff. You don't believe in that rubbish, do you?'

'Of course not.'

***

In another café in another town, a youngish man in a striped T-shirt is sipping coffee and reading the paper.

'You certainly drink a lot of caffeine.'

Looking up, he sees the slim, balding waiter who served him and notices that he is now the only customer in the place. It seems he is in for a conversation, like it or not, so he prepares to open up – but just a little.

'I don't sleep very well. Wake up tired,' he replies.

'Is that your van?'

The waiter is looking out of the window towards an old Volkswagen parked across the street. It stands proudly, like an oversized yet perfectly proved loaf of bread, the chrome work reflecting flashes of afternoon sun.

The man follows the waiter's gaze, then, reassured that nothing is amiss, turns back to answer.

'Yep. 1973 bay. Neptune Blue.'

The waiter smooths his linen apron and looks at the vehicle appreciatively. It is the colour of British seawater, topped with a pristine white roof, and is evidently well cared for, despite its vintage.

'Are you new in town? I haven't seen you around – until this week.' He smooths his grey-green apron once more.

'No. I live *there*.' The man nods towards the camper van. Small sets of patterned curtains hang listlessly at the windows as evidence. 'Just passing through,' he concludes.

He returns to the pile of papers and starts leafing through a local magazine. The waiter hovers, imagining a life on the road.

'Don't you get lonely?' he asks.

The man turns a page and spots an unusual story.

'That's near here isn't it?'

'Well, it's a local magazine.'

'Shilly-on-Sea – how far is that from here?'

'Not far, I suppose. It's the other end of the county but that's not so far. There's not much there, you know. Tourists usually give it a miss.'

'What's my best route?'

'Well, you can take the main road and turn off at Axworth, follow signs to Kembleton, keep going; it's not far from there. Or just follow the coast road. Shouldn't take too long.'

The man tears the article from the paper and rises from the table to leave.

'What about your toastie?' the waiter asks, in a worried tone of voice.

'Can you wrap it up for me to take away instead, please?'

'There's no rush, you'll get there long before nightfall.'

'Good to know, but I might make some stops along the way.'

A short time later, the waiter hands over the napkin-wrapped toastie and the man hurries towards the door. The waiter watches, perplexed.

'Places to go, weird shit to see,' he explains as he dash-es off.

Across the road he slides open the camper door, opens a wall-mounted cupboard and adds the torn magazine story to a collage of other tattered articles. Then he hops into the driver's seat and turns the key. The engine ticks over obediently and he sets off for the coast road.

CHAPTER 4

At the suburban semi, Matthew is watching the police come and go. He screws up his eyes in the sunshine, watching all the busy grown-ups walking past. Their heavy trudging feet dislodge gravel on the path.

He is sitting, unnoticed, on the front step, fingering the softness of the tiny moss forests that edge the stone. He stretches his legs out in front of him, enjoying the scrapey sound his shoes make on the ground.

He watches the adults above him, carrying mysterious things to their cars. The high sun soaks the thick lawn before him and forces him to squint. He looks across the wide, cherry-tree-lined street and sees a few more policemen talking to neighbours at their doors.

The gardens and verges shine bright, thriving with chlorophyll-bright leaves. Roots have pushed through the pavements, forming mountain ranges in the tarmac that kids step over like a game. A lone blackbird is raking beneath the bushes at the edge of their garden. The police are on their way out.

Matthew hears the thuds of car boots closing and the growl of engines being started. One of the police cars drives away, gently cruising around the corner and away from their street.

Just as it disappears, another car approaches loudly, bouncing along the road in a faint cloud of dust. He looks in the direction of the noise to see a scruffy Vauxhall Cavalier grumbling around the corner before halting abruptly by the kerb.

A bulky, unkempt man erupts from the driving seat. He is wearing a half-tucked shirt, and his dark curly hair seems to wobble around his head. His huge feet land on the pavement, clad in big, casually laced boots. He charges to the boot of his car and grabs a box full of computer disks, balancing a chunky beige keyboard on top. After slamming the boot shut, the man advances up the front path, looming larger with every step.

At the same time, a lanky policeman emerges from the back garden. He is rolling up police tape and carries a register under one arm. The man fixes him in the eye and commands: 'Don't move anything!'

'And who are you? The ghostbusters?' the policeman retorts, jutting his pointy nose into the air. The bulky, unkempt man gazes skywards, invoking the patience he is constantly striving for. Before he can answer, the constable gets official.

'Stay where you are; we need to register you in the Scene of Crime log.'

'That won't be necessary, Sergeant Brooks. It's not a secured scene anymore,' asserts Chief Inspector Barrow, passing his subordinate on his way to the Rover 800 series parked at the kerb.

Spotting the small boy watching from the front step, the bulky man marches across the front lawn towards him.

'Do *you* know anything about this?'

Matthew stands and his eyes well up with tears. The young constable loiters, watching, ready to interpose his weedy frame if – but hopefully not – necessary.

'What's it to you, anyway?' he demands, feebly.

In one motion, Matthew launches himself at the big man, flinging his arms around him at beer belly height. The man, in turn, drops his box to the floor. The keyboard bounces on the lawn. He hugs the child back protectively, one large ham hock of a hand on the boy's head.

Sergeant Brooks stands watching hesitantly, his reedy question still hanging on the air.

'I'm his uncle,' the man announces with a proud stare.

Brooks backs away down the path.

Just then, another figure appears at the front doorstep from inside the house.

'Dan!'

'Sarah,' he acknowledges.

The siblings regard one another, with similar blue eyes.

***

Not far away, a dark truck wobbles across an uneven track and reverses quietly to a low, graffitied building with a rolling metal door. Crunching over sparse, scattered gravel, steel toe-capped boots advance toward the doorway. Muscular hands work the key in the padlock then push up the dirty steel shutter. It moves with a shriek and stops with a clang.

***

Further along the coast road, a blue-and-white camper van beetles along under the late-afternoon sun. The strains of 'Wichita Lineman' spill from the open window. The youngish man, singing along with the radio, is taking in the views.

The ribbon of pale sea road he is following carries a thin sheen of sand and dry summer earth. The shining blue-grey of the sea is pricked with the sunny peaks of waves, and gleams in the distance. Sunlight is bouncing from the bonnets and windshields of passing traffic, so he reaches past the road map for his sunglasses and puts them on.

The route meanders between the sight of sun-speckled waves and inland strips of quaint hamlets and sleepy villages. Unshowy yet rich people live here in comfortable bubbles, warmed and buffeted by salty sea air.

As the van chugs along, he taps a finger on the steering wheel, in time to the radio. He passes a patch of trees that catch a gust and shimmer in the field. An expanse of grass waves ruffle along the hillside, as if pushing him on.

He rests an arm at the open window, his shirtsleeve gently flapping against his arm. The Indian summer sunshine threatens to tan his pale skin.

Cresting a small rise, he finds himself slowing the vehicle at a junction where a row of detached houses lines the road ahead. He notices one of the houses hosting what looks like a family gathering in the garden and slows to look as the van rolls past.

He sees a large house built of pink-red stone, its roof dotted with pitched dormer windows and edged in painted wood. It's the type of residence that wealthy owners call a cottage but is clearly a big house.

The large envelope of garden is defined by a low picket fence, painted duck-egg blue, and he can see an assortment of happy people eating, drinking and playing in the grounds. He can't help but swallow as the smell of barbecue wafts near.

The man drives a bit further along the village street and curls the van into a parking space shaded by a tree. He turns off the engine. A perfect spot for a nap.

***

Closing the heavy door behind her, Zoya calls into the house.

'Hi, Dad. I'm home!'

She walks through the hall.

'And I've brought some of Rhoda's cakes!'

She turns into the kitchen and places crinkly shopping bags on the countertop. At the same time, her dad enters the open-plan space and shows off with his trademark wheelie.

'Hi, love. How was your day? Did you give Alan the jelly mould back? What's new?'

Zoya bustles around the room, putting things away, circling Richard's chair which he spins this way and that with his habitual exuberance.

'I did. Not much. I forgot to tell you this morning, the Audobons have been flyering for the fair they're organising – they asked me to invite you. Tom and Rhoda went up to Axworth for another appointment. Carl stopped by to say he's still on for backgammon on Friday. Oh, and we've got a town ghost!'

Zoya busies herself putting the cakes away in the kitchen, getting out pans and looking in the fridge.

'I know – a poltergeist, no less!' Richard says, chuckling.

'How did you…? Ah… Is Vanessa staying for dinner today?'

Shaking his head, Richard explains. 'No, she's cooking for Frank. Sounds like someone broke into the vicar's house and pulled some crazy prank. Though it could have been a real ghost, being a vicarage and all…' Richard says, dark eyes twinkling.

'They haven't lived in the vicarage for years, Dad, that old manse is now Sunnyview Lodge. You know – Carl works with them. So, what do you fancy?' Zoya asks, looking in the fridge, 'I think we've still got some…'

'Hold your horses, love. I've got it covered. Moroccan stew coming up in…' – he checks his watch – 'twenty-three minutes. I'll have it on the table by the time you come back into the kitchen.'

'That's great, Dad.'

She bends to kiss his cheek and then hurries off to a far corner of the house, saying, 'Then I'll just go out and say hello.'

CHAPTER 5

I open my eyes to see the beech trees waving their branches above me, dappling the sinking afternoon sunshine in ripples across my face. The papery rustle of their leaves is the only sound I can hear.

I lift my head from the pillow and run a hand through my hair. There is a clammy feel inside the van, the cotton sheets, now wrinkled beneath me, no longer cool against my skin.

I get up and pull open the door to feel soft, salty breezes drifting towards me. With bare feet, I hop onto the sun-warmed paving flags and walk along the street in my shorts.

I head towards the fancy cottage. Not a soul to be seen. The only movement catching my attention comes from the undulating grasses and crops in the surrounding fields.

I vault over the low fence, as neatly as I can. The slats wobble a bit and my feet land on spiky, buzz-cut grass. Bare patches are threatening to form in some places, suggesting a summer's worth of fun played out all over the lawn. Some of the bedding plants bear small flowers; others have already bloomed and gone.

Once inside the garden, I see that I was right. There, in a corner of the patio, is a large barbecue flanked by tables of cooked meat, burger buns, paper plates, napkins, iced bottles of beer, and jugs of lemonade and juice. No people, of course.

One gauzy curtain is flapping lazily outside an upper window, having been tugged out of place by the wind. I take a plastic cup from a stack and fill it with fruit punch.

I now see a small, white-edged pool set in landscaped paving and flanked by sun loungers. I crouch and stick my hand into the water, which laps feebly against the tiles. The surface jiggles slowly, reflecting multiple suns in its craters and carrying a couple of children's floats across the pool.

There is a noise. It startles me and I lose my footing: the splash is louder than you'd think.

My head goes under. I right myself and gasp. I see that it was just the stack of cups falling over on the table. I'm an idiot – a wet one. My cup is now spinning at the other end of the pool.

I catch my breath and then haul myself out onto the side. It's not deep but I am sodden and surprised. I feel weak. My wet feet slip-slap watery puddles over the paving and the lawn feels sharp under my soles.

I move my soggy, sorry self back to the deserted barbecue and heap a plate with sausages, burgers and chicken legs. It all looks delicious. Plenty of food to spare.

Shadows are starting to form between the fence posts, and the sun hangs lower in the sky.

I take my meaty treasure to a lusher corner of the garden and sink down into the daisy-dotted grass.

I grasp a fat, sturdy sausage between my fingers and close my eyes as I eat it, savouring the flavour. The sun's rays fall over my face and I stretch my legs out to dry off, listening to the softest lullaby of the sea beyond the hills.

***

After dinner, Dan Mather is boarding up the broken pane on his sister's kitchen door. The smell of ravioli coats the room and one upper window has been opened in an effort to dissipate the condensation. Outside, the garden is catching grey shadows. Inside, the kitchen light casts a warm orange glow to all but the corners of the room.

Dan has been allocated a square of newspaper to stand and work on. As he taps the board into the wooden frame, Sarah is carefully putting away the last few items from the strange arrangement on the counter, inspecting each one in a new and mysterious light.

She clears the final piece and turns to find her son lingering in the doorway.

'Time for bed, young man.'

The boy hesitates, already wearing pyjamas, watching as his uncle taps in the last nail and then rises, a little sweaty, to his feet. He notices how big his uncle seems in their kitchen and watches intently as Dan puts away his tools. They make small, metallic clangs against the box.

'Will...?' begins Matthew in a small, uncertain voice.

'Yes, you can have a story,' Sarah answers, assuming the question her son can't spit out, but Matthew keeps staring across the room towards Dan and tries to find his words again.

'Will...?'

'Yes, Uncle Dan will still be here in the morning. He's going to stay with us for a while. You'll soon get used to him.'

But that isn't his question either and so he blurts out, more loudly: 'Uncle Dan?'

Dan stops what he is doing with the toolbox and arranges his face into what he hopes is a kindly, avuncular, encouraging smile.

'Uncle Dan, will *you* read me a story?' Matthew manages, the childish request hanging for a moment in the tomatoey fug.

Beaming now, Dan responds.

'Aren't you a bit too...? Of course. I'd love to. Let me have a wash and I'll be right in.'

Shortly afterwards, he is sitting on the foot of Matthew's bed, pink and shiny from his wash. Matthew's fuzzy pyjamas have rockets all over them and his soft, clean hair sticks up in tufts.

The evening is still light beyond the cotton curtains, but the bedside lamp softens the boy's room with its glow.

Matthew is propped up against a pile of pillows at the head of the single bed, his slender legs forming a tiny mountain of duvet. The other end of the mattress sinks to a dent beneath Uncle Dan, who sits hunched over, the small paperback in his hands.

The curtains ripple gently by the open window. Passing cars and footsteps can be heard from the street. Grown-ups are putting their bins out and calling their children in.

Dan is reading from the place that Matthew had got up to. The book is *Matilda* by Roald Dahl and the boy is listening, rapt. After the passage where Miss Honey tells Matilda her secret, confessing her desperate need to tell someone about her childhood, the reading comes to a natural rest. Dan pauses, looking over at his nephew. He folds the book around its bookmark before carefully placing it on the bedside table.

'It's better to share things with other people instead of carrying secrets around with you,' he says. 'Have *you* ever felt a desperate wish to tell everything to somebody?'

Matthew shakes his head.

'Well, you know you can tell me, or tell your mum, anything at all, don't you?'

Matthew nods, and a tuft of freshly washed hair bounces on top of his head.

'Anything at all.'

'Yes,' his nephew says quietly.

'*Is* there anything you want to tell me?' Dan asks, holding the boy's gaze.

'Just that…' he whispers.

'Yes?'

Dan assumes the expression of avuncular encouragement once more.

'Just that… I'm happy you're here.'

***

I'm resting my hands on the fencing, looking out to the distant sea. Breezes tickle my follicles, flutter my night-dress, catch my hair.

The choppy moonlight and soft twinkle of the town lights below me make the night seem enchanted. The streetlamp glow collects on the patchwork of buildings; corners and crevices cookie-cut from the night's shadow by a warm, blue tinge growing in the sky.

The townscape lies like a valley beneath my vantage point up here on our hill. The sea shuffles in the distance, pinpricked by moonlight – a shimmer at the edge of the world.

I close my eyes.

I feel the gusts lapping my curls and sculpting my hair above my head in tendrils and tentacles that furl and float and fall. I feel the smooth wooden railing at my fingertips, and the grooves of decking under my bare feet.

I hear the hum of street-channelled winds swelling up towards our house. I hear the crisp flutter of fine leaves from the shawl of delicate birch trees swaying nearby. I hear their branches playing at the fence like a xylophone.

Everything is warmth and every part of me feels cosy, contented and alive. Happiness spreads through the nerves and veins and cells of me, along every inch of my skin. I feel a gentle, happy glow in the deepest part of me and the caress of softest cotton against my thigh. I can smell the salt on the air again and the rich, green scent of the bushes below.

Everything is calm here. No sounds but the whoosh and shush of trees.

***

Just before dawn, a bulky shadow strains to arrange boxes in an empty room. The final load lands on the dusty floor with a thud, and heavy footsteps scratch across the concrete floor. Gloved hands yank down a rolling, screeching, metal door and, in the glare of a head torch, secure a shining padlock. An engine growls into life. Tyres turn slowly and the vehicle crunches across unlit, uneven tarmac and escapes the hastening day.

CHAPTER 6

The kettle boils and Zoya pours water into a couple of mugs. Vapour spirals up to her face. She wipes away a blob of sleep from the corner of her eye and looks through the window over the front garden that slopes down to meet the street. She listens to the radio for a minute, letting the tea steep.

'... the latest in a spate of goods vehicle robberies in the county. The driver sustained minor injuries during the incident but did not require hospital treatment. The police are appealing for witnesses. In good news, we have two community events coming up in Shilly-on-Sea. Teams are reminded that tomorrow is the closing day to register for the Porden County Community football tournament. The first match will be held in the town on Saturday the sixth of October in aid of the Sunnyview Lodge charity. A town fair will be held on the Glebe on Saturday the twenty-second of September...'

The toast pops up.

Zoya slaps the toast onto a plate, butters it and bites a slice, before turning her attention back to the tea. Dispensing with the tea bags and adding glugs of milk, she places everything on a tray and heads upstairs via the ramp. Spiralling upwards in slippered feet, she reaches the storey above, negotiates the parlour furniture and continues on up to the top floor. She crosses the wide hallway and knocks gently on her dad's bedroom door, opening it enough to place the steaming tea on a low unit just inside the room.

'Bath's running, Dad!' she calls through the opening, then crosses the landing to deposit the breakfast tray on her own unmade bed.

She nips back along the hallway to check on the running bath, plunging her hand into the frothing water to test the temperature and encourage the bubbles. Richard appears at the doorway in pyjamas, wheeling with one hand, cradling his tea with the other.

'Child, I can still manage to run myself a bath.'

'I know, Dad, but I like looking after you.'

'Okay, but I'm sorted from here on in. You go and enjoy your breakfast.'

'Okay, but shout if you need me.'

She pads back to her bedroom at the back of the house and collects the breakfast tray. She carries it across to a small doorway in the far corner of the room, where she climbs a few curving stairs into a round turret room crammed with pictures, cushions and all sorts of… *stuff*.

Contained within the smooth plaster walls of the curved room are a muted riot of colour, textures and shapes. An old wooden desk stands where you might expect to find a corner – replete with an intermittently dusted, chunky typewriter in pride of place. There is no paper in the platen.

An old travelling trunk, oily with age, lies by the wall, a paint-splattered easel nestling behind it. Low bookcases are flanked by stacks of towering, shelfless books and prints, and a sleek metal telescope stands proudly by the window.

Zoya carries her breakfast across the room, the sturdy floorboards emitting the usual creaks in the usual places. Mismatched rugs haphazardly carpet her route through the clutter to a small sofa covered with throws and cushions in silk and linen and wool. It faces the sash window, tall and wide and gazing south towards the sea.

She sets down her tray and starts to pull the sash cords until the opening feels vertiginous, and cool morning air fills the room.

The walls are dotted with a smattering of prints and paintings as well as photographs that range from sepia to black and white to Kodachrome. Framed book covers convey a sixties and seventies aesthetic. There are pictures from Africa featuring animals, people and sun-baked landscapes.

There is a large portrait of a young woman. Her ash-blond hair is pinned up in the style of the day, but rebellious tendrils fall beautifully around her calm, happy face. There is another, smaller, more impressionistic, painting of the same face, the sitter now an older woman with shorter hair. She is accompanied in the painting by a younger man, wearing his hair neat but natural and looking equally happy. They are holding one another and smiling, their love-infused happiness depicted in bright, lively daubs of bold paint.

Zoya is now settled on the sofa by the telescope, which is aimed at the pink, fluffy morning sky. The constellation maps pinned to the nearby wall patter gently in the breeze. Foliage and traffic and sea salt scent the room and mingle with the kaleidoscopic traces of typewriter ribbon and perfume and cigar smoke; with oil paint squirted on canvas and wines drunk and spliffs giggled over; with years and years of meals consumed.

Zoya leans forward to remove the lens cap, munching on a triangle of buttery toast.

The strengthening daylight is beginning to flood the town's nooks and crannies and she puts her eye to the viewer, turning the scope through an old, familiar path.

There, just down the hill, are the stuffy-looking rows; tall, grey Victorian town houses ratcheted along an elegantly curved street that leads to the small, formal park. She turns the focus knob and sees, almost predictably, the figure of Carl putting what looks like a bag of balls into the boot of his car. He has been friends with her dad since before she was born and looks set to never really retire.

She swoops the telescope around to look at the centre of town. She pauses and sits back for a slurp of tea. The noise might have echoed round the curved walls of the room but for all the photographs, paintings, star charts and paraphernalia softening the sound.

She sees a seagull swoop past the window and loves the feeling of being up as high as the birds.

Setting down the tea and putting her eye back to the telescope, she adjusts the controls for a clearer look at the old town hall. She can make out the range of philanthropic figures sculpted into the building and alights on the back of the Ephraim Alderney statue placed dutifully in the square. A few people are cutting this way and that across the space and a car is driving down the long, straight high street towards the sea, disappearing now and then behind the ash trees planted along the central verge.

Angling the telescope slightly, she moves her gaze down the high street to a row of pubs. It's too early in the day for anyone to be about.

Wheeling further to the right, her lens finds the imposing Methodist church steeple and the old manse next door. A space in front of it, crested by the odd ancestral sycamore tree, indicates the flat, grassy green known to locals as the Glebe.

Her gaze swoops slowly over rooftops but she can't spot any adventurous cats.

She checks the seafront, a long way ahead of her, and notices the beach café shining in the sun. The many windows allow the glow to pass right through the corner and it looks more inviting than it ever does when she arrives for work.

Continuing the slow sweep eastwards, past the police station across the road, she explores the ornate part of town. She spots the curved facade of the old theatre slumbering there, between the brass-handled shops and elegant squares.

Adjusting the focus further, she peers at the distant seafront promenade. She can just about make out the edge of the lido, more from local knowledge than visual clarity. She looks towards the grand hotel situated at what was once the edge of town. The telescope has reached the limits of its focal capacity and the grand old dame of Edwardian tourism remains a neat shadow in pride of place by the long beach.

The viewfinder fills with a blur of blue and white and she readjusts the focus to try and keep the vehicle in range. She tries to trace its journey as it drives along the coast road and down into the town.

She manages to pick it out again as the van pulls up at the beachside, just beyond the café, and has plenty of time to refocus as the driver parks up. She watches for a few long minutes. Nobody emerges from the camper. She leans back on her sofa and polishes off her toast.

CHAPTER 7

That afternoon in the beach café, the youngish man sits at a table by the window, cradling a cup of coffee and looking out at his camper van parked by the sea. The sunlight is slowly sliding around the bay.

There is a breath of condensation creeping up the plate-glass window behind which he sits sheltered cosily from the buffeting breezes that play along the coast. The broad, sand-sprayed road corners around the building to run beside the grey seascape along the front. He can hear the muted swelling and falling of the English Channel edging the shore.

He looks to his right and sees a distant pedestrian making their way along the beach-softened promenade. He notices the rust-speckled railings stretching westwards along the walkway, the pale windblown sand and the ever-moving waves beyond.

The glass-panelled door swings open to his left as someone blusters inside. The gentle click-clack of comforting café noises is punctuated by the sudden caw of gulls and splash of waves against rock.

He looks eastwards, beyond the cake-wedge porch at the corner. A few cars follow one another around the bend there, having reached the end of town. This seaside place feels alive, but ever so quietly. He relaxes in the wooden booth seat.

He picks up the last mouthful of his bacon roll. Chewing, he brushes tiny crumbs from his fingers onto the plate before swirling the last third of coffee around in his mug. He enjoys the play of liquid and gravity and the tiny motion it requires of his arm.

A conversation breaking out behind him catches his attention because the harsh tone seems out of place.

'Can't you get rid of it?' asks a woman's voice, perhaps the neat, beige-clad figure he hadn't paid much attention to as she made her way in.

There is the sound of someone brandishing something made of paper; the 'thwop' of a magazine being thrown down on the counter.

'I mean, why do you even stock it anyway, Tom? It's nonsense,' the voice continues.

'I quite like the quirk,' counters a slower, smilier-sounding man's voice in reply. He switches to a more serious tone to elaborate. 'Look, it's a useful magazine, Sarah, with articles and events listings across the county. Local advertisers. And it's free.'

The youngish man pays closer attention, his crinkled paper napkin slowly unfurling on the tabletop.

'But it's libellous!' Sarah asserts, the sibilants exploding from her controlled, quiet voice.

'Look,' – Tom tries again – 'it doesn't mention you by name... It doesn't give your address. I wouldn't worry about it if I were you. Just a kooky little article that most people wouldn't even notice.'

'That's not even my kitchen in the photograph!' she complains, tapping a fingernail at the open page.

He looks closer at the faint crosshair pattern on the table in front of him and listens harder to the conversation taking place behind.

'How did they...? How did they even get the story?' queries Tom's deep voice, calm but puzzled.

Lowering her voice with effort, Sarah continues. 'Well, that's another thing. I never told him he could put it in the magazine.' Her tone snaps back to exasperated defeat. 'So, you won't get rid of it? Even for me?'

After a pause that may have accommodated a small sigh, Tom replies. 'Sorry, but it's useful for people.' Then his voice becomes exaggeratedly friendly. 'Don't worry, tomorrow's chip paper and all that.'

'Fine. Look, I've got to get off to school anyway,' comes the reply, and Sarah weaves between the tables and chairs towards the café door.

'Will we see you and Matthew at the fair?' Tom calls after her, but she doesn't seem to notice and bustles away.

The youngish man takes a look at her as she leaves, his eyes tracking her as she walks away down the street. Then he calmly drains the remains of his coffee, slowly stands, and goes outside. Turning town-wards, he can still see her marching into the distance and sets off, following her route.

***

A short time later, the woman is waiting alone at the busy school gates; cars are arriving, parents chat on the pavement and children are spilling out onto the street.

The primary school stands at a broad four-way junction and the man is lurking at the red-brick corner of a building across the street. He peers around the edge of the wall.

The school itself is an extended jumble of low buildings arrayed behind a protective stone wall. A curtain of railings sprouts from the perimeter and encircles the site. The playground gradually fills with chatter and movement as the children emerge and flow out through the gate, their small feet clattering on the paving slabs.

When the woman turns, he darts back behind his corner, then tries to look casual by leaning a foot against the wall.

Some of the rowdier kids kick a hacky-sack across the tarmac and shout to one another. Most greet their mums with soft voices and begin the slow walk home.

The man leans a shoulder against the bricks, maintaining a position where his gaze can skim the corner of the building and keep the woman and son in his sights. He watches her relieve the boy of a small rucksack and take him by the hand. They are just across the road from him now and he hears the boy ask: 'Mum, can we get a dog?'

Then they set off walking at a slow pace.

The man hangs back a while, leaning and watching, until they are just about to round a corner. Then he sets off, following them, his scuffed Converse padding casually along the pavement.

By the time they are passing a row of suburban shops, he has almost caught up with them. He is close enough to hear their conversation about what the class did at school.

A slow-moving parade of schoolkids meanders past shops that are busy with colourful signs and packed windows. Mothers set the pace for the little ones, while older shoe-scuffling dawdlers trundle along in clumps.

A car parks illegally on the kerb outside the newsagents while children emerge, clatting gum and dribbling over sweets. A clump of white dog poo is narrowly avoided by shiny, new-term shoes, the potential culprit barking in a garden nearby. A few local adults are popping in to pick up basic provisions. The man has no reason to feel so out of place.

The woman tuts to see an empty wrapper left on the pavement, stoops to pick it up and deposits it in a bin. They are nearing the end of the row now.

Then he sees the child freeze in his steps, his hand-holding arm going taught.

A broad-shouldered man wearing an asymmetrically collared jacket, walking in the opposite direction, is looking the boy full in the face. This man keeps walking for a minute before sneaking a look back at the mother and child. The youngish man notices a flash of submerged fear playing across the square-jawed, stubbly face.

He pauses. He feels like turning on the spot to follow this new mark. He stands stock-still on the street, pulled in two directions. He makes up his mind and carries on tailing the woman and the young boy.

The school crowds thin, forking in different directions, peeling off for home and calling goodbyes. The woman and boy enter a quiet, tree-dotted street where roots distort the pavement and younger children play in front gardens within sight of their mums. He feels out of place here, but continues onwards, hands in pockets, not breaking his casual gait.

At one semi-detached house, opposite a junction and next to a wooded path, the woman and child turn into the garden. The front door is being opened from inside. A big, curly-haired man takes the shopping bags from the woman and pats the boy on the back as they file past him into the house.

The youngish man pauses to light a cigarette and risk a further glance, but the large man in the doorway is still there and seems to be looking intently back at *him*.

He continues around the corner and out of sight. He gets his bearings then starts walking in the general direction of the sea.

CHAPTER 8

That evening, the youngish man is walking about the town centre, popping into restaurants and pubs. He paces up and down the busier streets, looping around and learning the layout of the town. He studies the faces of men who pass by.

He finds himself at The Ship's Wheel, a brick pub with age-yellowed net curtains hanging at the upstairs windows. It is the first in a row of three pubs.

He pushes the door and goes inside. The place isn't full, but pockets of men are hanging about, nursing pints. A few clumps of blokey mates are rooted here and there, none too rowdy – though a bark of raucous laughter bursts forth every now and again.

He pauses to spot if any one of the men wears a green jacket with an asymmetric collar or sports the stubbly square jaw and hard stare he should recognise from the street. He tries to blend in.

The pub has a dark-patterned carpet, worn thin and shiny near the bar, dartboard and gents. The wood panelling looks tobacco-stained. Perhaps this place once wore its nautical theme more overtly, he thinks, but he can only spot a browning print of some ship sailing the seas hanging, long-forgotten, on the wall.

Scanning the pub and not seeing the face he was hoping to, he gradually realises that the barman is staring at him.

'What'll it be?'

He dutifully approaches the bar before anyone else notices him and sees several drip trays, perilously close to overflowing. They offer a pungent aroma of lager and cider and ale.

The barman has picked up a clean glass in readiness – whatever it would be, was apparently meant to be it in a pint glass.

He is a thirty-something with a ponytail and shrinking Star Trek T-shirt featuring Spock, Spock's iconic hand gesture, and Captain Kirk. The Enterprise hangs in the space-sky behind them. The man wearing this T-shirt is looking a little bored and a lot impatient. The youngish man keeps looking around.

'Can I help you?' queries the barman.

'Just looking for someone,' he explains.

'Drink while you wait?'

'Maybe I missed him… Taller than average, broad, shaved head? Maybe you know him?' he ventures more boldly.

'That could be anyone. What's the name?'

'Never mind,' he says, backing away and knocking into a darts player as he goes.

'Hey!'

'Sorry,' he says over his shoulder, making his escape from the pub.

He goes straight into the place next door. This is a larger establishment, all plate-glass windows, laminated promotional signs, quiz machines and sports TV. He sees that it has been unimaginatively named Shilly Sports Bar.

It's a chain pub packed with smart shirt wearing lads. Herds of young men are standing around, giving the place its base note of stiff shoes, hair product and overdone aftershave.

A long wooden bar with a proliferation of shiny beer pumps and fixtures is being tended by a team of uniformed staff. Uninspiring contemporary music is being piped around the cavernous room from expensive speakers, causing the patrons to raise their lager-loosened voices almost to shouting.

He would never choose to spend an evening here.

He circles the bar, checking faces, but doesn't see anyone he recognises. He soon retreats to the street and the late-summer evening outside.

The third pub in the row, The Admiral and Smuggler, is another traditional 'old man's pub' in the mould of the first – except this one is green-tiled with red woodwork and seems even quieter inside.

As he walks in, he feels the same suddenly-deafened sensation you get from diving into water. This pub is emptier and airier than the first, and chunky, bottle-bottom windows keep the street sounds outside. He can't hear any traffic and the sports bar no longer seems to exist. The familiar fragrance of beer and cigarettes can be detected but the desperate reek of aftershave is gone.

He notices a run of plush, green, stud-pinned seating running in a broad wheel around the corner of the bar.

Warm lamps bathe the interior in a soft glow and the tables are sturdier, like dining tables, though alcohol stains have removed some of their sheen.

He almost does a double take upon seeing the barman: a thirty-something man with neck-length hair. This one is wearing a vintage *Empire Strikes Back* T-shirt depicting all the main characters grouped on the snow planet Hoth, and a streak of orange for the sky. If he wasn't scrutinising faces this evening, he would have thought it was the exact same guy.

Three customers mosey out of the place, leaving the man and the *Star Wars* fan alone. It feels like time for a sit and a drink by now, so he sidles up to the bar.

'Pint, sir?'

'Yeah, no, have you got any porter?'

'Fuller's, do you?'

He nods and the barman begins to pour.

'Fine choice,' another, croakier, voice says, sounding lived-in but well projected and strong.

He looks over to see the speaker sitting at a cosy booth at the corner and finds a twinkly-eyed gent of indeterminate age. His face and physique don't quite match, making him seem either younger or older than his years. He looks like he leads a healthy, outdoorsy kind of life.

Right now, the man looks perfectly at home indoors, though, a regular fixture even, and is holding up his own glass of porter in acknowledgement. The youngish man nods at him.

The barman sets his drink down on the drip tray and he hands over the cash.

'Thanks. Erm, I'm looking for someone. Problem is I can't remember his name…'

'Try *him*,' the barman advises firmly. 'Carl knows everyone around here. Especially the do-gooders and the, er, troubled. Which is yours?'

He scouts about in his brain for something convincing to say.

'Hey!' pipes up the outdoorsy man, addressing the bartender with friendly authority. 'We like to give people second chances in this town.'

The barman wanders off to change a barrel in the cellar, muttering. The older man, 'Carl' apparently, gestures for him to join him at the booth table. He picks up his porter and obliges.

'So, let's see if I do – know your man, that is.'

'Okay, thanks. Erm, big, bigg*ish* guy, maybe not that big, quite broad though, thirties… or forties? Bald, no, shaved head, I think.'

The older man chuckles. 'You're going to have to be a bit more specific. Who is he? How do you know him?'

'Do you know what? I can't say. Doesn't matter.'

'Wears a green jacket?'

'Yes! I think so, you know him?'

The man guffaws. 'Nope. Just a lucky guess! You young men are all wearing them,' he answers, and he gently slaps his hand on his thigh. He seems delighted to have amused himself so much.

'Okay, well, thanks for your help,' says the youngish man, getting up to leave.

'Hey, that porter's too good to waste,' Carl interjects, flashing the eye-twinkle. 'How's your backgammon?'

He is opening up a board and tipping the blots out onto it.

'By my reckoning, it takes a game per porter.' He fixes him in the eye. 'And I should know.'

'Okay, but I'm not very good.'

'Neither am I, young man, at least, my long-standing opponent is beating me at the moment, so I need all the practice I can get.'

'Where is your opponent tonight?' he ventures.

'At the top of a very steep hill.'

The man watches his new companion in puzzlement, waiting for an explanation, but he only chuckles. He watches Carl set out the blots in a perfect mirrored arrangement.

'Black or white?'

He shrugs and the local relents, preparing to offer more information. Getting him to open up about the town would be a very good move.

'I play every week with an old, old friend – lives in that crazy house on top of the biggest hill.'

'I've seen that house. There's something on the roof, isn't there? What is it?'

'Exactly what it looks like.'

'Some kind of whale?'

'A minke whale; well, a sculpture. The ancestor who built that house was a Dutchman with the same name –

Minke – and, upon visiting the town, there was a rare sighting off the coast. So, this Bartholomeus Minke, an eccentric fellow, decided it was some sort of "sign" and settled his family here. Built the big house and, later on, his son stuck a massive whale on top. Why not?'

He chuckles again.

'Yes, that's quite eccentric.'

'I suppose we're all just used to it round here. Always been there. We just call it Whale House and that's its name. You won't see any sign with that painted on it, but, with a house like that, I suppose they don't need one.'

He rolls the dice and makes a split move without having to think about it. The youngish man emulates with a move of his own, several questions bubbling up in his mind.

'Fine people,' the man continues. 'Calliope was a lovely woman, but sadly no longer with us. Richard's going to live there the rest of his days, no two ways about it.'

They shake and move their blots in turn. The rattle of dice in the wooden tumbler reverberates intermittently around the empty pub. The youngish man sips his drink and places the glass on the tabletop.

'Does he live there all alone?'

'Oh, no. His daughter lives there too, and they have visitors all the time. And that's where I play most of my backgammon. We've a tournament been going on for over twenty years; we'll know the winner when one of us dies!' He chortles. 'Of course, the walk up there didn't used to bother me.'

'It looks like a really steep hill.'

'I was always a sportsman, but age catches up with all of us – enjoy your body while you can.'

The youngish man wonders if he should feel self-conscious about his own slim frame.

'Richard uses a chair now, but at least he gallivanted around Africa in his youth.'

'So, what sports did you used to play?'

'What sports *didn't* I play? Taught most of the county to play 'em too. What's *your* sport?'

The youngish man catches an involuntary laugh and transforms it into the beginnings of a sentence.

'Do I look like…?' Then he composes himself further to come up with a more polite answer. 'I'm not really into sports.'

'You look like a runner,' the older man announces.

'Skinny, you mean?'

'Or a cyclist,' he suggests, sending a blot to the central bar.

'I used to cycle. As a kid, quite a bit, but now it's just… walking around.'

By this point, the backgammon champion is amassing blots in his home board, while he is failing to escape the bar.

'You're new in town then?'

'Just passing through. So, you *do* know everyone?'

'I know a few.'

'What did he mean, saying – you know – "especially the do-gooders and the troubled"?' he asks, looking back over to where the barman is leaning, reading, no other customers in the pub. Bearing off a couple more blots, Carl sits back and looks him in the eye.

'I like to give back, that's all. And I help drifters stop drifting. Not everyone around here understands. Most people like to judge before they've walked that mile in someone else's shoes.'

Then, lightening up, he says: 'They're not walkers like you and me.'

He smiles a twinkly, collaborative, sort of smile.

'What is it that people are judging?'

'Oh, we've got a halfway house here now. Not a bail hostel – a charity place I'm involved with. Somewhere people can stay while they get back on their feet. Doesn't matter what they've done or who they've been. We like to give people a second chance. Gets them onto a better track.'

'Sounds very honourable. Do you run it?'

'Not the accommodation, but I organise a lot of events for the lads who live there. Maybe you want to join in?'

'Oh, no, I'm not...' He stammers, reaching for the right words, annoyed at being taken for a potential reform project. 'I'm already on a good track. Just passing through.'

'Are *you* going to stop drifting?' the older man asks, earnestly.

'No plans to – but I think I can stay put until the end of the game.'

***

Later, in a wood-covered shadow, well away from the nearest street lamp, broad shoulders lean against a garden fence. The figure stands just beyond the pool of light illuminating the path.

The tree canopy shifts the shadows in the night breeze. Only the tallest cedars, towering over him, catch the blustery wind; the low bushes sheltering by the fencing seem to avoid its touch. There is the song that urban birds sing when they have lost all sense of the dawn.

A very distant car hums quietly in the background. Nobody seems to be around.

Steel-toe-capped boots edge along, squelching the soft soil underfoot. Gloved hands feel for the loose section of the fence and find it. The bulky figure moves the wooden plank aside and squeezes through the gap into the dark suburban garden, the rough edges grazing his jacket.

In the bushy corner, he is hidden from any prying eyes inside the family house, although the brick-built semi looks quiet, the windows blank. The garden smells of compost and creosote and cut grass.

It all feels deathly quiet – no signs of life in the house or the streets; the in-between small hours when everyone is asleep.

Beyond the bushes and grey blooms stands the shed. The intruder sees its pitched roof – a black profile blocking the orange glow of the streetlight. Thick fingers grip the bolt cutters more securely and the man moves like a shadow around the corner, readying himself for the bleak task ahead.

Bright light shocks him; a pair of headlights suddenly revealing a vehicle at the junction across the street. The beams are trained on his position, directly pointing at the spot. The man drops to the ground, flinging himself onto the turf with a muffled thud. Blades of grass scratch at his face.

He wriggles over the soft soil back to the hidden corner, listening intently to the sound of the vehicle which is *not* driving away. *What is the driver doing?* he thinks. *Watching the house?*

The trespasser sneaks his large frame back through the fence opening and slinks through the darkness beyond. He avoids the well-lit footpath to dart through the wooded border, sticking to the step-muffling earth. His scraping, scrabbling, sinking feet run as fast-yet-quietly as they can.

Where the trees abruptly run out, the figure emerges and slows to a deliberately normal gait. Leaving the alley, he walks between concrete bollards to a dark van parked on waste ground nearby.

Back at the street, the headlights move on, as the vehicle eases around the corner to park opposite the still-sleeping house.

CHAPTER 9

I get out of my van and stand in the road. I look up and see stars. There is less light pollution by the sea. The night sky is still dark but about to turn – that flip from yesterday to today that I've become so used to, living as I do.

There is little to be heard except a faint breeze rustling some of the trees. I check for telltale signs of life in the house that I followed them to – nothing so far.

It stands in grey stillness, the modest front lawn rippling slightly, making the house seem deader. The soulless windows look back at me, unblinking. I pace across the gently cambered road and push open the low metal gate to the path.

'Hello?' I call out, just in case.

I walk on up towards the house and can't see any movement inside. The path passes along the side wall to the back, where a garden with a shed can just about be made out. A set of tall cedar trees sway above the rooftops, casting shadows as they move. Let's see what I can see.

I go straight up to the front door. As I push it open, the draft excluder sweeps the plush carpet as if to say 'hush'.

'Hello?' I say, loudly, like a question, and go inside.

I step into the hall. Small picture frames have been hung on the walls and a bunch of flowers arranged, quite precisely, in a vase.

So, who do we have? A child, his mother and father – that man who saw me and stared? I wander through the ground floor to find the kitchen, talking as I go.

'Hello. I loved your work, the sculpture thing…'

As expected, nobody and nothing there.

Everything seems neat in the kitchen except for a board nailed over a pane in the back door. It smells of food and cleaning products. There is nothing and nobody here.

A faint light is expanding over the property. I can see quite a large back lawn bordered with well-established bushes and plants.

I knew it would be like this but had to give it a try. Maybe someone will appear. I try to walk heavy – to attract attention, my trainers tapping across the linoleum floor.

'Hello? Is anybody here?'

I trudge around and find myself in the front room. An array of cotton bedding is piled on the sofa. Is the dad in the dog house, I wonder, but I don't wonder about it for very long.

I climb the stairs to the first floor, passing a door all stuck with stickers and drawings as I go. The boy's name – it has to be – 'Matthew', is written at the centre. I push open the door; nobody there.

Then, I shuffle to the doorway of the master bedroom for a perfunctory look. It's pretty much as predicted, one double bed positioned between fitted wardrobes. One side of the bed is neat, the other ruffled. I close the door and move on.

Well, this has all been very disappointing, not that I actually had my hopes up, but still.

So I call out: 'If you're there, I only want to meet you!' – but there's nobody anywhere, of course.

From the upstairs landing window, I can see a Vauxhall parked in the drive. It gives me an idea and I bounce down the stairs again. I walk out, through the kitchen, onto the back patio. Everything out here is rendered a collage of greys. There is a hint of some tree trunk creaking in a neighbouring garden.

'Are you out here in the garden?'

Apparently not.

I go over to the shed. The grass is longer here, and I wade through it, ankle-deep, like walking along a shallow shore.

'Don't mind if I use a bit of engine oil, do you?' I say out loud, pulling open the timber door.

It's dark and fusty inside the shed. I stop to ignite my lighter so that I can see. Another disappointment; it's empty, apart from some rags or clothes on the floor.

I close up the shed and stride onto the back lawn. It would all be such a waste of time if I didn't have so *much* of it to waste.

I look up and pinpoint the constellations again, spinning slowly as I gaze. I turn in a spiral, looking up at the stars. My feet tread a flattened crop circle into the long leaves of springy grass, which crumple and uncrumple beneath me, stars spinning overhead.

'Hello?!'

I'm shouting this time.

'There's nobody here, is there?'

Then, more quietly to myself, but I can't help saying it: 'Never fucking is.'

***

In the dawning light, a man in a dark truck arrives back home. He drives it quietly to the end of a cul-de-sac that is scattered with similarly downtrodden bungalows and parks on a patchy scrap of land. The low buildings here each sit in their own square of garden, most are pebble-dashed and double-glazed. The end house glowers from behind an overgrown privet hedge, somehow looking scruffier than most.

The man picks up a green jacket and some kind of empty sack from the passenger seat. He steps out of the vehicle onto scrabbly ground. Birds chatter in some nearby bush and a low buzz of traffic is building at the main road. His boots crunch and scuff quickly over the wide, mossy path as he makes his way to the door.

He hears the muted double ring of the telephone coming from inside and, after fiddling with the key at the lock, opens the door and rushes in. The ringing phone becomes louder and more insistent the moment he gets inside. He sprints through to the cluttered kitchen to pick up before the caller rings off.

He knows who it will be.

Daylight is now falling through the back-door window, showing up the unwashed crockery by the sink. He grabs at the wall-mounted handset, its long loop of curly wire tangling as he paces the small room.

'Yeah?' he answers gruffly, flinging the gear in his arms onto the floor.

'No. I couldn't. *I couldn't*. Someone was watching. Turned up to watch the house just as I was about to... No, they didn't see me, I'm not an idiot... I don't know, couldn't see them for their headlights – pointed right at me. Do you know something I don't? Because I could have sworn... I'll sort it. Don't worry... Tonight... Yes... It was *you* that dropped the... No... No, don't... What's DN?... Didn't even draw blood... Yes, I'll deal with it... Who? Who's been asking about me?... About *me*? Are you sure?... Probably looking for someone else. You're being paranoid... Yes. I'll let you know.'

The man hangs up and sinks heavily onto a creaking chair. Dust motes float in the pale morning light.

CHAPTER 10

Dawn has now broken, and the households are starting to stir. Bright beams of sunshine bathe the wide suburban street, the shadows, collecting by its brick walls and thick hedges, softening as the day swells. In the van, the young-ish man turns the keys and the vintage engine stirs to life. He looks across the street again at the house, that garden shed still visible at the side. Its roof is starting to catch the morning rays slipping through the cedars.

A light goes on in the bathroom.

The engine rumbles softly, expectantly, and his gaze drifts back to that strip of garden. His left hand slips its grip on the handbrake. He pauses and doesn't drive off.

He turns towards the unassuming house, still not able to stop wondering. Will someone emerge from their sleeping place in the garden shed? Who? Why?

Looking along the road, he can see pairs of identi-cal modest family homes snuggled together, two by two. Cherry tree roots crack the pavement between coloured chalk marks from children's games. He decides to turn off the engine.

He unearths a battered Marathon bar from the glove compartment, peels the wrapping and takes a chewy bite. He adopts a sideways position – better for keeping watch – curling his long legs around and resting one foot on the dashboard. He fixes his eyes on the shed door.

***

Inside the house, breakfast is up and running. Matthew is quietly munching through a bowl of Coco Pops and chocolatey milk. Sarah is busy assembling the school backpack and squeezing in a sandwich box of carefully prepared lunch. Her own breakfast plate and mug are already rinsed and neatly placed by the sink. Wandering around with a mug in the midst of all this, Uncle Dan wears a brown terry-towelling robe and tries to find somewhere to *not* be in the way. He shuffles on through to the front room, where everything is tidy except his mess of bedding on the sofa.

He takes up a position at the bay window to sip the hot, reviving tea and familiarise himself with the morning outside. A clear, bright day, crisp yet warming, is unfurling in front of him. Curls stick up on top of his head.

He notices an interesting-looking vintage van parked across the street. It wasn't there yesterday.

***

In the camper van, the youngish man pulls on a jumper and shifts position, determined to keep watch. The scent of garden grass begins to soak the air. He hears the faint rumble of traffic, the clunk of car doors, the scrape of bags being set down on driveways, and the foley taps of shoes treading well-worn paths from doorstep to commute. He hears the chirruping of bush-hopping birds. A cyclist glides by.

***

Dan draws back the net curtains for a better look at the world outside. Other brick semi-detached houses face Sarah's from behind similar blocky front gardens. There's nothing much to see. A shard of sunlight shines in his eye, making him squint, the reflection bouncing from a window of the house across the street. He sees a neighbour plodding around the corner and notices the gleam of the van parked outside number 32. He sees a jumble of curled shapes at the driver's-seat window, but the reflection makes it hard to see who.

A man, dressed for the office, closes his gate and heads to a car.

Dan's tea is now firing up his brain. Sunlight twinkles off the chrome wheel trim and he finds himself admiring the distinctly seventies shape of the camper parked across the road.

***

From his vantage point inside it, the man maintains his vigilant watch, unaware of anyone in the front window of the house. The smooth leather of the car seat squeaks as he moves his leg and the indents of the headrest are pressing lines into his cheek. Nobody comes out of the garden shed.

***

Dan can hear crockery and cutlery being stacked by the sink and Sarah getting Matthew ready for school. Dan registers that the person in the van seems to be staring at the house. From this distance, through the haze of hot tea vapour, he can make out a figure hunched up in the driver's seat, his body twisted, a collection of folded arms and legs. Don't those vans have beds in the back? Isn't that the point of them? And what's he staring at?

***

A car pulls away further down the street. Still, the youngish man stays put. He watches and waits and wonders, considering how long to give it, but somehow not able to tear himself away.

***

As the sun moves a tiny fraction, the windows no longer reflect its glare. Dan has a clearer view of the watcher now. He stares straight out of the bay window at him. The person may or may not be staring back.

Things have moved on in the morning routine now and Sarah is zipping Matthew up in a lightweight jacket that he won't need for the late summer's day ahead. She checks a shopping list and snaps it shut in her purse. She might have given Dan some instructions that he didn't really hear and is helping Matthew into his backpack by the door.

Dan shuffles around them in the hallway, sets his cup down on the telephone table and fastens the tie of his robe. He finds the opportunity to ruffle his nephew's hair and tell him to have a good day at school and then Sarah and Matthew are off down the path and onto the street.

Dan steps out of the house in his slippers to see them off as they go. He can hear Matthew asking her something.

'Mum, can we get a rat?'

***

In the camper van, the man's attention is diverted from the shed to the three people appearing at the door. He sees a woman and boy, ready for the day, and a man who has evidently just got out of bed. As the woman and child march off away from the house, the man stays in the garden.

He notices the boy turn around to gesture at him, drawing a curvy, horizontal line through the air. The man in the robe is doing the same in return. A 'wave', he realises. Very clever. They are 'waving' each other goodbye.

He watches the woman and child walk off down the street, walking in the direction of school. He turns back to the house to resume his watch on the shed, but the big man in rumpled bedclothes is standing on the path, glaring right at him. He shrinks in his seat.

***

Anger is growing inside Dan. He can now see the stalker clearly. He clocked him watching his family walk off and now recognises that slim, observant face from hometime yesterday.

***

And then the burly man in slippers is marching across the street towards him. His adrenaline builds to fear. No time to react. The van door is wrenched open. Big hands grip his shoulders and haul him out into the street.

CHAPTER 11

In a different town, another man in slippers is knocking at a neighbour's door. He shifts his weight on the black and white lino tiles, almost pacing the floor. He wraps himself tighter in the brightly striped dressing gown and tries again. The brass knocker seems quite ineffectual, creating a soft, muted tap against its plate. He starts to bang on the door with his fist.

'Donna!' he calls through the door. 'Are you home, princess? I've got your guitar tuner. Wanted to return it before you went to work – because, remember, I'm going away.'

He is holding a small metal device in his other hand. Donna doesn't answer. The shared hallway remains quiet. A brown leaf falls from one of the dying pot plants onto the pile of old leaflets below.

Robin furrows his brow. He hears the growl of traffic from the main road outside and the slam of the heavy front door as a neighbour leaves the flats. He knocks on the door again.

Jude appears in the hallway, sporting her practical haircut and comfortable shoes. The aroma of baking bread wafting from her kitchen smells delicious but he is too worried to feel hungry. She smiles at Robin and notices he is trying to fit something through Donna's letterbox.

'She's away, isn't she? Said she had to go out of town to see someone. Seemed quite serious about it, like not a fun trip.'

Jude scans Robin's expression to see if any of this information helps.

'She said she'd be back yesterday,' he replies, looking at the door as if to assess how easy it would be to get in.

Then, gesturing with the guitar tuner, he explains: 'Doesn't fit'.

'Maybe she's gone to work early? Here, I can take that and give it back to her later,' Jude suggests kindly, holding out a hand.

***

Inside the kitchen sit Dan and the youngish man, facing each other with matching suspicion. Two fresh mugs of coffee stand steaming and untouched on the table between them.

The scallop-edged blinds are raised and everything in the kitchen is clean and neat – except for the two men. Dan, still dressed in his T-shirt, pyjama bottoms and dressing gown, presents an intimidating pile of simmering accusation, whereas the stranger slouches, defensive yet preoccupied.

'So, you're not going to tell me?' Dan says, not taking his watchful gaze from the quiet man's face.

From his position at the table, the man still has a clear view of the garden shed and clings to his stubborn obsession by mostly staring out of the window.

'What?' he replies, questioning the question and returning Dan's unwavering look with his own calm gaze.

'Why are you watching the house?'

It's not the first time he's been asked this in the past ten minutes. He turns back to watch the shed.

The sun is peeping above the wavering treetops behind the hedge, sending dappled sunlight into the kitchen. A lone blackbird is raking through the undergrowth somewhere nearby.

Without turning his face from the window, the slim man replies in a clear, relaxed voice.

'I'm not. Why did you drag me in here?'

He throws a sharp glance at the heavy-set man in pyjamas who sits watching him, legs splayed, fists resting on his chunky knees.

Dan takes a moment to respond. The fridge-freezer begins to hum.

'I've seen you,' Dan replies, not quite a threat. 'First yesterday, after school, and now today.' He fails to elicit an answer. 'Looks like you've been there all night?' His deep voice is rising but under control. Dan leans forward on the table. 'Look at me when I'm talking to you!'

Casually doing as he is told, the man thinks for a while before replying without defensiveness or urgency. 'I live in my van. I can park it where I like.'

'Not outside, my, er, my *sister's* house, you can't.'

'I'm not hurting anyone.'

'Aren't you? Looks like you've been following my nephew around,' comes the deep voice – but Dan is finding this casual interrogation difficult with someone who seems much more interested in something else outside. He changes tack. 'What do you keep looking at out there? Never seen a garden shed before?'

Who is this person sitting quietly across the table, seeming perfectly happy to be there; nothing to hide, nowhere to be?

The clock ticks quietly on the wall. Delicate bedding plants sway beyond the patio, fluttering their tiny flowers. A magpie alights on the shed roof, caws noisily and then flies off to the high trees.

The stranger looks pensive for a while longer and then fixes Dan directly in the eye.

'Who sleeps in that shed?' comes the unexpected question.

'What? Nobody. Why are you following my nephew? Look I'm treating you fairly, haven't jumped to conclusions – most people would – made you a nice coffee. I'm being polite. I don't *have* to be polite, you know?' Then, remembering to breathe: 'What *are* you staring at?'

The man looks down to the table and reaches long fingers for the nearest mug. Picking it up, he leans back again, the wooden chair creaking as he moves. He blinks slowly a couple of times as he takes a welcome slurp of the coffee. It feels like some sort of answer might be forthcoming, so Dan sits back and watches him think.

'Nobody's in the shed?'

'No!' Dan booms, then switches to a tried and tested persuasive tone of voice. 'Just tell me what you are up to. I'm a nice guy, you can tell me. What do you want from us?'

He leaves the question hanging in the air – most people feel the need to fill awkward silences.

'Are you sure?' his subject asks confusingly, making Dan retrace his own statements in his mind.

Now lost in the tangle of questions, he settles on the man's accent, mentally registering that he's probably not from around here.

Just then, the front door opens and Sarah bustles into the house. Carrying a small bag of shopping into the kitchen, she pauses upon seeing the pair of them before setting it down on the counter.

She looks warily at her brother – still not dressed for the day – and at the lanky, unfamiliar man who is looking out of the window, tree-filtered sunshine lighting his pale face. Nobody speaks and she begins to wonder what exactly she is interrupting.

'What's this? What's *he* doing here?'

She is questioning her brother but watching the other man intently. She has never seen him before.

Dan looks at her. 'Calm down, this is just someone I'm… interviewing…'

'About what?' she snaps, and then turns to the stranger. 'What are you doing in my house?' He doesn't answer, so she tries Dan again. 'You never asked my permission. What's all this about?'

Dan takes a breath. He never meant to set her off with worry.

The stranger suddenly speaks up. 'Your brother here thinks I've been stalking you.'

Dan looks like he really wishes he hadn't said that.

'What? Why? I'm calling the police,' Sarah announces, marching into the hall.

The big man in the bathrobe and the slim stranger in the stripey jumper look at each other across the table.

'No, don't do that,' Dan calls after her, raising his hands in a gesture of emergency placation. 'We're just talking. Nothing we can't handle ourselves,' he remonstrates, leaning back in his chair to see her by the telephone in the hall.

She isn't listening. 'I'm calling the police.'

***

In a small, open-plan office cluttered with desks, piles of files and teacups, the light clatter of fingers on clunky keyboards is sliced by a ringing telephone. A young woman answers.

'Hello. Advo-case?'

A man wearing cords and carrying some papers picks his way through the mismatched furniture, papery stacks and filing cabinets to arrive at the pair of desks where she sits. He places a report on the unoccupied desk and catches the young woman's eye.

'Sally – is Donna in yet?' he whispers across the desks to her.

Sally asks the caller to wait a moment and cups the phone. The man continues talking.

'We were meant to be going over the file before our meeting with social services this morning. She's back today, right?'

Colleagues stretch over the furniture, handing papers in peeling file covers to one another – a feat made possible by the cramped layout.

'Yes, she's normally in early but I haven't seen her yet,' Sally replies, looking up. 'Maybe she's been delayed…?'

She punctuates the conversation with a short smile before returning to the paperwork in front of her and the caller on the phone.

'Yeah. Let me know when she turns up?'

Chief Inspector Frank Barrow is standing in the kitchen. A subordinate skulks by the door, clutching a notebook and pencil. He hasn't yet made a single mark on the page.

Dan and the youngish man are still seated in their chairs at the kitchen table but are both now turned respectfully towards the tall policeman with the Easter Island face. Sarah is pacing in the background.

Things seem to have escalated quickly, but what those things are, nobody seems sure.

'So, which is it?' Frank commands, in his warm yet effortlessly authoritative tone. 'Either *you're*' – he turns to the mild looking stranger – 'a stalker, or *you're*' – he turns to Dan – 'holding this person against their will?'

The stranger is getting that friend-of-the-family vibe from Frank Barrow's presence – or else why would a senior officer have shown up?

He glances out to the garden while Dan pipes up in his own defence.

'Hey, I'm just asking a fella some questions over a nice cup of coffee. He's free to leave but doesn't seem to want to – just keeps staring at that shed!'

'Did you have anything to do with the break-in the other night? Just be honest, son. Your fingerprints will find you out.'

The chief inspector probably *is* old enough to be his dad. The stranger splays his hands in a dramatic gesture and asserts his position.

'I'm the innocent party. It's *these* guys who are imprisoning someone in their shed.'

Sarah halts her pacing to look from face to face to face and Dan runs a hand through his hair in exasperation. The constable starts writing the word 'shed' in his notepad.

'What's that?' Frank queries calmly, advancing fractionally towards the witness. The morning isn't making any sense. 'What makes you think that?' he asks the out-of-towner.

The man takes a moment, swallows and wets his lips. 'There's someone in there,' he begins conversationally, 'but *this* guy keeps denying it.' He jerks a thumb towards Dan. 'And *she's* over-reacting about *something…*'

Then, having released this morsel of information into the world, he sits back in his chair.

Chief Inspector Barrow slowly turns, looking at everyone, choosing his words wisely. He rests his hands on his belt and addresses the accuser. 'Now, don't go throwing accusations around, son. We can all resolve this nicely.'

He pulls up the chair closest to him and sits down in front of the stranger, a calm but imposing presence. 'Listen, I've known Sarah for many years, and she wouldn't harm a fly.'

He delivers an expression that shows he expects his listener to comply with this assessment, but the man first closes his eyes and shakes his head before glancing round the room. He leans forward to reply to the policeman.

'Then someone's hiding in there without their knowledge.' He speaks as plainly and rationally as he can. 'It's weird,' he adds, with a shrug of his shoulders. 'I just wanted to know what's going on.'

At this, Sarah is gathering the collar of her cardigan about her neck and gravitates to the window to look hesitantly at her own shed.

'What? Someone's here?' she mutters to the pane.

The police constable crosses out the word 'kidnap' on his pad and scribbles 'hiding' followed by a neat question mark. Dan bangs his hands on the table.

'He's talking nonsense! There's *nobody* hiding in that shed.'

With a gentle scrape of the chair legs on the floor, Frank Barrow slowly rises from his seat. His wide shoulders tower over them then sag slightly as he exhales a sigh of resolution.

'Only one way to find out.'

***

A short time later, the five of them are standing in the garden looking at the shed door. Low flowering plants wave stalks of petals towards their shins. There is a shiny padlock on the bolt.

'You must have the key?' Frank suggests, turning towards Sarah, who hovers at the edge of the group, closest to the house.

She doesn't take her eyes off the shed door. It stands solidly in the frame, the thick steel padlock looping the catch.

It's quite pleasant in the garden. An unseasonably warm September day is well underway. A giddy bee buzzes in and out of earshot. The breeze ruffles overgrown privet fingers that point towards the wooden shed.

'Well, I suppose, somewhere. I never really used the shed. It was Paul's domain. But I don't remember him ever locking it, even when he still... lived here.'

'Well,' Frank prods, patiently, 'would you mind looking for it?'

'There'll be a drawer somewhere, forgotten keys and useful bits of wood,' Dan adds, encouragingly. 'What did he keep in here?'

He nods towards the windowless shed.

'Just... tools... I suppose. I don't know. I never really went inside. But I think he took them when he moved out.'

She trails off, lost in thought, remembering.

'So... could you go and find the key?' the chief inspector instructs, patiently.

***

Soon, the semi-circle numbers seven with the addition of two more officers – one carrying bolt cutters.

With a nod from Barrow, Sergeant Brooks dons protective goggles and advances slowly toward the locked door.

They watch the development silently, each confused – in different ways – about the turn of events.

Justin Brooks, the same sour-faced officer who Dan saw yesterday, steps towards the door. He reaches out to grasp the padlock with the cutters and everyone braces. He raises the tool into optimum position.

'So, you really can't find the key to this?' he says, breaking the taught silence, turning back to ask.

There are several terse shakes of the head.

'Looks like a new padlock, though? What are we trying to retrieve anyway? Must be important.'

The onlookers barely respond, except for the youngish man. 'It might be,' he says, softly.

The policeman turns his attention back to the lock.

'We don't know there's *anything* inside,' blurts Dan, shooting the stranger a sideways look.

'Or any*one,*' counters the man who nobody knows.

'Do be careful with those. Should we stand back? Don't damage the shed,' cuts in Sarah, causing Sergeant Brooks to look around at her.

'Just get it open, Justin. We've been here a while.'

'Okay, boss, here goes.'

Soon the shed door flips open and seven eager faces peer into the darkness within.

A small gust from the swinging door lifts particles of dust and a certain smell begins to spread towards them. Eyes begin to adjust and make out a shape inside. The semi-circle inches closer. The smell leaking into the garden becomes pungent, like rotten eggs. Then, in the same moment, they all see it; a loose shoe, a pallid foot pointing towards them – a body on the floor.

Mouths drop, expressions twist and eyes look away. Sarah gasps audibly and clamps a hand across her mouth. Dan scoops her under his arm protectively, and she looks back towards the normality of the house.

Most of the group shrink away from the morbid surprise; the dark, unnatural shape at once recognisable as a human body but unnervingly unfamiliar in this state. Even the police see few bodies around here.

'What do we do?' Sergeant Brooks asks, panicking.

Frank interposes his frame between the discovery and the civilians and switches gear.

'First, get this door closed again. Sarah, Dan, I advise you to go back indoors. Kate, call the team in. Justin, bring him in.'

'This one?' Justin queries, pointing at the stranger.

'Yes, this one,' Frank directs, as if addressing a simpleton.

'But I didn't do anything!' the stranger protests. A bemused expression is vying with shock across his face.

'Then how did you know?' Dan asks, accusingly, in a booming voice from the kitchen door.

Sarah, sheltered in the crook of her brother's arm, also pauses to look at him. 'Are you psychic?' she implores in a subdued voice. 'Tell me, are we in danger? What's going on?'

Chief Inspector Frank Barrow once more takes control. 'Dan, Sarah looks like she needs a good cup of strong sugary tea and a sit-down. Sergeant Brooks, get him in the car.'

The youngish man goes willingly, following the gentle pressure of the officer's grip on his shoulder. They put him in the police car and lock the door.

CHAPTER 13

At Whale House, Zoya is pouring the tea. Richard and Carl, at their backgammon table, each smile at her in thanks.

She leaves them, playing and chatting among the pot plants and sunshine in the conservatory end of the parlour, and carries the teapot across the room. She settles on the window seat where she and Vanessa are set up for afternoon tea and chat and views across the town.

The dice shaker rattles in the background.

She pours the golden tea into two more cups and places the pot, once her mother's, on the table by the milk jug. She nestles into the cushions. Beyond the town lies a spectacular view of the bay.

Vanessa Barrow is adding milk and selecting a chunky biscuit from the plate. Richard has chosen something classical from the vinyl collection that crowds the player by the wall. Teaspoons clink, wooden blots slide and a piano softly scores the scene.

Zoya gazes across the bay where the sun glints from the sea.

'So, I'm not supposed to say anything…' Vanessa confides, glancing to the men across the room, as if she is about to share a secret.

Vanessa enjoys a gossip, Zoya knows – everyone knows – so she prepares to play along. 'No,' she concurs, fulfilling the required conversational prompt.

'But it looks like Frank is going to be a little busier than usual. He called about dinner. Something big happened... They found a... well, I shouldn't say really.'

And she really shouldn't. The wife of the local chief inspector isn't actually on the force.

'That's okay,' Zoya says, 'I understand. Police confidentiality is important.'

Vanessa would never take the hint. 'But I can probably tell *you*. I mean, it's a matter of public safety. And you're a young woman too. It's just that... Don't be alarmed... It's just that they found a body this morning. In a garden shed. Apparently been there for days.'

Zoya is listening intently, her biscuit hovering above her teacup. It seems insensitive to go for a dunk now. This talk of a dead body is more than she bargained for. She places the biscuit back on her saucer.

'What, really? In Shilly? Was it an accident?'

Vanessa looks up. 'Can't be. Nobody knows who she is. The dead woman, I mean.'

'Did you say she, er, the body, was in a garden shed? Whose?'

'Oh, I really can't say.' Vanessa takes a gentle sip of her drink. 'I mean, I don't know yet.'

Zoya would have wanted to laugh at Vanessa's reasoning – if the subject matter wasn't so serious.

'But I do know it's shaping up to be a proper murder investigation,' Vanessa says, nodding for emphasis. 'Looks like she was suffocated and locked up in a tool shed. The people who live there have never seen her before, don't know anything about it, and Frank believes them. I mean, apparently we *know* them.'

Zoya sits back in the pile of cushions to let the news sink in. Her dad and Carl are laughing and bickering in their usual comfortable way.

'That's horrible,' she states. 'Poor woman. Is it…?' She pauses to consider how best to phrase her question. 'Have there been any others?'

She feels silly even suggesting it, but it was Vanessa who brought up the topic of public safety and now it is swimming around in her mind.

'Not as far as I know. But they have someone. In custody. A drifter who lives in a van. Won't say why he was watching the house. It's all very…'

Vanessa breaks off to find the right vocabulary and take another bite out of her biscuit.

'A VW camper van, by any chance?' Zoya finds herself asking the question simply because the memory of watching one drive into town flashes through her mind.

'Maybe, why?'

'Oh, probably nothing. I just saw someone driving one, but that was only yesterday. You said this woman had been dead for a few days…?'

But it seems the chief inspector's wife has her mind already made up about the perpetrator as she leans in conspiratorially. 'Well, look, keep all this under your hat. I wasn't meant to say anything, but do you think he was…?'

'Yes?'

'Returning to the scene of the crime?'

CHAPTER 14

Moonlight falls through the small, high window and casts a sheen across the tiles. I am lying on a slim cot in a narrow cell, one arm bent under my head. I hop off the bed and pad across the smooth concrete floor to the painted metal door. It hangs heavy on its hinges as I swing it open.

Out in the corridor, I see that one way leads to the holding cell and the rest of the custody suite, and the other leads to another metal door and, I suppose, the secure parking bay outside.

I turn that way and my rubbery footsteps squeak along the corridor. Then I pull open the heavy door. It makes a discordant, clanging creak.

A couple more turns and a couple more doors and I find myself in the warm night outside.

Stepping across the tarmac, I look up at the sky. I see a sprinkling of stars and a big bright moon.

I reach the high street, turning around to see what I can see. I need to get to know the town and I want to see if anyone is here.

I was in a daze on the way into the police station and didn't notice much, but now I discover that the station stands across the street and down a bit from that café I know.

The evening townscape is moonlight clear. I pause to listen to the waves.

The glittering midnight sea beckons me to the beach end of the road so I start walking. I pass the empty café, which stands at the corner junction, and stare out at the dark water.

Then I turn back towards the town. What can I see?

Along the waterfront to the east of me stands a large shadowy box that can only be a grand old Edwardian hotel. It would give me a great vantage point so that's the direction I pick. I curl my arms around myself for comfort, the wool of my jumper fluffy against my palms.

After a few minutes' walking along the promenade, over rasps of stray sugary sand, I encounter a large open area with stacked deckchairs and an old lido reflecting a watery moon. I walk along the low wall of the pool, careful not to fall in. After the lido, I see the hotel ahead of me – perfect for a rooftop view.

Grey in the light now, this grand establishment is pretty much what I expected – elegant striations of old-fashioned luxury finished with fine metal-worked balconies on the side by the shore. I find a service door and quickly locate some stairs. After some determined climbing, I reach the small door at the top. It opens outwards and reveals – like a theatrical curtain – an extensive starlit scene.

I make my way out onto the flat roof and find a path between the vents. I can see the whole town.

Splashes of silver and lines of shadow pick out an array of buildings that stretch as far as the hill. I find a spot among the ventilation shafts and sit down, resting my arms on my knees.

From my sheltered spot I hear the swell of the English Channel, muted by the roof behind me. Nothing else seems to stir. Looking above, I can make out smoky, starless smudges that must be drifting clouds.

I push my sleeves over my elbows and attempt to get my bearings on the town.

Now I pick out the coast road that I drove in on, curving over the hill to my right. I work out that the road runs through a smart district and emerges at the junction with the high street near the little café. I drove into town that way and then parked by the waterfront. The road continues westwards, further along the coast, but I haven't gone that way yet.

I look inland and locate the biggest hill, the one with the house with a whale on the roof. The hill makes for a good reference point as I construct my mental map of the town. Approximately halfway along the imaginary line from here to there, but a little to my left, I find what can only be the town hall. From my wanderings the first night, I deduce that the cavernous space running to the right of it and towards the seafront must be the wide high street. I haven't walked the length of it yet, but I figure out that if you start at the beach café junction and walk north into the town centre, the road broadens and becomes dotted with trees.

Somewhere in that direction is the backgammon pub and its neighbours. I'm starting to piece it all together.

I let myself enjoy the high breezes for a while and then get up and take the stairs back down to the ground.

This time, I walk inland from the lido and rediscover the upmarket streets and squares I thought I remembered. These buildings seem to be of a similar vintage to the old hotel, topped with Edwardian embellishments and presenting tall shop windows at pavement level. One building stands out – an old theatre, but I can't tell at this hour if it is operational or abandoned.

I walk a vaguely diagonal route towards the main drag, passing expensive shops – a formal dress shop, wooden rocking horses, speciality toffee, a French patisserie – that kind of thing. When I reach the broad artery that is the high street, I make a right turn towards the town hall. Out in front stands a typical Victorian statue – some philanthropic-looking man. It is surrounded by a small square of benches and modest planting. I walk up to the stone steps and imposing porch of the civic building and find myself opening one of the giant wooden doors.

Once inside, the stone changes to marble and I am in the grand entrance hall. It is a tall space bounded by a staircase, wood-panelled and floored with endless squares. You can practically hear the dust falling. The walls are adorned, as they all are, with portraits, carvings and other civic dignitary stuff. I shuffle back out and pull the oak door closed behind me. It reverberates with a thud.

The high street leads further inland, towards that weird house on the hill. I cross over to the east side of the main street and see the familiar row of pubs. I step into The Ship's Wheel, pick up a dart and throw. It bounces off the dartboard and I sigh. I retrieve it from the sticky carpet, put it back where I found it and continue with my walk.

The bright moonlight is now picking out the roof sculpture of Whale House. I feel sort of drawn to the place, but the steep road leading up there puts me off. Instead, I veer off to explore the north-eastern quarter of the town. Following my nose, I find neat residential streets of brick terraces, stone townhouses and well-established trees. A small park opens up before me.

Iron railings mark the perimeter and breezes race across the grass. I push the gate open and discover the usual parky things. There is the obligatory bandstand, the duck pond, spiky roses, gravel paths. Stone steps sweep up a small rise between two low buildings. One looks like a bowling club hut.

I crunch my way along a path to reach a metal bench. I lie on it and stay there, looking at the stars. I should know all the constellations by now, but I don't. There is quiet bubbling coming from a small stream that must empty into the pond. I think I can hear the flapping of a tethered flag somewhere nearby.

I sit up and get going, taking the path to the slope. Trudging up the flight of steps, I discover a small museum of sorts. I give it a pass and leave the park by the north gate, finding myself walking uphill. By the time the townhouses phase out and the road levels off, I already have a far-reaching, lonely view over the whole town. I press on and there it is – the strange old house that I've been gravitating towards all along.

It stands at a dusty junction where a narrow lane flows away from the road. I stop in front of it to have a detailed look, and also to catch my breath. The air seems more earthy than salty up here. I feel the soft kiss of a gentle breeze.

A copse of birch wood presents a calmly rustling shadow beside the house and the building itself rises above me, like a mountain begging to be climbed. It isn't as imposing as I had expected, and the rooftop whale sculpture seems perfectly at home.

A small garden banks up to a wide front door. The residence is tall, maybe three or four storeys, though it's hard to tell because the asymmetric windows aren't regularly spaced. There is even a rounded turret bulging at the top right of the house. It seems to be a house worth exploring but first I take stock of the grounds.

Flanking the house look to be tall wooden fences, reaching above the second floor. Nobody has fences that tall – are they hiding something back there?

I find it intriguing and want to take a look.

I go over to the slatted fence, stretch my legs and start to climb. The construction offers easy hand- and footholds and I soon find a rhythm, slowly but surely, climbing up. Barely two metres off the ground, I actually start to feel a little smug, but then, looking up for my next handhold, I am shocked by something new suddenly above me – something waving in the breeze.

A full head of abundant curls is hanging down towards me and a face, hidden in shadow, is peering at me from the top.

I freeze in place and catch my breath.

I hear a voice.

'Hello?' it says.

A woman's voice is calling down to me, clearly and calmly. I lose my grip and fall.

I land softly on the grassy slope and tumble back a few paces. It doesn't wake me up. Finding my balance, I scarper back to the empty road. And, yes, I *still* see the person watching me, her hair moving in swirls on the night air. I feel I ought to say something, but my mouth hangs open and, instead, I turn and run, my solitary footsteps ringing out in the deathly-quiet street.

CHAPTER 15

The next day, Zoya is at work in the café, pouring two take-away coffees at the counter and talking to Frank Barrow.

'What, no doughnuts?' Ray jokes from his regular table by the wall.

'Very funny,' Frank replies, giving Zoya a bored look across the countertop.

She can make out Vanessa through the window, hair perfectly coiffed, sitting in the passenger seat of their car. Beyond that, she notices a tall, slim man walking out of the police station: someone she half recognises from somewhere she can't place.

'Is that... is that the man?' she asks Frank in a low voice.

He follows her gaze, turning around to the street and craning to follow the figure as he walks towards the beach. Then he sighs and looks to the ceiling.

'I told Vanessa not to say anything.'

'No, it's just that I saw him drive into town the other morning and I was curious. Who is he?'

Frank Barrow places his hands on the countertop and leans forward to speak quietly. The words coming from his firm, letterbox mouth are hardly audible above the clatter of crockery. She catches a whiff of his recently applied aftershave – no doubt Vanessa's favourite. It goes well with his fresh, smooth shirt, which she knows Vanessa will have pressed with scented ironing water, and love. They seem to be on their way to a nice day out.

'Well, between you and me…' – he fixes her with a look that apparently doesn't work on his wife – 'You don't need to worry about that man. He's got an alibi; we've got him driving on traffic cameras exactly where and when he said he was.'

Then he reduces the soft, measured voice to an actual whisper and continues.

'And it doesn't fit with the forensic pathologist's time of death for the body.'

Hearing this from the chief inspector makes it all seem much more real, and, when he whispers that word – 'body', she gets chills.

He relaxes and picks up the coffees.

'You might see him around a bit, because I've got him reporting in every day, just in case… just because when somebody is of no fixed abode it's hard to find them again otherwise… I mean we'd do it but… resources. But I'm only telling you this as a close family friend.'

He touches her on the arm.

'Zoya, you're like a daughter to me and I don't want you worrying. Whatever happened, it looks like a one-off thing.'

He checks his watch.

'Look, we best get going – we've got tickets for *Phantom of the Opera*. Got to keep the little lady happy.'

He smiles. She knows he means it – keeping Vanessa happy is Frank's main purpose in life.

'Okay, thanks, Frank.' She smiles back. 'Enjoy your coffee.'

The big policeman leaves, looking like an old-timey boxer out of his uniform, and, minutes later, they drive off down the street heading toward Axworth. Zoya wipes down a table by the window and sees the same enigmatic man sitting on a bench, contemplating the sea.

She finds herself whispering: 'But what were you doing in my dream?'

CHAPTER 16

I'm sitting in a chair on the decking outside my room. My robe feels extra soft and silky against my skin. At the corner, the birch wood sprinkles feathery leaves over the veranda fence. I like the rustling sound.

I look up at the heavens. Pinpricks of light grow brighter as my eyes adjust to the stars above.

Then I hear a voice.

Someone is shouting up from the street.

'Hello? Are you there? I didn't mean to run off last night. Are you awake?'

It's a man's voice.

Then I remember. I get up and move to the corner of the walkway that peeks out at the side of the house. I see him immediately, standing awkwardly in the middle of the road.

I have the oddest feeling, like I've just seen an old friend, and notice that I'm smiling. I try to make out his moonlit face better.

'I'm here!' I say, throwing my arms out dramatically. I hear myself laugh.

The man steadies his feet and seems to break into a laughing grin of his own. We've never met before – but I saw him, didn't I? – climbing our fence and then running off down the hill.

I can feel his eyes fixed on me as I watch him wrestle with a spreading, vanishing, beaming smile.

He clears his throat and calls, clearly. 'Hi.'

'Hi,' I reply. 'I'm glad you came back to visit.'

'Me too. What are you doing up there?' he asks, simply, curiously.

'Just enjoying the night.'

I shrug and then take in the sweeping vista, before quickly returning my gaze to the visitor, for some reason wary that he might suddenly disappear.

'It's a nice evening,' he answers, agreeing with me. 'I bet you can see all the way to the sea?'

'I can. I love it up here. Views and breezes and moonlight on the waves. And calm. And solitude, well, until *you* turned up.'

I grin.

'Oh, I'm sorry,' he almost stammers. 'Do you want me to leave?' His body language seems genuinely crestfallen.

'Don't be silly. Hey, weren't you climbing up the fence last night?'

'I, er…'

'So, what's stopping you?!'

'Okay. I'll give it a go!'

He seems excited and jogs towards the house. Taking a position with a firm grip, he looks up at me to say something.

'But if you watch me, it might put me off. Don't watch, I'll just meet you up there.'

'Okay.' I laugh. 'I won't watch.'

I step back, away from the edge, and sit on the floor to wait. I can hear him climbing up. Strangely, I'm not a tiny bit concerned about who he is or why he's here.

The fence wobbles a bit and then his head appears over the top. He sees me and then looks at the veranda, evidently surprised.

'Wow, you've got a whole platform thing up here. A sky kingdom! Like the Ewoks!'

I laugh. I know the film he's referring to, but never made that connection before.

'Yeah!' I see his hands gripping the top rail, the knuckles looking whiter than white. 'Feel free to climb over! It's safer on this side.'

He nods and swings his long legs over and onto the decking.

'But don't worry,' he says, as he pulls himself over the top, 'I can't get hurt.'

He stands on the deck and I get up. He takes a few steps, looking around before taking in the view of the bay.

'You are not wrong. That view is *amazing*!'

I gather my robe around me and lean against the fencing, observing my night visitor.

'So, aren't you the one...', I ask.

He turns around to face me.

'... with the VW van?'

I couldn't say anything about a 'body', right now, because everything feels so light and free and exciting. I remember my conversation with Frank as I watched him leaving the police station. That did happen, didn't it?

'I am,' he answers, taking a few steps towards me. 'Nice of you to notice.' And then he pulls a cute little expression that might be his way of styling out a touch of embarrassment. 'The whole town talking about me, eh?'

Or it could be a genuine question. He seems adventurous but unsure of himself. I quite like looking at his long face with its ever-changing flow of expressions. Then I realise that that face is looking back at me and one of us should blink. Or look away. So I start walking and talking.

'No. Not the *whole* town. Just some of it.'

I dart a look at him. I find I really want to know, though, so I go for it and ask.

'So... Did you... Were you there when they found that dead body?'

We have reached the garden furniture by the house. He sits on the sofa.

'Yes, and it was horrible.'

I choose the chair opposite, watching him talk.

'But I didn't have anything to do with it! I was just... *there*.'

He is looking at the loop of walkway that circles the garden. Then he looks up at the roof. You can only see a little of the whale sculpture from back here, but he will have seen it from the street.

'Why is your house so weird?'

'I don't think it is.'

He holds my gaze for a moment, then nods slowly, looking around again.

'You're right,' he says after a while, like someone who really means it. 'It's interesting.' He smiles and his hands spring to life in gesture. 'Nothing wrong with interesting!'

'Nothing wrong with interesting,' I agree. I laugh, putting my feet up on the low coffee table. '*You* seem interesting. Are you?'

He puffs a little air into his cheeks and then blows it out. 'Hard to know how to answer that one.'

A comfortable pause stretches out between us and the wind weaves through the trees.

'Listen,' he says, breaking the silence, 'do you often come out here like this?'

'Like what?' I don't understand – he can see the furniture and cushions.

'Like *this*. All alone in the middle of the night.'

'Hmmm. Never thought about it.'

And then I start to.

'I suppose I do. But this is a dream, isn't it?'

'Do you ever see any people, apart from me tonight? Any animals?'

'Animals?'

I look down at the garden and try to see into the adjoining field. I slowly scan the sky without spotting or hearing any birds. Then I look back at his expectant little face. I suppose my own is crinkled up, confused.

'It doesn't matter,' he says, and sits forward, offering me a handshake. 'I'm Reed, by the way.'

I take his hand. 'Zoya.'

It's daytime at the beach café. Dan sits at a central table, flipping through a pile of scrawly notes with his left hand and penning an article on a pad with his right. A big, floppy hat and a plate of crumbs are also on the table in front of him.

'So, you're a journalist?' Ray says from his regular table.

'Features mainly,' Dan replies with only a cursory look around.

'Hey, written any ghost news recently?' Ray asks, chuckling in his limitlessly jolly way.

As Dan turns this time, he sees that Ray is holding up the latest copy of *The Porden Chronicle*.

'No, that was actually my editor. That one wasn't meant to be… Look, well, never mind.'

Dan sees he has lost Ray to his own mirth, which is just as well, as he wants to finish writing the piece. Soon, he stops writing and packs away his papers.

As he settles back to sip from his mug, he notices some-one familiar walking towards the café – the loner with the camper van who was watching the shed; the one with the alibi, according to the police. He watches as the man walks in, letting a salty gust through the doorway with him. He sees him slide his lanky frame besides the window table, run a hand through his wind-tangled hair, and study a menu.

Zoya is also watching. He's just the same as he was in her dream. She feels nervous for some reason.

'Lee, I'm just getting more napkins from the store,' she mumbles and disappears out of the room.

'Okay,' Lee replies, amid a swish of hair, approaching the window table to take the order.

Dan watches. The man orders something then looks out to the seafront. Beyond the pane of glass, giggling children play, and couples walk arm in arm.

The day feels softened, no sudden moves.

'So, you're still hanging around?' Dan asks, projecting his voice to the window table and causing Reed to look up.

The combination of Dan's bulk, expansive posture, loud voice and direct demeanour make him very hard to miss.

Reed smiles ambiguously. 'Yep, well spotted.'

Dan grins a little with one side of his mouth. 'Helping the police with their enquiries?' he probes.

Reed scans the room, but nobody is paying attention. He relaxes again, pleased to see his presence going unnoticed. 'Well, I'm a very helpful chap.'

Realising this is all a touch too confrontational, Dan decides to change tack. He gets up and carries his hat, briefcase and mug across to the window table where he squeezes into the opposite seat. Reed does nothing but raise his eyebrows ever so slightly.

'Look, I think we may have got off on the wrong foot,' Dan states, opening a new conversation. 'I'm Dan Mather.'

A small crumb falls from the corner of Dan's mouth as he smiles. He reaches into his pocket and places a business card on the table. He saves his new companion the bother of reading it by reciting – 'Dan Mather, sceptic investigator and journalist' – before adding some biographical details not stated on the card. 'Grew up in the next town over, love real ale, no time for mumbo jumbo.'

Dan studies the intriguing man who looks back at him. The man's composed expression doesn't give much away. He tries a broad smile and jokes: 'Hey, this is like a very one-sided date!'

'Pleased to meet you, Dan,' concedes Reed.

They both look out of the window where they can see someone explaining the rules of a game to an assorted group of men on the beach. Reed recognises Carl from the pub.

'You like this town?' ventures Dan.

'I do. Nice and close to the sea.'

Reed nods, his manner very laid back.

As it's a Sunday, there are extra cars in the promenade car park and a sandy picnic rug is being shaken, powdering the wind with sand.

'Police say you're a drifter. Live in that old van. You don't *look* like much of a hippy.'

Reed is wearing dark jeans, skateboarder trainers and a two-tone vintage bowling shirt under a jacket that he hasn't taken off.

'Do all visitors to this town get this kind of grilling?'

'Sorry – occupational hazard,' explains Dan. 'It's my job to get information out of people.'

Reed looks down at the business card, bemused as to what it might mean. A hand places a plate of breakfast on top of it and Reed looks up to say thanks.

Dan lays a palm lightly on Lee's arm to ask – 'Excuse me, do you do those American-style refills here?' He waves his empty mug.

'We do now,' Lee says, smiling, 'be right over.'

Dan acknowledges this kindness with a small wink.

'So, you're investigating me?' Reed asks, in a faint echo of Dan's opening question, prompting the bigger man to lean forward on the table.

'Look, I'll level with you. I need to know what's going on.' Dan's face falls into a serious expression. 'That's my sister and nephew in that house. They're frightened and I think *you* know something.'

Reed chews on a slice of toast with the hint of a frown on his face. Finishing his mouthful, he replies – quite calmly and deliberately – 'I don't know anything about that woman.'

Dan notices the careful choice of words. He sits back, scrutinising Reed. 'But you knew she was there.'

Both men leave the statement hanging – halfway between an accusation and an observation. It doesn't get an answer, though Reed shakes his head slightly and resumes looking out of the window.

Reed isn't unsympathetic, but isn't about to start explaining himself – how could he? He's tried opening up, but this is as far as it goes.

Dan, meanwhile, is watching him and registers the closing up. He sees the eyes gazing off into the middle distance.

Someone arrives with the coffee pot – Zoya, but she doesn't say a word.

Dan smiles and nudges his mug towards her. Reed has pressed his eyes closed as if thinking through a puzzle. Zoya takes a good look at him while she has the opportunity, and then she zips back to the counter to serve another customer.

When they are alone again, Dan breaks the lull. 'Okay, okay, you're the moody, silent, drifter type – but at least tell me why you were there, watching the house. I'm not going to press charges or anything, but I need to know. What brought you to town? To my sister's house?'

His earnestness, if not desperation, demands some kind of answer, so Reed opens his eyes. 'I saw your article and I was curious.'

'Now, hey...' Dan snaps into defensive mode. 'That was my editor. I never told him to print that stuff. It was just a message about going out of town for a few days. Sarah was very angry with me... but...'

'No big deal. I just look out for stuff like that.'

'*Paranormal* happenings? Poltergeist activity? Let me tell you, after many years of scientific investigation, there isn't any such thing.'

Reed shrugs gently. 'I never said there was.'

'But you think you're psychic?'

'No.'

'But you '*know*' things?'

Reed shakes his head, subtly, his eyes growing sad. He doesn't respond.

'Listen.' Dan almost spits out the word, frustration and anger underlying friendly advice. 'If you're hanging around here because you think you're going to find some paranormal shit, you're wasting your time. It's always some kid messing around. That body? That's some awful kind of random coincidence. But I just need to *know* how *you* knew about it. For my family's peace of mind.'

Taking his time to answer, and raising his palms as he does, Reed eventually replies: 'Sorry, I can't explain.'

'You mean you *won't*.'

They both sit there, quietly, slumped now, at opposite sides of the table.

'I'm sorry,' Reed continues. 'I truly am.' He does seem genuine. 'I'm sorry for what happened to that poor woman. I'm sorry that your family are scared. But' – he holds Dan's eye – 'I really can't tell you how I knew somebody was in that shed. I would, if I could…'

'… but you can't.'

Dan nods bleakly.

The sun beams onto their faces and a bout of laughter breaks out at the far corner of the room. The frivolity is nothing to do with them.

'Look, I apologise,' Dan begins, brightening. 'I'm sorry for spoiling your meal. I'm sorry for coming over here, asking you questions and taking up your time. It's just how I'm made. I need to understand everything. That's why I'm in the line of work I do. I notice things.'

He looks around for an example.

'See that corkboard over there? In amid all the community notices and posters and lost and founds, there's a weird... bulletin, profiling someone in the town.' He nods to support what he's saying. 'Every day, a different bulletin, like a public notice but... weird. Something about someone running a football hooligans' club.'

Dan gets out his notebook, flicks a few pages and reads: *'Which sports fan is in the secret family CLUB? Be careful he hasn't HAD you ON because he is BUZZING around bringing hooligans to town.'*

He changes his intonation to convey the random capitalisation of some of the words.

'You look at it.' He points at the café's noticeboard. 'Clearly batty. *That's* the kind of thing other people never notice, but *I* can't get out of my mind.'

Reed doesn't need to check up on what Dan is saying about the noticeboard because he's already spotted one of these bulletins himself, this one warning the ladies of Shilly-on-Sea that a notorious philanderer had come to town, intent on defrauding them – or some such. 'Which trophy-winning philanderer wears... shiny shoes?' He tries to remember the bizarre wording. He had written it down. Weird, indeed.

Just then, Reed notices something else: an older guy sitting alone seems to stiffen up in his chair. Is he listening in? But Dan is now getting up from their table, leaning on the back of the seat. His voice is back to charming and placatory. He is gathering his things.

'I'll let you get on with your day, but if you know anything' – he gestures with the hand holding his big hat – 'hard facts not silly spiritual stuff, mind, please let me know.'

Reed smiles up at him. 'I get it, you're a man of science – but what's with the wizard hat?'

Dan follows his gaze to the hat in question, then he places it proudly on his head. 'This, my friend, is a wide-brimmed fedora. And I wear it in honour of my hero, James Randi, magician and scientific examiner, greatest sceptic investigator of us all.'

He pauses, tilting his head. 'Nice talking to you...' he says, leaving a name-sized blank to be filled in.

'Reed,' he obliges. 'You too.'

Then Dan almost bows and walks out of the café.

Back at the counter behind them, a flash of cocktail party syndrome has given Zoya goosebumps. That's the same name he told her in a dream, isn't it? How could she have known *that*?

She busies herself elsewhere in the café, not looking at him at all. A while later, someone leaves – an older man – but then, not long afterwards, she senses *his* familiar figure getting up and walking out into the street. She confirms that the window table has been vacated and goes over to wipe it down. From this position at the corner, she watches him – Reed – walking up the road into town. She jumps a little as a voice at her shoulder says something. Lee has sidled up behind.

'Why do you keep staring at that man? Do you know him or something? Hardly the man of your dreams, is he?'

Reed follows the older man down the road, hanging back at a distance. The man is walking with purpose and veers off into a side street. Reed catches up by extending his stride. He reaches the corner and sees the man walking ahead of him. Resuming his normal gait, he follows the man through a few back streets before emerging at a rectangular expanse of grass.

Reed pauses at the shaded corner and watches as the man makes his way around the pavement to the long edge of the clearing. He passes the large, spired church and approaches the matching stone house. Reed takes a seat on a bench at the opposite side of the park. The man walks up the steps to the front door.

The bench slats feel hard beneath Reed's thighs and the grubby wooden bin emits a sandwichy, faggy smell.

At the door, the man seems to be flicking through a thick ring of keys, but then it is opened from within. A couple of men walk down the steps, one lighting up a cigarette. They don't stop to chat.

The man he is watching catches the door before it closes and goes inside.

Reed stays put on the bench and has a look around. Several benches line the perimeter and there are a few old sycamores studding the lawn. And that's it.

A couple of wood pigeons flit through the trees nervously, cracking branches and flapping wings among the broad leaves. When they erupt from their hiding places and fly off, the boughs reverberate in their wake.

Reed takes out a small notebook and opens the worn leather cover, turning to a blank page. He sketches a rudimentary map of the location and how to find it again from the landmarks he knows. Then he draws a cross by what he now assumes to be the old manse, although it doesn't look like it's used as a vicar's home anymore.

As he has the notebook in his hands, he flicks back a couple of pages to find the note he had copied down:

Which trophy-winning philanderer wears shiny shoes? Ladies be warned, this man is CONSTantly ABLE to DANCE away with your hearts and your money.

He puts the notebook away and looks across the park. He sees a modern extension protruding at the rear of the building, but no more people coming and going, for now. He spots a small sign fixed by the door and resolves to read it later.

***

Later on, when the evening is still light, Zoya is in her corner bedroom, organising things. Partly drawn curtains hang at her window, pale in the evening light. 'Free Fallin'' is on the radio again.

The music has to compete with the clump and bash of equipment that Zoya slings out of the cupboard, tossing it onto the bed or propping it against a wall. She has already extricated a rucksack, several suitcases and various zippered bags.

The organised chaos covers the room with colourful Gore-Tex, rough canvas and metal attachments that rattle like chains. A pair of skis lean against the wall, and, on the carpet, a climbing harness and snorkelling mask.

Zoya sits in a spiral of footwear, re-lacing a hiking boot.

The telephone rings.

She can hear the one in her dad's room, out of sync with the one downstairs.

It goes unanswered.

'Dad, can you get that?' she calls, even though he's probably too far away in the house to hear.

The phone rings on. She scrambles to her feet and dashes into his room.

'Hello, Whale House?... Hi Cara, how are you?... I was just packing for my trip, actually.'

The excitement vanishes from Zoya's face.

'Oh... I've a feeling you're calling to tell me that the itinerary's changed? Cancelled? Shit. Can you book me onto another one? No, it has to be when Auntie Abigail's here.'

She almost stamps a foot.

'Sorry Cara, I know it isn't *your* fault. It's just... yeah, I was really looking forward to getting away.'

As I stand outside the house tonight, the whale looks friendlier, somehow. I suppose it has one of those faces that looks different, depending on your mood – if sea creatures even have faces. I cup my hands to my mouth and call up.

'Zoya! Zoya!'

Nothing.

'Are you awake?'

I wait, hoping.

'Are you there?'

She pokes her head out of the turret window, flapping an arm at me and hissing.

'Shhh, I'm here. Shhh, you'll wake my dad.'

'We won't. Don't worry about that.' I hold out my arms. 'Shout as loud as you like!'

'Really?' She moves back from the window, perhaps listening inside the house. 'Because this is a dream, right?' she says, as if catching on.

I look down at my toes, thinking. 'Sort of.'

'Why *are* you in my dreams?' she asks, curiously.

I walk on up to the house – just to see her better. 'It's not really like that.'

'What's it really like, then?' she asks. Her eyebrows are knitted a little, but she still looks playful. 'I saw you today in the café, didn't I? Talking to that journalist. That was really *you*, wasn't it? And you were there when they found that body.'

She pauses for me to respond. I nod, gently.

'What's going on?' she exclaims, bemused. 'Do you have magic powers?' she asks suspiciously, pointing a hand at me. 'I heard him calling you a psychic! Why are you *here*?' She throws her arms up in emphasis.

It feels like a whole load of questions I can't answer – or not right now, anyway – so I just end up smiling up at her. 'No, none of those things.'

I look around at the sky, which is getting lighter.

'I can't stay long tonight because I have something to do, but I just wanted to come and say hello and… check that you're real.'

'Stay there, I'll come down,' she instructs.

'Down the fence?'

'No, I think the front door will do. Wait for me.'

With that, she disappears from the window, so I wait.

I cross the garden towards the front door and stand about casually, studying the moon-grey leaves. I'm still waiting maybe ten minutes later, wondering why it is taking so long. I lean back against the wall and look out over the distant lights of the town. I see a broad sweep of rooftops, sepia in the light. Nothing in particular catches my eye.

Should I shout up again?

I adjust my position, transferring my weight. I bend a knee to rest my foot against the house.

She still doesn't appear, either at the door or the window or up on the decking. I don't know how long it has been. I take a seat on the smooth stone wall at the road end of the garden and look for lights and movement in the house. I could go in there myself, but I wait outside, politely. I should really get going.

'Hey?!'

No response.

'Where did you go?'

I realise I'm probably talking to no one, but continue speaking, just in case.

'You probably can't hear me anymore... but I have to go somewhere... I'll come back tomorrow night though.' I stand up. 'Promise.'

I drift to the empty road, still looking up at the silent house.

'Okay...? Okay...?'

I start my journey down the hill by walking backwards, not giving up on a glimpse of her.

'Bye.'

It seems odd – or does it? I've never met anyone this way before.

I walk on, down into the town, feeling like I know my way around. I spot the spire of the church I'm heading for and keep going in the general direction. The sky is definitely lightening now. Soon enough, with the aid of a little brisk walking and my sketch map, I find my way to the green space and cross it to the stone steps of the manse.

The screwed-in sign reads 'Sunnyview Lodge' – which doesn't give much away, but, having met the old sporty guy, I have a pretty good idea what this place is. I almost forget but fish out a thin pair of gloves from my jean pocket and tug them snuggly over my hands, wriggling my fingers. I don't normally do this, but I've never had my prints taken by the police before, and, well, I just don't know. If Zoya were here with me, this is when I'd be saying 'Don't worry, I'm the good guy' and hoping she believed me.

I push at the door and, of course, it opens.

I step up and over the threshold, letting it close behind me. I switch on the light.

The strip blinks into life, antiseptically probing every corner and making me squint.

My eyes adjust and I find myself in a broad corridor. A few foam-filled chairs and a low table with magazines make it feel more like a waiting room. There seems to be a fire door between me and the hall stairs. A run of rooms stretches away from me along the ground floor. I go that way first.

I enter the lounge. It looks like a common room. I look around and find chairs, sofas and shelves crammed with board games and books. There are shiny patches on the cushion seats, a magazine stand spilling with newspapers and a wonky picture on the wall that nobody has bothered to straighten. There are 'no smoking' signs but the faint aroma of cigarettes lingers on.

A large television fills one corner, the screen lined with a border of dust. I don't dwell too long in here. I've got a job to do.

I move on and find a large kitchen with too many ovens, sinks and toasters. A long wooden table is positioned in the centre of the room. The walls bear a range of notices, including rotas, fire safety information, a flyer for a local football tournament, sign-up sheets for various activities and team sports, and a colour poster for a town fair to be held on the Glebe outside. It makes me think of a holiday camp, not that I've been to one. Well, not with anyone around.

A door at the back of the kitchen leads to a boxy extension. Here, I systematically work my way along a corridor of single bedrooms, opening every door. From the clothes I discover in each identikit bedroom, I confirm that the residents are all men.

Some rooms seem more established, with more possessions and more adornments on the wall. Some of the beds are covered in patterned duvets – like that of the Watford fan whose room is plastered with yellow-and-black Hornets paraphernalia, with football fanzines piled by the bed. Other rooms seem more temporary. I wonder what the requirements are for staying here.

From what the man told me over the game of backgammon, I know it is a charity of some sort, but it's the residents that interest me. I press on.

I don't find anything too unusual: a tin lined with joints, which I take; dog worming tablets hidden in a sock, which puzzles me until I poke around and discover some doggy treats and a scruffy lead. This guy must have a secret dog, quartered somewhere nearby. Fair play, I think. It must be nice to have a pet.

Other residents of the extension block seem to be: a big George Michael fan who has posters and cuttings all over the walls; a Simpsons aficionado whose windowsill is crammed with yellow figurines; and a keen sewer with a homemade quilt and a sewing machine in the wardrobe.

I have worked my way to where the extension joins the main house and find that a fire door opens onto what they might call the back stairs. I go up them.

I find a very different layout here. Some partition walls divide up the larger rooms, but it basically follows the original plan of the house. I still discover some of the same job-lot bedlinen and standard-issue storage units, but, on the whole, it feels less 'institutional' here.

In one neat room, I discover an array of ballroom dancing trophies and framed photographs. The pictures seem to be of the resident through the ages, with different dance partners, or else the loves of his life. Opening the narrow wardrobe, I see a beautifully pressed suit and clean, well-shined shoes. There are also lots of medication bottles with serious-sounding zed-heavy chemical names. It makes me sad for the guy and all his strongly felt romances now sadly confined to the past.

The other room of note is that of a northern soul fan. I spy his small record player, first of all, and eagerly fall upon his box of vinyl. My rifling turns up not a few hidden gambling slips tucked between the papery sleeves and gatefolds. I put it all back in place and move on.

At the end of the corridor, at the gable end of the house, I find a room that is larger, yet dowdier, than the others. Spotting that same, shabby jumper slung on the back of a chair, I know I'm in the right place.

This one has a stove, kettle and sink kitchen and a small bathroom to itself. There's not much in the way of personal touches.

A brown fug seems to hang over it now as the dawn's light grows beyond the thin, drab curtains. The walls here were painted some kind of muddy, neutral colour a long time ago and don't seem to have been refreshed any time since. The bare floorboards fail to disrupt the colourless theme. A distant, whirring hum of some cranky old boiler seeps into the space. It all reeks of tobacco, singeing and marsh-dark, over-brewed tea.

There is an annoying creak as I step across the floor.

I spot a shelf with some ring binders on it. They mostly seem to contain checklists and manuals and updates of rules. The thick ring of keys I saw hangs on a nail.

Moving through to the bedroom, I find another single bed. It is blanketed in a heavy, crocheted throw of coloured hexagons that brushes my shin like a cat. Wrinkled pyjamas peek over the covers. I suppose the old manse might get a little draughty. Looking through the clothes, I find brown overalls – the type that caretakers wear, because that's what he is, I surmise, or some kind of warden: the man with all the keys.

Perhaps he has a home, and even a family, elsewhere, but I get the impression that this is it.

I open some drawers and cupboards. What does he do in his spare time? Even some of the tinier dorms manage to reflect their residents' personalities – football and film posters, books, guitars, a collection of small rocks, a set of inherited war medals: little bits of life. Nothing here.

I'm disappointed. I can tell the sun is properly rising now. A lonely ray pushes through the cotton curtains, pointing to the far side of the room, where there could easily be another window, but isn't.

I start thinking about the pilfered spliffs in my pocket.

Then I see a corner of white paper sticking out from the wood panelling. I investigate and find out that the panel is actually another door. It pulls outwards into the room and I can see why. There's only a tiny space behind it, and it is filled with a desk and stacks of paper. I identify a small printing press, inkwells, rulers and scissors.

A neat space on the desk has been kept clear for working. I peer into the gloom and pull on the string light switch. A sheet of crisp paper lies in the centre, words neatly printed. I lean in and read:

'Which birdwatcher is hiding shameful surveillance secrets under their mattress? TAKE CARE that they don't take their cameras to work or EAVESdropping on your children is the least of your worries.'

It is printed in lower and uppercase letters, exactly like the other weird notes I've already seen. I pick up an inverted letter block and run my finger over the shape.

'Bullseye,' I say to myself.

CHAPTER 20

Chief Inspector Barrow opens the door to the incident room and makes eye contact with the detectives. They come over to where he stands.

'Alright, boss?'

'Good weekend?'

'Very pleasant, thanks, lads. *Phantom* at the Playhouse,' Frank replies. 'Have you got everything you need?'

The detectives look around at the team and the room, nodding assent.

'Now, what have you got for me?'

The officers look at each other, until one volunteers a summary.

'Not much so far. Died from asphyxiation. No sexual assault. Victim hasn't been formally ID'd but there's a missing-person report up at Axworth: female, 38, five foot five, blond, so...'

'Seems to fit the description.' Frank nods solemnly. 'Any ties to Shilly?'

'Not that we've pinned down yet, boss, but it's only a drive away.' The detective looks at his notebook. 'No family. Just a mother who died last year. Both lived in Axworth all their lives. Might not be ours anyway. We've tracked down a neighbour to come in and take a look later today.'

'Who's community liaison on this one, sir?' the second detective asks.

'I am,' Frank confirms. 'Okay lads,' – he starts to close the door again – 'keep me informed.'

***

Not too far from the station, Reed is walking through the town centre when a car pulls up beside him. A lumbering, rust-prickled Cavalier trundles past and bounces to a stop by the kerb.

'Hey, what are the chances?' Dan says, leaning over from the driver's seat, smiling.

Reed leans a hand on the car roof and bends down to speak to him. Inside, the car seems to be strewn with food containers, discarded clothes, papers and wires. He spots the ever-present big black hat.

'How's your day of being mysterious going?' Dan asks.

Reed laughs and thinks up a suitable reply. 'Fine thanks. How's your day of sceptic investigating panning out?' Reed notices a load of technical looking boxes on the passenger seat.

'Just on my way to an interview, as it happens. Off to see a man about a "ghost". There's an *Anomaly* article in it – if it turns out to be what I think.'

'With all your…'

'Personal computer. Yes, that's right.'

Dan also has an electro-magnetic field meter, motion detector, audio recorder and infrared camera in there, but doesn't go into detail about any of that.

Reed decides to risk a question, seeing as it's been playing on his mind all morning and here is someone who might know.

'Do you know anything about a birdwatching caretaker? Amateur photographer, maybe?'

'Not sure, what's he done?'

Reed twists a little and shrugs off the question.

Dan continues. 'I do know a few people round here, through my sister, but, honestly, I haven't been here for… quite a while… so… Why? Where did you hear about him? Is it something about the murder?'

'No. Nothing important. But I think you might be hearing about him soon.'

Dan responds with a waggle of his head and imploring hand gesture – as if to say: 'And you're not going to tell me anymore?' – but that's all the information he's going to get.

'Okay, well, be sure to thank your crystal ball for me, won't you?' Dan says and resumes his position behind the wheel.

'Will do,' Reed nods, smiling. 'And I hope you're Truth-a-Tron 5000 comes up with the goods today.'

Dan sighs and drives away, shaking his head. Reed can see him doing it through the rear window. The tyres scratch at the road and the engine chugs away. Reed watches Dan's car disappear around the corner and finds himself alone.

***

But someone is watching him. Across the road, wheeling a bike with a box of bunting in the basket, is Zoya, feeling her adrenaline spike.

Him again. She spots him through the gap between leafy ash trees. Should she go over to talk to him? She can't help feeling she wants to resume the conversation they were having last night, while she... slept? Another dream of another night visit – but then what happened? She can't remember – but it left her with a strong sense of unfinished business, like a conversation interrupted, something that drifted beyond her grasp.

The morning felt too sudden and too soon and she's been carrying around a sense of incompleteness all day. It feels like she was all geared up for going somewhere or doing something that never happened. Maybe it is just her cancelled trip.

He's still there; across the street. She feels like rushing over to talk to him because, whatever it is they end up saying, how wrong could it go? She feels the urge to close the distance – to look into his eyes and feel like they are... friends.

And why shouldn't she? He is only a person and she's usually pretty good at talking to those.

What would she say? 'Hey, I've been dreaming about you...' – bit off-putting – '... for the past three nights in a row'? No, absolutely not.

There's a strange aura about him. She feels a pull and a push. Like magnets. Something makes her want to avoid him, but she can't move away. A weird affinity? Yes. A crush? Absolutely not.

And, anyway, it isn't quite *that*. She's not *attracted* to him – but it's something she can't explain.

While she is stopped in her tracks, not knowing what to do, Reed starts walking away down the street. She watches his ambling gait as he wanders off.

Zoya rolls her eyes – why is she even thinking about him at all? Her bike rattles back to life, the box of bunting shaking in the front basket as she pushes it along the alleyway towards the Audobons' townhouse.

'Hey, stranger. I've been seeing you in my dreams.' How would that go down? The very idea makes her cringe.

***

Just west of Whale House, a lane splits from the road and runs alongside the wall. Mrs Wood is walking Grumbles, a fawn-coloured pug, and chuntering to herself about that crazy house she has to look at every day. *Why is that sculpture stuck on top of it, and anyway, it shouldn't be allowed.*

The lane plunges between the boundary wall and a line of thickening trees. The townscape gradually disappears behind tangling branches. Finely veined leaves pattern the copse with colour that ranges from fresh summer greens to early-autumn reds. The little dog is investigating plant matter which lies, decaying, beneath the blackberry bushes and nettles. He seems to find the scent fascinating.

Mrs Wood periodically yanks the lead to keep Grumbles on the path, where it is clean. Unlike the dog, she isn't interested in the growing symphony of foliage that edges the path home.

'We've got a system, Grumbles, remember? You do your business on the back garden, where nobody can see me scoop it up.'

A slave to the intriguing smells, Grumbles keeps trying his luck.

Mrs Wood lets her pet peeve fester, spinning out her disapproving thoughts for yards.

'Blot on the landscape,' she mutters.

Grumbles looks up at her, doggy eyebrows flexing. He doesn't understand. Maybe she is talking about food.

'Someone should tell the authorities. The planners should make them put it back how it was. It must have once been a handsome, upstanding sort of house, and in such a prominent position too. Shouldn't be allowed.'

Then she spies it, ahead of them in the path.

'There it is again.'

She keeps seeing that small van here, driving down the lane.

She checks her delicate little watch. *Is it here every day?* And such an odd place to park it, too. They must be up to no good.

She picks up her walking speed, and Grumbles bursts into a run. His tongue lolls out of the side of his mouth and his little eyeballs bulge.

The small van drives off before they can get there. Something untoward, she decides. Her mind is quite made up about that. They reach the place where the van parks and have a look, and a sniff, around. For the first time, among the lush foliage, she sees a heavy green gate tucked into the old stone wall. It is wide and made of metal. How has she never noticed it before?

Something underhand is definitely being perpetrated.

Then she notices Grumbles sniffing and biting at a small quantity of fronded leaves that have been trapped in the gate.

'Don't touch those, Grumbles!' she says, yanking him back by the lead.

She picks up a leafy twig and holds it at arm's length.

'Ha, drugs!'

I'm standing at the corner of the veranda, waiting. I am warm and calm but feel the tingle of electric anticipation. Something is going to happen.

'Zoya! Hey! Are you awake?'

And there he is – in the street, shifting his balance.

'I am!' I call back. 'Ready and waiting.'

I feel my cheeks ripening with the super-wide smile I don't like so much in photographs – but I can't help it. He seems to be beaming too. We are ready to spring into action.

'Wait, I'll climb up!'

I lean forward and follow his figure as he jogs towards the fence.

'You know there's a door, right?' I say. He pauses.

'You know what? Wait there – I'm coming down.'

'But it didn't work last time – I waited by the door but you never appeared.'

I tighten the laces on my trainers.

'But if *you* can climb the fence, so can I. Let the adventure begin!'

I swing my leg over the rail.

Reed steps back and covers his eyes melodramatically. Then he parts his fingers to watch me as I find a foothold. I don't know how much of his reaction is a joke and how much is genuine fear for my safety.

'Don't worry, I know what I'm doing.'

'Okay.'

He adopts another comic pose of knees knocking and finger biting. I am clinging onto the slats. As I climb down, the wood wavers a little, flexing away from the metal frame beneath. I keep moving.

He relaxes.

'Expert climber, huh?'

'No, but *you've* been doing it so… how hard can it be?' I tease.

'I'm being stupid' – his voice sounds earnest again – 'you must have done this a thousand times before.'

I reposition my foot.

'Be careful!' he calls.

'Nope, I never thought of it,' I tell him, 'until now.'

'But… you're a rock-climber?' He's guessing.

'No, had one weekend on a climbing holiday, which was fun – but that's about it.' My muscles are beginning to tire. 'Funnily enough, we didn't climb any fences though.'

I'm nearly at the bottom.

'Why would I have to be careful anyway? This is the dreaming, isn't it?'

I land on the grass, secretly pleased I didn't mess up my dismount in front of him.

He grins at me – with what seems like admiration – and then dives into some answers.

So, I listen.

'Well, first of all, I don't know that I – *we* – *can't* get hurt in this... *dreaming,* as you call it. And secondly, if you fall...'

'... you die?'

'No, you *wake up*. If you fall, you wake up in real life.'

We have started to walk down the hill.

'If you dream you are falling, you usually wake up, don't you?' he says, looking down at me.

Our paces sync up in rhythm, even though he is taller than me.

'Yes, I think everyone has that.'

'Well, it can be quite handy if you *want* to – I sometimes fall over on purpose if I want to wake myself up.'

I pause, half expecting him to do it right then and there, but he keeps on talking.

'It actually takes a bit of learning – because all your instincts are to *stop* yourself falling over, but I suppose it helps knowing that it doesn't hurt.'

He senses I'm about to give it a try and takes hold of my elbow.

'Don't try it now – you'd disappear! And I don't want you to.'

'Nor me.'

We carry on walking.

'So, where are we going?' he asks, after a few quiet seconds.

'Everywhere!'

I fling my arms out and start to spin around. He laughs.

***

Soon, we are running down the high street and, I'm not sure, but it feels like boundless energy. We just kind of went for it, starting at the top of the steep road and not stopping at the bottom – sprinting instinctively to the sea.

I must be quite fit from all the cycling and everything and he looks, well, you might say *wiry*, but I think that the dreaming is giving us an artificial boost. Never has running felt so free and so fun. I slow up – not from tiredness but because I have a million questions bubbling up in my mind.

'Do you usually run about all night like this?'

He catches his breath. 'No – not so much fun on your own.'

'Why don't you drive your van around?'

'Hmm, it's complicated. Not everything seems to work. Like, when I'm in this…'

'… dreaming?' I suggest, finishing his sentence.

'Okay, *dreaming* – I never had to name it because I've never had anyone to talk about it with before… So, not everything works. Electricity but not electronics, I think. I don't really get it, but some things work, and some things don't. But anyway, apart from that, with driving there's a safety issue.'

'But there's literally nobody else on the road!'

'Look, I'm not sure how much you've processed about what's happening yet…'

'Well…' – I walk along purposefully, considering – 'I have questions.'

'Okay, shoot.'

'Well… what if I *did* shoot you – with a gun – would it kill you in real life?'

'That's pretty dark!' He pulls a jokey expression at me. 'That's the first place your mind went to? Should I be scared?'

I laugh. 'Just an example! What I really mean is – can we get hurt?'

His eyebrows flex. 'I don't know – I don't think so. At least, I've always woken up fine. I'll warn you – there might be lots of questions I can't answer. It's hard to figure out.'

He takes both my elbows to engage my full attention, standing in front of me, face to face. 'Physically… we really *are* here.'

He says this like it is the most serious thing in the world and then watches my expression as I take it in.

'How do you know?' I ask eventually – just a question, not a challenge.

'Well, we can move things, and they *stay* moved. Except for, our bodies are still wherever we are sleeping in real life. That's where we will wake up.'

I look down at myself. 'So, we aren't really here at all?'

'But if it *feels* like we are, and we can *act* like we are, then maybe we *are.*'

'Or maybe you are just moving the things that stay moved *with your mind*,' I suggest.

He looks like this has never occurred to him before and I realise I shouldn't expect him to be able to explain it, and how could he anyway – how could *anyone*?

I stare at my hands in front of me. It really *feels* like I'm really here.

'We can touch things,' he continues, taking my hands for emphasis on 'touch'. 'We can eat.'

'Eat?'

'I do a lot of eating in this... dreaming thing, actually.'

'But eating in the dreaming can't feed your actual body, though? I mean, you do seem kind of... slender?'

'Hey!' he protests, but I can see that he isn't really offended.

As we walk on, nearing the seafront, I can see him puzzling things over, like maybe reassessing his entire life.

***

Later, we are standing outside the fancy French patisserie. Reed already seems to know his way around town.

'So, let's see what you think.' He gestures formally to the upmarket cake shop like a stiff waiter.

'But...' I begin.

'Oh, that's another thing,' – he places a hand on the sculpted brass handle – 'we can open all doors.'

And he does so, holding it open for me to go in.

Somehow, it doesn't surprise me – this whole thing feels so limitless and free. We're not really here, but we absolutely are.

Dazed, I walk inside.

The interior of the patisserie is all smooth marble and glass cabinets. There are elegant round tables for two, flanked by French patio-style chairs and matched by the vintage till at the counter – altogether posher than the one we use at the beach café. The cakes themselves are perfectly round or perfectly sliced, ornate creations, an enticing parade in paper cases; cream-piped, cherry-topped and chocolate-swirled.

I seem to be creeping gingerly, like a reluctant burglar, but Reed's footsteps across the shiny floor are loud. He doesn't even lower his voice.

'So, what do you fancy?' he is saying, moving towards the softly humming display fridges.

He starts pointing out the options by naming the cakes with made-up names.

'We've got… Stripey Slices… Far-fetched Fancies… Lemon Nostrils… Builders' Fingers… Puffy Fluff-fluffs…'

This isn't what any of the cakes are really called, of course. I stifle a laugh. 'Shh, someone will hear,' I whisper, pretty sure that the owners live above.

'They won't.'

He looks at me.

'They really won't. Oh! I love a Belgian Elbow.' He points at a caramel confection. 'Want one?'

I must look very hesitant.

'Relax, we're only going to sample one each.'

I raise my eyebrow. 'So, you're a food thief?'

'Only a little bit. I like to spread it around. Nobody notices a tiny bit of cereal missing, a slice of bread, the odd
sausage…'

He opens the chilled cabinet door and a sugary scent
drifts out. The aromas of strawberry, lemon, caramel and
chocolate mix in the air around us.

Reed has picked up a couple of eclairs and hands one to
me. We peel back the paper casing and look expectantly at
each other. This shouldn't feel so exciting. And then we go
for it, stuffing the chocolatey, creamy cakes into our faces
and laughing with our mouths full. The eclair squishes between my fingers and oozes gooey deliciousness onto my
tastebuds, the cream still cool from the fridge against my
tongue. Yes, it feels like *really* eating, and the chocolate
also seems to be sending endorphins to my brain. But then
it has all felt this way, all evening; like a sugar rush.

'What else do you steal?'

'Nothing! The odd bit of change…'

'But you spread it around…?' I say, cynically.

'I'm a good person,' he says, over-emphasising closing
the cabinet door to prove it, 'really, I am. I'm just redistrib-
uting the wealth.'

We wipe our mouths and walk out to the street again
and he drops our cake wrappers and napkins in a dustbin –
another exaggerated act of good behaviour for my benefit.
I smile.

'From a lot of people to yourself? Not quite Robin
Hood is it?'

We are pacing in the same who-knows-where direction together, across the well-kept paving slabs of the small Edwardian square. An elegant fountain bubbles away beside us.

'I like to think of it as the common weal. I would never take a lot from any *one* person. And I never take anything important.'

'What's stopping you from robbing a bank?'

***

So, a short while later, we are standing inside the bank. Actually, we are standing in the vaults because when he said we can open all doors, he meant it.

'We just walked right in!' I whisper. 'Unbelievable.'

I catch him up.

'And the security cameras won't pick us up?'

'No: electronic. It's like we're here but also *not* here.'

We walk slowly through a suite of safety deposit boxes.

'So, like, this is all really happening in our minds, but, like, in *both* of our minds?'

I stop abruptly.

'What's the matter?'

'Just… my brain hurts from thinking about all of this.'

He comes over and places a warm hand on my shoulder.

'Best thing: don't even *try* to understand it. I've never managed to – and I've been doing this all my life.'

'Zen and the art of dream-time wandering, eh?'

I nod, then shake my head. Reed is watching me, smiling.

We walk past more shiny boxes, across immaculate dust-free floors. I can almost feel the weight of the building above us. Everything feels stagnant and smells of metal.

The safety deposit boxes clang as we take them out, poke around and then put everything exactly back in place. We discover jewellery, of course, and ivory ornaments, keys, gold nuggets and commemorative coins. Some of the contents are quite surprising and perplex us. We find computer discs, a small Jesus figurine, pebbles, puppets, a glass eyeball and one shoe. Some of the metal drawers contain other boxes, one is jade, another dark walnut inlaid with a pattern. There are antique knives, a toupee and a monocle, lockets stuffed with hair.

Then we replace everything just where we found it. Nobody will ever know.

'But it would be useful to know the rules…' I say, having thought about it.

Reed instantly understands and starts to summarise for me. 'All doors are open. If I fall, I wake. It's all real.'

'We,' I say.

He nods. 'We.'

He takes off the diamond headpiece he's been wearing ridiculously, and puts it gently back in its box.

'*See*, I'm not a thief,' he says, showing me his empty palms, like a magician.

'Well, we're not stealing people's possessions, but we are sort of stealing their privacy,' I say, instantly regretting my seriousness – but I do have a point. I notice that Reed even seems to agree with me.

'Yes, privacy. It *is* an issue. I don't snoop around the houses of people I know.'

He takes the safety deposit box and slots it back into place.

'But what about your fingerprints?'

'I never used to think about it, but now the police have them on file, so I might have to.'

'But if we leave fingerprints, then I suppose we must really *be* here.'

'Yes, but then, my prints should have already been on that shed, where they found the…'

I nod briskly and he gets my gist and doesn't finish the sentence.

'But, the point is, the police never placed me at the scene because of that, so maybe we *don't* leave fingerprints at all.'

'You were there the night she died?'

'No, another night, and I didn't know she was there. So anyway, I don't know if we leave fingerprints or not.'

'You're right. It's best not to overthink it. Let's get out of here. I could do with some air.'

We make our way through some heavy-duty doors, closing them behind us. I decide to recap, getting it straight in my head.

'We can open doors and move stuff. If we fall, we wake up. We don't get picked up on security cameras. We *proba-*

bly don't leave fingerprints.' I think for a bit. 'What do you mean '*it's all real*'?'

'We're in real places,' he explains. 'This is the real bank. I haven't imagined what I *think* the bank vault *might* be like – this is the real one. If we could come back when we're awake, it would be exactly like this.'

'I don't think we'll be able to manage that,' I say, 'but let's test it somehow.'

'Okay, where do you want to go?'

We reach the street once more and close the imposing doors of the bank behind us, with some effort, and then sit down on the broad, stone steps. They drop away neatly to a colourful pattern of tiles that pave their way into the small public square off to our right. The stone feels pleasantly cool at my fingertips, his leg, warm at my thigh.

After a few minutes just sitting there, quietly enjoying the glimmer of dawn, he turns to me.

'I bet there's somewhere you've always wanted to have a nosey in?'

'Yes,' I reply, 'there is.'

CHAPTER 22

'You've never been to the theatre before?' Reed asks, dubiously.

'Of course I have! But never behind the scenes.'

We are standing in front of the Titania Theatre on a dusty patch of pavement, looking at the blank marquee.

'Nice little theatre.'

'Well, it's the only one we've got.'

We approach a pair of doors and he goes to take the handle, but I cut in. 'Allow me.'

I open it for him. We nod, formally, as he goes inside.

At first, the foyer is murky and grey. Then the ceiling bulbs blink, sequentially, to life. Reed has found the switch.

There isn't much to see: burgundy carpet, empty poster hoardings, an abandoned wheel of cable and an empty cloakroom. Some of the hangers have fallen to the floor. I've been here for cinema screenings, comedy gigs and live music – but not recently, I note.

We swing open the doors to the auditorium and find it blanketed in fusty grey nothingness. There don't seem to be any light switches on the wall.

'What we need are the houselights,' Reed suggests.

We figure out that the control room must be on the upper floor and rush upstairs to find it. Then we just turn *everything* on. We play around with combinations of switches, laughing at the disco-tastic light show we are inadvertently creating. He starts singing a Bee Gees song.

Back down in the auditorium, now modestly lit, we walk up the aisle. The rows of curled seats present a sea of red waves. You can just tell that their hinges recoil with a squeak and a bang. The place smells musty.

Reed is wheeling around to look at the ornately decorated ceiling and balconies with a sense of curious awe. I'm noticing the fraying fabric, crackled paintwork and flaking plaster. I feel a twinge of sadness about the state of disrepair.

We walk right up to the front because, of course, we have to go and stand on the stage. We walk across the wooden boards that are marked with scuffs and stains and speckled bits of paint. There is a safety curtain hanging high over our heads. Peering up into the shadows, I see ropes and gantries and lighting rigs. The velvet curtains hang in swoops and there are draughty wings, cutting away to darkness, at the sides.

Once up here, the stage feels smaller than it looked. The empty seats seem to crowd us expectantly as we stand there with nothing to do. Suddenly, the whole surreal everything catches up with me and I get into an uncontrollable fit of laughter. He laughs too but then looks concerned as I have to lie on the floor. I can't stop my breathless laughing and I feel I might pee.

Reed sits down beside me, to check that I'm okay. His eyes are bright, watching me, and he keeps catching my contagious laugh.

I gather myself.

'Shhh!'

He looks intrigued by my sudden seriousness.

'Someone lives here.'

He immediately looks over his shoulder into the wings, like I might have just seen something behind him.

'No, not like *Phantom of the Opera*. Just old Quentin, the impresario. I think he owns the theatre. I think he has an apartment here somewhere.'

'Don't worry, we won't disturb him.' Reed hops to his feet. 'Come on, you said you wanted to nosey about backstage.'

He offers his hand and pulls me to my feet. Then we wander off into the wings, weaving between curtains and flats and rows of tethered ropes and pulleys, careful not to trip over anything.

As we go, I tease: 'Never had you down as a disco fan, never in a million years!'

'Well, people can surprise you.'

He flashes a cheeky grin.

We explore the warren of stores and discover a treasure trove of props: painted backdrops, trees, furniture, a cut-out of a passenger train. By the time we reach the costume department, we have run a bit out of steam. We stroll through long breeze-block rooms lined with bustling rows of colour, clothes on hangers jostling for space. Heavy brocade hangs next to shiny nylon, soft chiffon by starchy netting, peasants, princesses and popes. Full skirts and scratchy petticoats catch at my jeans as I pass.

It would be too overwhelming to choose something to try on for fun so, instead, I sit on a large trunk. Reed reappears and joins me at the doorway, plonking himself on a box, all knees.

'You know what?' I say, leaning back on the cold wall. My voice echoes in the stairwell.

'What?'

'I don't really feel like playing dress-up, after all. I'm just happy being me.'

'Me too.'

Then we sit there noticing the set of steps that lead up.

'Come on, we haven't been everywhere yet,' he says, so I follow him up the stairs.

***

We find ourselves on the luxury carpet of a landing that leads to a single glossy teak door. The eaves curve to the ceiling. We must have reached the top. A polished console table has been adorned with a crystal vase of sprightly roses and the lock and handle are shining brass. It looks like we've found Quentin's apartment.

Reed has already taken hold of the door handle and so I whisper: 'No!'

I shake my head vigorously and widen my eyes at him. We shouldn't.

'Don't you want to see his apartment? I bet it's really kooky,' he says, in his normal speaking voice.

'No!' I hiss. 'We're not tiptoeing round someone's home. If we disturb him, he'll have a heart attack!'

He puts his hands on my shoulders and adopts a kindly teacher-ish tone. 'Listen to me. There's nobody there. There's nobody *anywhere*. It's like the whole world belongs to us alone. If we go inside that flat, it will be like he's just not home. He's probably sleeping, right? But, to us, it will be like he isn't there.'

I shuffle back a bit, away from the door. 'What if he's awake, though?'

'No, *really*, if he's awake, it will be exactly like he isn't even there, and if he's asleep – well, there's usually a clue. Easiest way to understand is if I show you.'

He gestures with a nod towards the door.

I hesitate. 'I don't feel good about poking around in someone's home.'

He looks at me a moment before replying.

'Fine, let's go...'

He moves to walk down the other, plusher staircase, the one that probably leads straight outside. He seems to just be respecting my wishes, rather than calling my bluff, but I find that I'm not following, and my feet remain rooted to the floor. I *do* want to go inside.

'Okay then. I want to take a look.'

One of us turns the handle and the other pushes open the door. Together, we peer into the cluttered living room that appears before us, and then we go in. It's everything I imagined of Quentin – and probably quite a bit more. Cleaner than I might have guessed but just as busy, with swishy drapes and swags and colourful theatre posters on the walls. The room is hung with framed black-and-white photographs – signed, as you would expect – but I don't spot any family photographs on display.

A couple of Victorian table lamps, already on, are giving the room a warm, cosy glow, though there is now also daylight filtering through the net curtains. It feels like a safe cocoon, filled with a life lived fully, and with just the right things. It is delightfully archaic, but then, so is he.

I notice a welcoming, luxurious musk; part aftershave and hair pomade; part meats, wines, sherries and cakes; part fresh flowers; part fireplace. The floor is soft with rugs.

Quentin certainly knows how to live.

He has himself shelves full of weird ornaments and a magician kit, a beautiful walnut drinks cabinet and a life-sized wooden carving of some pin-up showgirl type. A favourite armchair has been placed, with matching footstool, in front of the cosy hearth.

I'm surprised to see live embers, but then I think, *why not?*

It's not as though *time* has stood still. These glowing embers are just like the wind ruffling the trees and the waves and the advancing dawn. I realise then, that we *do* have a time limit, because at some point – well, at *any* moment – our sleeping bodies will wake up.

I continue creeping around the apartment. He has an upholstered telephone bench with a vintage phone. There is also a large, leather-bound diary scrawled with bookings, it pleases me to note. The kitchen is quite tiny, kind of 1950s in its sparseness and lack of fitted units. I expect he has rich, elaborate meals at the local restaurants, and, perhaps, also delivered in.

There's even some kind of roof terrace where, poking my head out, I see a large rabbit hutch. This pleases me too. I should make friends with Quentin and come visit. I haven't seen so much as a wedding picture, but I bet he has wonderful stories to tell. Perhaps there is something in the bedroom, maybe by the bed. I look over to the unexplored room. I do *want* to go in.

Reed spots my hesitation. He has been mostly delving into a box of tricks and inexplicable equipment. It seems like crossing a line until I observe just how carefully he does this, gently touching each object and placing it back exactly where it was.

He sees me by the bedroom door. 'It's okay,' he says encouragingly, 'there's nobody in there.'

So, I push it open and see a very well-dressed bed with a silk headboard. There are thicker curtains in here, shrouding the window and making it dark. I spot a tall, wooden wardrobe with a strip of mirror. I'm not going to go any further inside.

'So, you're saying that Quentin, right now, is sleeping there in that bed, and I just can't see him?'

I'm standing at the threshold.

Reed has remained in the parlour and is looking towards the hearthside chair. I see that it is flanked by a glass of sherry on a side table.

'Actually, I think he might be sleeping in that chair.'

I feel a bit freaked out by this as I've circled that corner a few times.

'Looks like a comfy spot,' I agree, 'but how do you know?'

'I don't *know* know, but I'd put money on it. See those clothes – that's what he's wearing.'

I look closer and notice that what might have been a throw is really a silk robe and pyjamas.

Reed goes on. 'We can't know for certain, but that's usually what it means. It *could* just be a pile of clothes someone left there, but… you have to look at the context.'

I close the bedroom door as I found it.

'Awake people are just invisible to us,' he explains. 'It's like… we are in the same place but a different dimension to them… or something – who knows?'

We mirror each other in a dramatic, palms-up gesture, rapidly developing our shorthand for discussing this phenomenon that only we know.

'But sleeping people look like little piles of clothes,' he concludes.

'But *we* don't wake up naked?' I point out, glancing down at my clothes.

'Well, we're not really awake,' he reminds me. '*Your* sleeping body is still safely tucked up at home and that's where you'll wake up. If you fell off the theatre roof you'd still wake up at home in bed.'

'And you've tried this?'

I move away from the disturbingly empty-but-not-empty armchair, walk through the kitchen and out onto the roof. I pass the rabbit hutch, which is all wood and chicken wire and hay escaping onto the floor. I can see lettuce leaves but no Mrs Miggles in there.

Reed follows me, his footsteps crunching on the gungrey weather-pocked felt. I'm standing by the railing at the edge.

'Please don't!' he implores. 'I'd lose you for the night.'

'But have *you* tried it?'

'I've tried lots of things.'

I stand there with my hands on a low railing, looking at the back streets below and thinking. 'But time still goes... normally?'

I'm looking up at the sky, but the narrow terrace is on the wrong side of the building to see any of the sunrise and, in fact, we are standing in shadow.

'Yes, normally. Or, if it's dilated in some way, there's no way of knowing. I just think of it as real world, real time.'

I recite the facts. 'We can open any door. If we move things, they stay moved. If we fall, we wake. Sleeping people – piles of clothes. Waking people disappear. Real world, real time.'

He gives me a wholesome, Agent Cooper-style thumbs up.

'If we wanted to, we could sit on that sofa and watch the fire going out, but I'd rather go somewhere to see the sunrise?'

He inflects his statement to ask the question of me. I smile and walk back inside as assent.

As we pass the armchair on our way out, I have to ask: 'Are you sure that isn't just a random pile of clothes he's just left there?'

'Well, it's just an educated guess. From all these years.'

I silently mull it over – how long has this been going on for him? How many places must he have been? I steal another glance at the chair.

Then I tell him: 'You know. This is all freaking me out. Quite a lot.'

'Yeah, me too.'

'But this is your life?'

'I just realised something,' he half explains enigmatically.

'What?'

'Tell you later,' he says, and sounds like he means it. 'Let's go and get some fresh air.'

Soon enough, we are down by the beach, sitting on the bench and looking out across the waves. The sun has barely risen, dashing out pinks and peaches along the bay.

'Warm, isn't it?' Reed asks me.

Although the sea breeze is fluttering my hair, I feel no early-morning chill to the air.

'Yeah.'

He's right. I look at him expectantly.

'Yeah, that's another thing. It's always warm in the… dreaming. It's one way to recognise where you are. You know: if you're awake or not.'

I hadn't imagined ever getting it confused.

'Not like you feel over-heated, just that little bit warmer, like always warm *enough*. It's an Indian summer, right, but this is England – it's always chilly at night.'

I nod to him, getting it. 'And not just warm, but sort of physically contented,' I add.

I didn't want to use the word 'sensual', for some reason, but that's what I mean.

'Yeah, I know what you mean.'

We sit there nodding and noticing our sensations.

'Why *is* that?' I wonder out loud.

'Who knows?' he answers in a comedy voice, and we both do the palm-shrug thing, without even looking at one another.

The wide bay curves away, indented with coves and clifftops and stretches of sand. The sea looks smooth in the distance but is choppier by the land, where rippling waves lap the rocks. There is a large canopy of clear, blue-ing sky above us and the sun peeps over the glowing horizon. Meandering sea scents reach us from the wet, plashing shore.

'So, what was it that you realised? That freaked you out back there?' I venture.

'Oh... nothing. It doesn't matter.'

'Hey,' – I take hold of his shoulder to make him look at me – 'we're in the *same dream*.' I hear wonder in my voice even though that's not the tone I was going for. 'Or whatever it is! It's like we're the only two people in the entire world right now!' I fling an arm out in gesture. 'I think you can tell me.'

He just looks down at his fidgeting fingers. 'Okay. I *will* tell you.' Then he glances at me sideways. 'But it isn't very nice.'

I turn my body to face him and lean my arm over the back of the bench. He warms up to whatever he's about to say. 'You know the little piles of clothing?'

'That's where a sleeping person is,' I say, as if trying to pass a test.

'I always thought so – and it's true – but I just realised: it also means something else.'

I just keep watching and listening.

'It must be the same for dead bodies.' His bright eyes look up at me to check my reaction. He bows his head. 'Like that woman in the garden shed.'

'Oh!' I almost put my arm around him. 'I'm sure Quentin is fine though!' And I do feel sure.

'Yes. But now I'm thinking of all those times – those little piles of clothes. Most of them – *most* of them – would have been sleeping, but some of them might – *must* – have been dead.'

I notice his skin has goosebumps and I know it cannot be from any kind of chill.

'And I never knew,' he continues, 'and I was right there. And I never did anything.'

What can I say? The places he's been, the night's he's spent like this, it's probably true.

'But you couldn't have known…'

All I can hear, like absolutely the only sounds, are the relentless waves of the sea crashing towards us. I feel the need to brighten the mood again. 'Best not to think about it too much!'

I'm sure he has said the same thing to me sometime this past night.

'So, *are* we the only two people in the world right now? In the whole entire world?'

'Put it this way,' he says, straightening up again, 'I've never once found another, erm… "dreamer" – until you.' He smiles faintly then looks back to the horizon. 'And I've been searching for a long time.'

'Now, *I've* got the chills,' I confess and gaze up to the fluffy clouds being moulded in the sky.

'Why aren't there any birds here?' I ask, because it is the oddest thing about the dawn today.

'No animals,' he states broadly. 'No people, no animals. But everything else is the same.'

'Who knows, right?' I say, answering my own next question, and then I stand up to stretch my legs, turning my back on the empty sea. 'I couldn't live in a world without animals.'

I stand on the bench and look up to my house on the distant hill. You can just about make it out even from here.

'You must have a cool family,' he tells me.

'I do,' I say, and plop down onto the sand.

He gets up from the bench and we start walking eastwards along the beach in the direction of the rising sun, pushing our feet into the soft give of the sand. The dawn light is picking out the reds of his hair.

'But it's just me and my dad now, at home. My mum passed away when I was quite young.'

'Oh, I'm sorry. Do you remember her?'

'Yes – and she was awesome.' I playfully kick a mound of sand. 'I was eight when she died of cancer.'

I don't want the conversation to drift into sympathy, though, and so I babble on.

'Did you know she was twenty years older than my dad? Other people seem to think that's odd or something, but they never cared.' I smile. 'They met in Africa, when they both had the wanderlust, and then came back to live in her family house, here. He worked at the zoo and she wrote novels. I still have her typewriter.'

Reed is watching me quite closely now. I wonder if he is having thoughts about the colour of my skin. 'Is your name African?'

'Yes, it is. East African. It means *dawn*.'

'It's a cool name.'

'That's my mum's doing. Zoya is also Greek for *life*, so she probably liked it for that too. But then she was called Calliope… so…'

'Calliope! That's a name and a half.'

I laugh. 'There's also been a Bartholomeus and a Michiel and an Egberdina – but that's because they were sort of Dutch, my mum's family. Great Aunt Jolien was the best, a sort of Edwardian adventuress. No, *really*! My mum based her first novel on her travels. Well, I'll tell you another time. Dad's from Manchester.'

'And your dad uses a wheelchair?' Reed asks, then explains: 'I met a friend of his in the pub, said you people at Whale House are "*fine people*".'

'Fine people,' I echo, nodding smugly.

'So, was he in an accident?'

'No. His legs used to be fine. It's a condition, well, disease, that made them weaken over time.'

'And he manages that steep hill?'

'We do have cars, you know. Actually, he doesn't go out *that* much; we have a lot of people round instead.'

'If I lived in a house like that, I'd probably stay at home a lot too.'

'But you can live in any house you want to – you can live in *all* the houses!' I say, suddenly realising.

'And so can you. So, what else did your mum write about?'

'Many, many things. She used to write in my tower room, *her* tower room. I have her desk and stuff.'

'Do you look like her?'

'Actually, I'm adopted. Mum was already, like forty, when Dad fell in love with her. But I was just a little, name-less baby when they adopted me, so they've always been my mum and dad. Okay, so, how about you?'

'I can see why you don't want to leave this place.'

'I will leave, one day.'

We walk on for a bit, past the old hotel with its wrought-iron balconies, the sunlight shining orange on the windows.

'What about *your* parents?' I ask again.

'I don't have any. I'm all alone in the world.'

He spins around to look at the empty town and stops ahead of me.

'Almost literally – apart from you.'

He's looking at me funny, searchingly, his face serious in front of mine. I think I shuffle backwards and feel something like driftwood rolling under my foot. And then I feel like I'm falling but I never hit the ground.

CHAPTER 24

Dan slaps a crumpled piece of paper on the counter for Chief Inspector Barrow to read.

Which birdwatcher is hiding shameful surveillance secrets under their mattress? TAKE CARE that they don't take their cameras to work or EAVESdropping on your children is the least of your worries.

'Look, I don't know who wrote this, or how they know, or even if it's true, but you have to go and check it out.'

Frank Barrow slowly leans forward for a better look, deliberately giving the signal that he won't be rushed. A tiny tear at the top of the page suggests that the message has been ripped from a pin board somewhere and there is a sweaty crease from Dan's clutch.

Frank knows Dan Mather a bit by now. It's good for Sarah's boy to have him around. Frank watches him pacing in front of the duty desk. He seems serious.

A colleague places a cup of tea by the chief inspector's elbow then returns to the bustling office beyond the security door. It closes behind him, sealing away the sounds.

Dan is waiting for a response.

There could be something behind this note, or perhaps Dan's desperation to explain the unexplained death is at play. Frank is feeling the burden of not being able to get the woman justice and not being able to put Sarah's mind to rest, but he doesn't express it.

'How are you getting on with the murder enquiry so far?' demands Dan, his sweaty fists resting on the duty desk.

Frank clasps his hands together, about to compose an answer.

'Thought so. Just go and question this guy.'

Dan emphasises his plea by jabbing a thick finger at the cryptic name on the paper.

'Mr Mather. Listen, I understand how stressful this must all have been for your family, so I forgive your brusque tone, but *I* instruct the police officers around here.'

Frank takes a plastic evidence bag, opens it in the approved manner and gestures for Dan to place the note inside.

'Thank you,' he says, sealing the bag.

'Do you know who that is?' Dan is expecting to be fobbed off with some empty reassurances but has to ask.

'Constable Walker. Get Brooks. There's someone we need to talk to.'

'Yes!' Dan exclaims, pumping a fist in triumph.

Frank doesn't look impressed. 'Calm down, Mr Mather, you'll be staying here with me.'

***

Soon, a police car is parked by the Glebe in front of Sunnyview Lodge. A curtain twitches at a window.

Sergeant Brooks gets out of the car. Constable Walker follows him up the stone steps of the old manse. Brooks rings the doorbell. On the second ring, the door is opened by a man in a scruffy jumper. He seems strangely excited to see them.

'What is it? Someone in trouble?' he asks.

'We just have some questions for Brian Eaves – lives here doesn't he?'

'Yes. What has he done?'

'I knew it,' his expression seems to say.

'You're Mr…' – the sergeant looks at his notes – 'Mr Derby.'

The man nods.

'You're the caretaker, is that correct?'

'The estates manager, yes.'

'Look, we don't want to make a scene at your doorway, Mr Derby.'

'Vince.'

'We know there have been naysayers and rumours spread, ever since this place opened up. Best if you just let us in.'

'Of course, officer, it's just that I don't think he's in right now. In fact…' – Vince focuses his eyes beyond them – 'there he is now.'

They look around to see a red Ford Orion driving along the far edge of the park.

'That's his car.'

Vince Derby is pointing at it with a yellow smoker's finger.

Then the driver pulls a sudden U-turn and takes off at a faster speed. Vince watches from the doorway at the top of the steps as the police rush back to their car and drive off. There's even a hint of tyre squeal, which pleases him to hear.

Vince watches even after all the vehicles have disappeared from sight, smiling. Then he kicks the doorstop away and closes the door.

***

Elsewhere in Shilly-on-Sea, a stakeout is taking place. In the single-track lane up on the hill, Mrs Wood and Grumbles the pug are waiting by some bushes.

She is spying on the gate in the wall. He is working on a dog chew.

Mrs Wood saw the vehicle go in earlier – but it hasn't yet come out. A clang reverberates along the wall. Grumbles pricks his ears.

The chunky little van emerges into the lane. Its tyres are smeared with squelches of earth, and scraps of foliage have caught in the wheel arches.

They spring into action. Straightening her back with a wince, and then galumphing along the path, Mrs Wood runs towards the van – very much on a mission. Grumbles trots along behind.

Up ahead, the van parks up and a young lad hops out to pull the metal gate shut. Walking back to the van, he double-takes to see a small, middle-aged woman standing in front of the vehicle. A small dog is sniffing away at a wheel.

'Stop! Stop right there, young man.' She yanks the dog closer by the lead. 'Don't go near him, Grumbles.'

'Stop what?' the lad asks, bemused.

'Whatever it is you're doing. Do you want me to perform a citizen's arrest?'

The lad bends down slowly to stroke the little pug, who is now busy sniffing his boots.

'Grumbles!' she commands.

A smile plays on Dale's lips. 'I'd like to see you try,' he says, without the slightest hint of aggression. He waits for her to see the funny side.

'Every day I see you, almost every day, parking in this lane with your van. I demand to know what you are up to.'

Dale kicks his boots clean at the verge and moves towards the driver's door.

'I don't know what you're on about. I just work for the nursery.'

Grumbles is now running up and down alongside the van, as far as the lead will allow.

'You expect me to believe that…'

'The horticultural nursery – you know, the garden centre?'

Dale has realised that this isn't a conversation he needs to be having and makes to get back in the van. The little pug is overexcited.

'You should control your dog better; I nearly stepped on him.'

'Don't you threaten us; I've made a note of your registration number.'

Dale rolls his eyes.

'And I'll be passing it on to the police.'

'Right. Fine. Okay,' he says, not rising to it.

It's a pleasant, sunny day and he's a level-headed young man.

'I'm just doing my job. I don't know what this is about. I think you must have got me mistaken for someone else.' He gets into the driver's seat and pulls the door closed. 'So, if you don't mind, I'll be going now.'

Grumbles has slipped Mrs Wood's grip and is running wildly around and around the van.

'Can you pick him up? I don't want to drive over him.'

'Don't think I won't be checking with your employer.'

Mrs Wood takes a swipe at collecting the little dog but comes up empty-handed. She follows him, circling the van.

Dale gets out of the vehicle again. Maybe he can pick up the wayward little dog and safely get out of there.

'You don't have to do that,' he replies, responding to Mrs Wood's statement.

He holds out a friendly hand to the wildly circling dog, who swerves past him.

'I don't know what it is you think I've done.'

They converge at the rear of the van by the freight doors. Grumbles is now jumping up and down to get a better sniff.

'So, what's in this vehicle? Grumbles seems to have got hold of the scent. If you're just an innocent gardener, as you would have me believe, why don't you open it up and show me?'

She taps briskly on the van.

'No, really. You *really* don't want me to do that.'

'Aha! Open it up this instant!'

'No, you really don't want me to.'

'I most certainly do.'

'No, you really *don't.*'

'I insist on it.'

'No, I'm saying, you wouldn't thank me if I did.'

'Go on, open it.'

'Believe me.'

'I'm waiting.'

'Look. I *can* do that, yes, no problem at all for *me*. But, trust me, you really don't want me to.'

'That's quite enough backchat, young man. Why don't youths respect their elders these days?'

'Okay then.'

Dale fits the key in the lock and turns it. Then he looks at her with an I-told-you-so expression already prepared.

'Here you go.'

He opens the doors and steps back to watch her reaction.

First, Mrs Wood's eyes widen in shock and then her face crumples in disgust. Grumbles turns and flees down the lane, his curly little tail bobbing in the distance.

CHAPTER 25

The next day feels unreal to Zoya, as if waking life is the dream.

She drifted through the motions of breakfast, errands, conversations, not altogether present, as if there and *not* there at the same time. She found herself at work in the café. Everything's the same. Everything's different.

She serves meals, clears tables, talks to regulars. And all along, playing and replaying the memory of last night.

When not daydreaming, she watches people, looking out for that one, tall figure, wondering where he might be right now. His shiny blue camper van is still there, parked by the promenade, but where is *he*?

The day wears on. Customers come and go. Eventually, the certainty of it all evaporates, the way dreams fade from waking memory, like cool mists warmed by the sea.

Then, she sees Reed walking towards the café and a bolt of excitement prickles her skin. Without thinking, she dashes outside, bumping into his body; surprising herself and unbalancing him.

They grasp hands to steady themselves and to lock eyes and to feel the physical reality of one another; right here, in the waking world. They whirl around and away from the doorway – an arm around a waist, a hand on a shoulder, tangoing footsteps, a scramble of interlocking limbs. Two people, one delirious motion. Tangled together, they settle in an embrace by the back wall; secretive whispers; infectious laughter; small, quick kisses.

They are talking over one another.

'So, it isn't a dream?'

'You disappeared! No, it's real.'

'I just woke up at home in bed. It really happened?'

'Yes, that's how it goes. So, you remember everything?'

'I remember it *all*. It all really happened?'

'Yes!'

They are resting against the wall, bodies folded into one another, eye inches from eye; gentle, instinctive kisses to test that the other is real. He exists and she exists, and they are really, absolutely, *here*.

She puts a hand up to feel the softness of his hair and they giggle at the preposterousness of their secret, shared experience and the very randomness of being alive in the world, and together. They are standing so close he can see his own face reflected in her shining, deep brown eyes. Here they are, two very different people, sharing the same feeling: where do I end and you begin?

'And I thought today would feel like the *comedown*,' Reed jokes.

She likes his bashful expression in extreme close-up.

'I know! It must look like we're high.'

They laugh and drag their gaze from one another. They seem to be alone.

They find themselves leaning on the back wall of the café, standing in the empty car park, a few metres from the grubby bins. There is nobody on the promenade.

'So, it's real. You physically exist,' Zoya reiterates, kissing his mouth to check.

'And so do you,' he replies, stooping to bury his face in her corkscrewing hair.

He brings his nose to her neck, inhaling. Zoya looks at the view in front of her; everything different, everything the same.

'We really *have* been hanging out in our dreams,' she murmurs, getting it straight in her head.

There's something to actually saying it – with her vocal chords, with her tongue and lips. There's something about releasing the words on molecules of air that drift past his mouth and cheek and ear. She can see the tiny hairs growing from his jaw. The two of them are really here, together in space and time.

There is a faint frying hiss coming from the kitchen window and a delicate distant sprinkle of waves falling over the rocky shore.

'You don't know how long I've looked for another,' Reed tells her.

He means another dreamer; someone to share it with. She understands.

They kiss again, kissing like lovers, then draw back to see each other, breath warm, eyes dancing. Wasn't it always like this?

A car chugs past, swerves to the wrong side of the street and brakes with an audible sigh. Dan is erupting from the open driver's door.

'I need your help,' he bellows, jogging towards them.

He grabs Reed by the arm and drags him back to the idling vehicle.

'Sorry sweetheart,' Dan calls over his shoulder to Zoya. 'I hate to interrupt a love scene, but I'll get him back to you in one piece.'

She stands there, watching.

Reed finds himself deposited in the passenger seat of Dan's car, his thoughts whirring to catch up.

'But where are we going? Is it about the murder?'

'Worse than that – it's Matthew.'

Zoya watches the rusty car tear off down the road and veer around a corner and then they are gone. She already misses his touch.

***

Inside the speeding car, Reed adjusts himself to the new scenario, absorbing Dan's worry and concern.

'Is he hurt?'

Dan takes another corner too fast. It flings Reed off balance. He grasps the handle and tenses his thighs, trying to stay in place.

'He's been seen talking to some man with a red Ford. We got a call.'

They speed along, heading inland and out of town. Reed doesn't know what to say. His body now feels drenched with anxiety, but, deep down, the warm feeling is still there.

Dan seems to be driving to a specific location, using shortcuts to get there as fast as he can.

'And *I'm* the muscle?' Reed asks, finally trying to ease the tension.

'I'm hardly in the peak of physical fitness myself, I just didn't have time to assemble the A-team!'

Dan swings the Cavalier around a corner into a retail park. Reed takes it in: wood-chipped beds planted with saplings; parking spaces marked with bright new lines of paint.

'There, a red Ford!'

Reed cranes to look and the car lurches to a stop. The retail unit nearby has tents in the window. They look at the car: there's nobody in it – no unidentified man, no Matthew either.

'What about *that* guy?' Reed pipes up.

A man in his forties is walking away from the shop, carrying some purchases in his arms.

Dan leaps out of the car to confront him.

'Hey, hey *you*.' He marches over to the man. 'I want to talk to you.'

The man stops in his tracks, staring at Dan with pinhole eyes. He looks worried.

'Yes, you! I just want to talk to you.'

Reed realises he should back Dan up and releases the passenger door. The man drops his purchases on the tarmac and starts to run. Dan follows. The man runs past the shop, tramples over the bedding plants and keeps going.

Dan, already panting, calls over his shoulder: 'Come on!'

Reed sets off; he has some catching up to do. One by one, they clamber over a waist-high fence onto fallow land. One by one, they weave through a thin copse of straggly trees, patter through a boggy patch and plunge into the deeply grooved ridges of a freshly ploughed field.

Reed's trainer squelches in the mud.

He sees the other two running away ahead of him, but slowly, the field slowing their efforts.

He keeps them in his sights, his long legs helping him to make up some ground, until he hits the worst of it too; wet ribbons of manure-rich clay that drag his heavy feet. The chase becomes slow-motion.

All three men are making comically laborious progress, chasing after one another, plunging their way through the energy-sapping mud. Reed finds it exhausting but keeps following Dan who keeps following the man, who keeps running – slowly – away.

He can hear a crow calling somewhere, and even a distant cow.

Up ahead, it looks like Dan is about to catch the man – but he executes a lunge that misses and lands on his belly with a splat.

Reed passes him, now only metres behind the man.

'Bring him down!' coaches Dan, struggling to his hands and knees.

Reed puts himself in range and flings his body at the man, the first rugby tackle of his life. He brings him down with an even louder splat.

The two of them lie there in the mud, catching their breath, their energy all spent. Reed can hear Dan panting, slipping and scrabbling up behind them. He is barking orders.

'Hold on to him. Don't let him go.'

The man doesn't look to be going anywhere – just breathing and keeping his face out of the mud.

Dan appears above them. Breathlessly, he gestures for Reed to get off the man and prepares to move in.

'Nice tackle,' he pants, 'and now for *my* skill set.'

He sits on the man's back.

'Sitting?'

'I'll keep him here. You go for the police.'

Dan and Reed are sitting in the peach living room, wearing dressing gowns. Reed has borrowed some pyjamas. Dan's curls are springing up as they dry, and Reed's face is pink and shiny from a hot shower. They are kicking back on the sofas, each holding a bottle of beer.

Reed looks around the room at the cabinets, ornaments and framed Bible quotations. The creeping glow of sunset colours the street outside.

Sarah bustles into the room and deposits an armload of bedding on Reed's couch.

'Your clothes will be dry by morning.'

He can hear the comforting hum of the tumble dryer.

'I don't know how you manage, sleeping in a car all the time.'

'Thanks, Sarah.' Reed smiles politely. 'You're very kind – and thanks for dinner too.'

'Yes, thanks, sis,' agrees Dan. 'It was delicious.'

They sound like naughty schoolboys trying to make amends.

'That's okay.' Sarah is standing by the doorway. She looks from one to the other, before fixing her gaze on the guest. 'I was wrong about you.'

She turns to Dan. 'Thanks for what you did. I know you were just trying to protect Matthew.'

She looks back at Reed. 'Both of you.'

Her words are heartfelt. She flashes a look at Dan. 'He doesn't know anything about it, by the way, so don't say anything.'

Reed sees Dan nodding, though he doesn't look that convinced. Sarah stretches her spine. 'I'm exhausted,' she announces, changing her tone. 'After putting him to bed, I'm going to have a nice long soak, I think. You gents finished with the bathroom?'

'Yep.'

'Yes – thanks. Enjoy your bath.'

Sarah returns Reed's smile and makes her way upstairs.

'Do you think she'll tuck us in too?' Dan jokes, stage-whispering. He chuckles.

Reed's face crinkles as he suppresses a laugh.

'You're welcome to move your van here too, park in the drive, use the facilities.'

Reed shakes his head.

'You want another beer?' Dan hops up and goes to the kitchen.

Reed sits there, feeling comfy and looked-after, watching the long shadows in the street.

'So, there's a girl?' Dan hands him a fresh beer, raising his eyebrows. 'That's what's keeping you in town?'

Dan sinks back down in his spot with a grin but, thankfully, doesn't follow it up with blokey banter. Reed doesn't want to explain.

'No,' he answers, 'the *police* are keeping me in town.'

Dan nods, but keeps the half smirk on his face and says nothing in reply. Reed tries to keep his own expression blank but just thinking of her brings a smile. He tries to straighten it out. He checks the alcohol content on the beer bottle and takes a swig.

'So, who is she?'

'I, er, she's great! It's not like that… It's… I don't often meet people I can connect with…' Reed lays a palm across his eyes, then pushes it through his hair and changes the subject. 'So, do you think it was this guy?'

'The murder or the one trying to get Matthew in his car?'

Oh, yeah, thinks Reed, *some serious stuff has been going on, best not to look so pleased with myself.* He tries to push Zoya from his mind.

'Either. What *did* Matthew say about it?'

He feels convinced Dan would have taken the child aside to find out.

'Nothing at all.' Dan's mouth flattens into a thin line and he slowly shakes his head. 'You know, we don't even know that really happened. Could have been any kid getting picked up by his dad. Sarah's friend thought she recognised him but… I think what's happened, has made us a bit jumpy – paranoid.' He snaps into a lighter mood. 'Maybe we just pushed an innocent man's face into the mud!'

They laugh. No more adventures for today.

'But why was he running away?'

Dan responds by widening his eyes and giving a slow shake of his head. The telephone rings in the hall so Dan goes to answer it.

'Hello, 393 8621?... Oh, hello, Inspector. Yes this is Dan... This might not be a good time. Sarah's just getting into a bath, I think... Oh, right...'

Reed is listening to the one-sided conversation with interest. Dan doesn't speak for a while, evidently receiving some news.

'So why did he...?... Nothing to do with anything?... Right. So... Is he pressing charges?... Good.'

Dan sounds relieved and Reed feels it too.

'I guess we owe the bloke an apology. Did he say why he was running away though? All *I* said was I wanted to talk to him.'

Dan falls silent again. Reed is intrigued.

'I get it... Yes, he's here now, actually. You want to speak to him?... Okay, will do. Right, thanks for letting us know.'

Dan sounds like he's trying to wrap up the conversation.

'Yes... Yes, we'll leave it to the authorities.'

That contrite schoolboy tone again.

'Yes, no more heroics. Okay, thanks, Frank. Bye.'

Dan reappears in the living room and Reed looks up at him expectantly.

'Are we in trouble?'

Dan shakes his head but looks as though he has some important information to convey. He flops onto the sofa, thinking it through.

'That *was* the police, right?' prompts Reed, eager to find out.

'Yes, turns out that bloke – Brian Eaves, he's called – hasn't done anything wrong. He's one of the residents of that halfway house, an ex-con yes, but seems to be living above the law now. The charity has helped him get work round here, bit of caretaking for the local schools. Never *hurt* anyone. Anyway, he's vouched for... So, the police were already looking for him – because of that weird bulletin you... *predicted*. Eaves just had a knee-jerk reaction to the cops calling round, turned tail and ran.'

'But *we're* not the police.'

Dan shrugs. 'He was already on the run.' Dan is looking at the patterned carpet now, a blank, dejected expression on his face. 'So... anyway... he wasn't anything to do with anything.' He flashes Reed a look. 'So, we had that mud-wrestling match for no reason!'

They fall about laughing, picturing the scene – the slow chase and the muddy foolishness. It doesn't seem real.

As the laughter naturally subsides, Reed turns thoughtful. 'I'm glad we tried to help, though.'

Dan nods.

'Oh, and Barrow said you don't have to report in anymore.'

'Good.'

Dan is suddenly very animated, his natural charisma switching back on. 'I apologise – I dragged you from the arms of a beautiful woman for nothing.'

This again.

'Literally dragged me!' concurs Reed, trying to brush Dan's interest off with a joke. He grins and wriggles his shoulders. 'I'll see her again.'

And he's planning to – right after he falls asleep on this very sofa.

They sit, amicably sipping their beers and thinking.

'You know, it's good to spend time with someone different for a change.'

At first, it's not clear whether Dan is offering some friendly advice, but then the meaning settles into place – he is talking about himself.

'I mean, different to me, different to my regular circle. We come in all shapes and sizes...' – Dan glances down at his bulky frame – '... but we're all the same. We love science, and science fiction and computers and... wear hats!'

They laugh.

'But you're a journalist. You must be meeting people all the time?'

'Meeting people, yes, but the people I spend most time with – we're the *same*. We go to conventions and swap theories and read all the same books, and comics...' He glances around the living room. 'You know, I haven't been *here* for a long time.'

'But you love them... Did you fall out?'

Dan wrinkles his nose. 'Not with Sarah. Although, we've never really seen things the same way.'

'Things?'

'Life, science, religion, politics,' he explains succinctly.

'What happened, then? To keep you away? Don't you live near here?'

'Next town over. It was the man she married. Paul. A religious type.'

'And you're a committed atheist?' guesses Reed, not having to go too far out on a limb.

'Agnostic, to be precise. But it wasn't that, it was the bloke's personality. He was one of these smug, superior types for a kick-off. And then he imposed all these petty rules.'

'No one likes a pendant.'

Reed adds a cheeky expression to underline his joke. Dan stops himself from correcting the word and adopts a crooked smile that registers amused admiration. He resumes his train of thought.

'I tried.' Dan sighs. 'He was my brother-in-law, after all. And, you know, it's just me and Sarah now, and Matthew, that's my only family, now our parents are gone. But I really... *hated*' – his hand makes a fist – 'to see them living under his stupid rules.'

'Was he... abusive?'

'Not physically. I just... I've always been annoyed by my sister not standing up for herself.'

'But she kicked him out eventually?'

'Nope. He ran off with another woman. A church committee type.'

He pauses, looking at Reed's outfit.

'You're wearing his clothes.'

Reed examines his paisley covered knees. 'What a prick!'

Dan chuckles.

'I don't know why we were surprised. That's what he was like, all surface appearances, but really selfish underneath...' Dan flashes his thick brows. 'But it was quite a scandal around here.'

'Seems okay now, though?'

'Looks that way, but I think it's still quite raw for Sarah. But at least everyone is extra nice to her now. Frank Barrow, that's the brother-in-law, has taken her under his wing. I just wish she'd had the guts to take control over her own life, and the boy's, before it all happened this way.'

'Still, it's good that you are with them now.'

'I'm doing what I can. Do you have family?'

Reed inhales a deep breath and resolves to keep it short. 'Not really; only child, orphaned young. Suppose that's why I'm happy in my own company, living on the road.'

'But you weren't born in that camper van. Who raised you?'

'Foster homes and...' He trails off, gives a slight shrug.

'Still in touch?'

'No.'

'What happened? Was it awful?'

'No, it was great.'

'So... tell me about it...'

Reed just sits and thinks.

'You know you said you had difficulty connecting with people...?' Dan says. 'Now's your chance.'

'Okay.'

Reed takes a sip of beer and moistens his lips. 'Here's the short version. For a while, I lived with... this family. They had a son my age and we were in the same class. We were sort of inseparable, always out on our bikes – Raleigh choppers. We had these little cowboy hats, his black, mine tan, and pretended we were out on our horses.'

Reed smiles at the memory.

'So, who was the goody and who was the baddy?'

'Neither. We were always both the same. Just a pair of little cowboy brothers, riding around looking for bandits.'

Reed leans forward on his knees and starts peeling a corner of the beer label. That's going to be the end of the story.

'That's nice. What happened to him?'

'Oh, nothing. We just... fell out... over a secret. And then I was moved elsewhere and that's that.'

'And you two couldn't make friends again? What was the bad thing?'

Reed begins to feel interrogated, trapped by Dan's hospitality, parted from his clothes and his van.

'It wasn't a bad thing. Nothing happened. Nothing bad.' He tries to wrap up the story. 'I just told him something he didn't believe and then we both felt sad.'

He shifts position in his seat, resting an ankle over a knee.

'Hey, you really do have a knack for getting people to tell you things. By this point, I'm usually out!' Reed rests open arms along the back of the sofa, forcing a casual pose.

Dan notices something and looks to the doorway. 'Hey, is that a little boy sniffing I can hear?' he says, projecting his voice towards the hall.

A little face peers around the jamb.

'Have you been listening?' Dan beckons his nephew into the room. 'Aren't you meant to be in bed? Hey, come here...'

He opens his arms, offering a cuddle. The child walks in lightly and snuggles into his uncle's chest. He has a wet face.

'Now, what's the matter? Don't be upset,' Dan says, in his most gentle and encouraging voice.

'I hope it wasn't my story,' Reed says from across the room. 'Don't worry; I'm fine now.'

'Yes, see, he's got friends now. *I'm* his friend. And *you're* his friend.' He wipes the boy's cheeks with the sleeve of his robe. 'There's no reason to be sad.'

Matthew nods and sniffs away his crying. 'Uncle Dan, you know you said I can tell you anything?'

Dan leans forwards and strokes the boy's arms, his face close enough for whispers. 'Yes, of course you can, what is it?'

'If *I* tell *you* a secret, will you believe me?'

'Of course I'll believe you. Now come on, dry your eyes; it can't be that bad.'

'Well, you know the ghost?'

'The...?' Dan's eyebrows shoot up and he cocks his head.

'It was me,' Matthew continues, 'I put all the things on each other. It wasn't a ghost; it was me. And then the police came and mummy was crying and now we can't go in the garden.'

Dan cuddles him and strokes his face, looking the child in the eye reassuringly. He also seems relieved.

'Well, thanks for telling me that, but it isn't your fault. None of that has anything to do with you. You're not in trouble, everything's fine. I love you... Mummy loves you...'

'But Daddy...'

The boy's face crumples again and Dan jumps in.

'He does. Your daddy *really* loves you,' – he enfolds the boy in a tight hug – 'and you'll see him again soon.'

Uncle and nephew stay locked in the loving cuddle for a while. Over the boy's head, Dan catches Reed's eye. He mouths something.

'*Always the kid.*'

Reed remembers.

'Uncle Dan?' Matthew says.

'Yes?'

He looks at the boy.

'Why were you all covered in mud?'

I swing my leg over the top of the fence and haul myself onto the decking. She isn't here yet. I see that the house remains lifeless and dark. My limbs feel a bit shaky from the climb, so I lie down and look at the stars. I can wait.

I think she'll be expecting me.

I make a pillow out of my arm and study the constellations. I don't know which ones I'm looking at, but it's captivating; the blanket of brightly speckled night. There are millions of them. The Greeks saw gods in the sky. I don't know why people have stuck with the old mythologies, though. We could make new stories of our own.

My pose is relaxed but I feel nervous. I get up.

I pace around the loop of decking, trailing my hand through the birch leaves at the back. I look down at the grassy rectangle of garden that lurks in the shadows below. It doesn't look like much.

A lamp goes on in her room and I see her moving. I walk back towards the house. I see her open the veranda door and step outside.

'Hey, stranger. What are you doing back there?' she asks me.

'Just waiting for you,' I reply.

I draw closer.

We don't touch each other, or kiss, but stand there, reading each other's expressions. Today – outside the café

– was that really me and really her? For a long time now, the dream world has seemed real to me – and the waking one, a fantasy.

'Hey,' she calls, softly, her mouth parting in that luminous smile, 'so what happened? Where did he drag you off to?'

'Oh, just a spot of mud-wrestling.'

She humours me by adopting a stagey, puzzled look.

'He thought someone was after his nephew... so we went to save the day.'

'My hero?' she ventures cynically, putting the attitude on for fun.

'... but he wasn't so we didn't and it's all fine. How are you?' I rest my hands on my hips, instead of touching hers.

'Great. I'm great. But my trip got cancelled and I couldn't book onto anything else...'

Is she nervous too?

'Hey, do you want to come with me to a festival? In a city, not a field.'

'I would!' I say.

Too sing-song?

'Still got to report to the police every day?'

'Nope. Turns out if you become too much of a do-gooding nuisance, they tell you to go away.'

'Is *that* how it works?'

'So, what is this Ewok village thing for anyway?'

'Best if you come round in the daytime to see. I know' – she's had an idea – 'take a seat.'

So, I find my way to the sofa and she rushes off inside. I hope the idea involves coming back. Then she reappears with a bottle of wine and glasses. I'm glad I didn't turn up here in those pyjamas.

'I thought we could do an experiment,' she announces, opening the bottle. 'You said you eat meals in the dreaming and feel full, so if we drink, do we get drunk?'

'I would say so.'

'And, if we move things, they stay moved?'

She starts to pour.

'That's about the size of it.'

'So, if we drink this wine now, it won't be there in the morning?'

She fills the second glass and hands it to me. I take it.

'Exactly.'

'And will we wake up with hangovers?'

'I think I can handle more than half a bottle of wine. That reminds me...'

I fish the tobacco case out of my jeans.

'I don't know if you'd be interested in sharing a little smoke with me? I don't much, but I found these and... I just thought... for the experiment...?'

Zoya agrees before I even finish the sentence. I pick a joint out of the tin and light it with the Zippo. It seems we are having ourselves a little party.

'I don't suppose you have a record player in the house?'

***

She does have a record player – and a nice bottle of whisky too. We are leaning together on the sofa, listening to records through the open window of her room. She has been playing me an LP by a new jangly-guitar indie band. The female singer has a beautiful voice that ranges from high trills to low cello tones.

'So, I think we've mastered the art of feeling here and *not* here,' I say, blowing smoke theatrically into the air.

We break into peals of laughter.

'No, I mean it, though.'

'I know what you mean.'

'Well, you're the only one,' I joke.

'I am, though. I'm the absolutely only other one!'

We laugh and I hand her the joint.

'I feel like I already know you – but also that there are so many things I want to ask,' I tell her.

'Me too,' she says, thoughtfully. The record ends.

'Listen – how quiet it is,' I say. 'You realise that, for tonight, we are the only two people in the world?'

'Is this you making a move?' she teases. 'Because I might – but only if you were the last man on earth!'

We laugh wildly at this, because, right now, I sort of am.

Then she runs off to change the record, commanding that we absolutely *have* to dance.

***

A short time later, things have gone very disco, and Donna Summer is blasting out of the house. We are both dancing like crazy – and I don't know quite how I've got to this point, because dancing isn't really something I do.

We're not even dancing together but are all over the veranda, really going for it, in our own separate bubbles. Like she said, if I can't dance like nobody's watching when we're literally the only people awake in the world, then when could I? And she's right.

I've lost myself in the music, letting the beats pulse through me, and now I can't stop.

And Donna Summer is *really* feeling the love.

I look over at Zoya. She is in the full flow of expressive dance. She's a really good mover.

She catches me looking and, for a moment, we are sharing the rhythm. Then, she gives me a look that changes everything, and we are kissing and grappling each other to the floor.

***

Later, we are lying on the sofa cushions on the decking, looking up at the stars. Everything feels fantastic.

'Beautiful, isn't it?' she says.

She feels warm and soft in the crook of my arm.

'Beautiful.'

I point at a scatter of stars.

'That's the Movie Director, and that's the Novelist and – see over there? – that's the Abstract Expressionist Artist.'

'What are you talking about?' She laughs, her eyes shining.

'I just think it's time we re-imagined the constellation stories because we don't live in ancient Greece,' I explain.

She giggles at my observation until a new impulse comes her way. She gets up, untangling herself from me, looking like she's had an idea.

'Let me show you something,' she says, all excited. She encourages me to follow her by yanking my hand. 'We can do better than this!'

I manage to scoop up my jeans and kick my legs into them without losing my footing as she drags me inside.

She pulls me into her bedroom, but I don't get chance to look around. She takes my hand again, leading me some-where else. We go through a small door in the far corner of her room and then spiral up a few steps. Then we're in the tower room at the front of the house. I love it immediately.

I look at the riot of unusual family heirlooms and... whatever else... Whirling around, I think I catch a glimpse of Richard and Calliope – in a portrait painted decades ago. The curved room envelopes us with colourful, cosy life-times and I see the typewriter that belonged to her mum. The walls are dotted with photographs and paintings and ink sketches, framed book covers and pictures of Africa – I don't know exactly where.

There's a lot of enticing junk in here but I don't get chance to examine it because she leads me across the room. She pulls me towards a cool-looking telescope by the win-dow. I notice the star charts on the wall.

She removes the lens cap and starts adjusting the position.

'I never knew you were a peeping Tom!'

Now she is opening the big window and fresh air is flowing in.

'Actually, I am. I love to watch Shilly waking up in the morning. I think I saw *you* driving into town.'

She says this without looking at me, turning her face to the clear night's sky.

'But we can also look at the stars,' she continues, 'sometimes even planets a bit.'

She beckons me over, excited to share, but I get distracted by kissing her neck. She turns around to kiss me and we are tumbling, falling over the furniture...

***

The next minute, Reed finds himself back in the sleeping bag in the living room. He has been woken up. Dan has rolled off his sofa and onto the floor with a thud.

Not now! Reed thinks.

There is a weedy strip of streetlamp orange between the curtains, but he can't see enough to tell if Dan's okay. He turns on the lamp.

Looking across the room, he can see the reason for Dan's sudden fall out of bed. Matthew is standing by the sofa and had been prodding his uncle awake. It isn't morning yet.

'Hey!' Dan shouts defensively, before waking properly and seeing the boy.

He softens his voice. 'Hey, Matty, what's wrong?'

Reed rubs his cushion-creased face. Dan gathers himself and the bedding into a sitting position and tucks his nephew onto his knee.

'I saw someone,' the boy says.

'Who, where?'

Dan looks around urgently, and Reed sits up in the sleeping bag. Dan is about to spring into action and start patrolling the house.

'No, I saw someone the night the door broke – a man that smashed the glass.'

'A man?'

Dan looks over at Reed then back to Matthew.

'Really? You were there?'

'I was hiding under the counter because there were scary noises outside. And then a big man fell into the door and it smashed and then, after a bit, mummy came. A big tall man with no hair. Is he going to come back?'

Dan just cuddles him.

Reed is thinking it over. *A big tall man with no hair.*

CHAPTER 28

The next day at work, Zoya is busy refilling the sugar bowls. There hadn't been any hangover and she remembered *everything* from the night before. She's been playing and replaying it in her mind.

That's why she volunteered for all the mindless little jobs today – little jobs and remembering. She's been trying to keep her smile under wraps, though, because there's everything and nothing to tell.

And she can't quite shake the edge of frustration. *Why had he just disappeared like that?* It was no way for the night to end.

The beach café has a muffled, sleepy feel to it today. A few customers are dotted around, eating and drinking quietly. They blur into the background.

Out of everything since Reed arrived, the disappearing is the only thing that jars. Everything else about the dreaming so far has felt good – normal – brilliant! Even seeing the town deserted just feels like people happen to be elsewhere.

But Reed disappearing was just disturbing. There was no magical flash of light or anything – he was there and then he wasn't. And she didn't even see it happen. She was with him and then alone.

She could reason that he must have woken up at that point – based on what he'd told her – but it didn't stop her feeling robbed of something. Of *course* she felt frustrated.

In the actual waking morning, she made a point of checking on the evidence. The things they had moved stayed moved and the wine they had drunk stayed drunk. *So, it had all been true.* In fairy tales, the heroes find whimsical treasures by the bed, not dirty ashtrays on the furniture. She had to laugh at the comparison.

Lee sashays past, curious about Zoya's laughter, but she turns away, hoarding her night-time adventures like secret treasure.

Then, suddenly, he is there, walking into the café with purpose. He seems bold and wild and excited; more dynamic than on any other day – and *here* and leaning on the counter.

'I don't have your number!'

He thrusts his notebook and pen towards her.

Zoya grasps his meaning immediately – he must be sick of the random disappearing too. She grabs the pad and jots down the phone number for Whale House as if he might vanish right there and then.

He reciprocates with directions: 'I live in the Neptune Blue camper van – parked just down there. If you need me, that's where I'll be.'

Then he leans right over the counter to kiss her fully on the mouth. She hears a light smattering of applause. Everyone is watching.

Then he tucks the notebook and pen into his jacket, thanks her and leaves.

Lee is standing, open-mouthed, by the kitchen.

'Hey! Where's *my* kiss?!'

***

Chief Inspector Frank Barrow leaves the police station and walks across the car park. A soft tea-time sun is striping the sky overhead.

The detectives are still at work in the inquiry room, but Frank has made a promise. He told Vanessa he would get home for dinner tonight; and she's making them pork cutlets. He heads for his Rover.

A small, buttoned-up woman is marching towards him and plants herself in his path. There aren't many residents Frank doesn't know, but she seems to be one of them.

'Chief Inspector! I must speak with you. My name is Mrs Wood. I am a concerned citizen and I must speak with you with some urgency concerning a–'

'Whoa, whoa,' Frank interjects, gently and slowly, 'is someone dying?'

The woman looks taken aback.

'Then, please, take a deep breath and start again. If you don't mind.'

'I have just come from your house.'

Frank looks mildly curious. 'That's funny, that's just where *I'm* trying to get to...'

'I'm standing for parish councillor,' Mrs Wood explains. 'And, speaking with your wife, it has come to my attention that, not only are local residents endangering the community, but – I am shocked to learn – that you *yourself*, have full knowledge of this transgression and outright danger to the town, and aren't doing anything about it.'

Frank Barrow shifts his weight and rests his big hands on his belt. He looks down at the woman. Years of accumulated gravitas are manifesting in his strong, gentle face.

'Now, just a second. What transgressive activity is this? Which local residents? If you' – he points a finger at her in a gesture few can get away with – 'are another one of those Sunnyview Lodge detractors, then I'm going to have to ask you to move along. And I would urge you to consider a more compassionate and tolerant outlook towards those people less fortunate than yourself. People's lives might take them down certain paths but...'

'I'm talking about those whale people!' snaps Mrs Wood. 'Of course!' She wags a finger of her own. 'About which something must be done! It shouldn't be allowed, what they are up to. Call yourself an officer of the law...'

'Now look here. See this warrant card.' He opens an official-looking wallet to show her his ID. 'This says I lead the local police force. Says I've served the force for thirty-three years. I've lived in Shilly-on-Sea my whole life and I've helped this community with thousands of problems.' He puts the warrant card away and points to the police station. 'Now, see those doors over there. You, and any of the citizens of this fair town, are welcome to go through those doors and talk to the duty officer about anything you want, day or night, and you will always be listened to. And we'll do what we can.'

Mrs Wood starts to speak but he just talks over her.

'But nowhere is there a law that says I have to stand in the street listening to your misguided perceptions about your neighbours – people who I happen to know personally and very much admire – and certainly not while my wife is waiting at home for me and my dinner is getting cold.'

Then he walks to his car. She watches him start the engine and turn into the street.

'The proper authorities will be hearing about this!'

***

The figure strides on in the night, choosing dark alleyways and shadowy lanes. He wears dark clothes and a woollen cap – too warm for the season.

He walks on, passing sleeping houses, then rounds a corner to be engulfed by the sounds of the sea. There is not a soul around.

The man scans the seafront, then sees it. It is parked just beyond the weak light of an old promenade lamp – a lone camper van by the beach.

He takes another look around. All clear. Then he advances across the road and onto the sandy tarmac. The wind picks up and scrapes a crisp packet against the concrete wall. The fag butts and squashed cans of underage locals have collected there too but, by this hour, the youths are all tucked up at home.

A fine veil of drifting sand moves across the car park. It is deserted apart from the van.

The figure pulls thick black gloves out of his pocket, eases them on and flexes his hands. He looks over the sleeping vehicle. All seems lifeless and still. He moves quietly towards it. Big boots are planted silently by the wheel and a gloved hand grasps the sliding door. The night slumbers on around him. Then he wrenches it open and bursts inside.

***

Fear runs through Reed's body as he watches the shadowy figure break into his van. The man goes inside. His wide eyes don't deviate for a minute as he watches the invasion from his secret spot in the dark. He is sitting on a rocky perch by the outcrop, dangling his legs in the slapping, hissing sea. The cooling water rises and falls in foaming waves. His instincts tell him to freeze.

The man emerges and takes off at a jog, leaving the door flung open and the little van vulnerable and exposed. Reed waits longer than necessary, then picks his way over the sharp, barnacled rocks to the sandy shore. He pads uncertainly up the beach.

He reaches the cabin and peers inside: ransacked, but not much. It obviously didn't take long for the intruder to discover that Reed wasn't inside. He swings the door closed, though the locking mechanism now seems busted, and jumps into the driver's seat.

He scans the scene, checking every direction, peering into the darkness where it pools. His hand shakes a bit as he turns the ignition key and then, with a quiet engine, pulls away onto the road. He drives the van timidly at first – a circling route to nowhere – then recognises the suburb gliding past the windscreen and knows just where to go.

He pulls up outside Sarah and Dan's place. The Cavalier is parked on the street, so he swings the camper into the driveway and right up to the house. He switches off the engine, leans back and slows his breath.

CHAPTER 29

The next morning, Reed wakes to the sound of light tapping on the window. His breath has condensed on the glass as he slept. His body feels frozen in its twisted, uncomfortable position and he's ineffectually clutching a jumper around his neck.

At the other side of the glass – Dan's smiling face. He is waggling a steaming mug at him. Reed begins to unfold himself. He winds the window down and the smell of freshly brewed coffee flows in.

'You always sleep in that position?'

Dan hands the mug to him. Reed takes it gratefully and sips the warming drink. Thin morning light is wafting over the tall trees behind the property, weaving light shadows over the driveway. He shakes his head, either in answer or dismissal, it isn't clear which. While he is pleased to see a friendly face, it's far too early for a Dan-style interrogation.

Dan, meanwhile, glances along the vehicle, cupping his own morning mug.

'I thought the point of these things is that they have beds? Mind if I take a look inside?'

'Come on in.'

Dan opens the door to the cabin, calling helpfully: 'Hey, I think your handle is broken.'

The inside hasn't been tidied since the break-in, but it only looks messy. Reed twists around in the chair to talk to him.

'So, you decided to take me up on the offer? I meant you could sleep in the house.' Dan sits down on the bed. 'You should have turned up earlier in the evening – we'd have let you in.' He has a wry smile on his face.

'I was…' – Reed grasps at one of several passing thoughts – 'delayed by someone.'

'By who?'

'Whom.'

Reed grins.

'No one likes a pendant,' Dan replies, quickly.

Reed smiles to hear the callback, then wonders just how much to say. He catches sight of people walking down the street.

'You know, I think I'd like to leave it here for a few days, if that's okay,' Reed asks, 'until I can get the handle fixed. It won't be an imposition, if you can spare the drive space, because I'm going away for a couple of days – with my friend.'

'Dirty weekend, eh?' decodes Dan, flashing his dark brows.

'It's not like that.'

'No problem at all, my friend, and I'll have that all fixed up by the time you get back. Hey, why don't you get changed and come into the house for some toast or some-thing. I'm sure Matthew will be pleased to see you.'

Reed agrees. Shortly afterwards, he is stepping out onto the driveway, having changed out of the salt-stained shorts. Matthew whizzes past and into the van.

'Morning, Uncle Reed.'

'Oh, morning.'

Dan has appeared at the doorway too. 'Sorry, he wanted to come and check out your "road house".'

'Hey, look what I found,' says a young voice and Matthew pops his head out with a small tan cowboy hat that fits perfectly.

'Bit small for *you* though, isn't it?' Dan teases, addressing Reed.

'Just kept hold of it for some reason. Had it since the seventies,' Reed explains.

'Now, Matty, don't you spoil that.' Dan addresses his nephew, removing the felt hat and placing it gently on the bed.

'Time for school,' Sarah announces, appearing at the door of the house. Matthew joins her and takes his bag.

'What are you doing today?' Dan asks Reed.

'Um…'

'Great. You can help me upgrade the garden fence.'

'I'm not much of a…'

'Don't worry. It's not a big job, there's a loose panel and it all seems a bit rotten down the side there, won't take long to fix.'

Reed smiles, showing his palms. 'Happy to help.'

***

'Thanks for the lift,' Reed says, hauling his bag out of the Cavalier.

'No problem. Have fun!'

Dan leans towards the passenger seat window to wink then drives off down the hill. Reed looks up at Whale House and neatens his shirt.

Zoya opens the front door long before he reaches it and bustles him inside. Her expression keeps defaulting to a mischievous smile as if she has some kind of surprise in store for him. He walks on into the house, up a slight ramp and into an open-plan kitchen. It's not what he expected, for such an old house.

Zoya leads him through to the back – into a room with picture windows that look out into the garden. He is intrigued to see something big moving out there. Then his mouth drops open and his weekend bag falls to the floor. Zoya is behind him, laughing softly.

There in the garden, quietly munching on a pile of saplings, is a small brown rhinoceros.

'She's called Molly.'

Reed looks agape at Zoya. Then his eyes snap back to the hefty little creature standing only a few metres away, on the other side of the glass.

'Why didn't you tell me about *that*?' he exclaims, his voice a whisper, his eyes lighting up.

Reed gets closer to the window for a better look. Yes, it's a rhino.

She is about armpit height and has hairy reddish skin, small intelligent eyes, and ears like petals. The mouth has curvy lips that come to a point in an overbite that looks very handy for grasping at foliage. She is busy chewing. He looks at the horn. That is definitely not a small horse.

'I told you it was better to come round during the daytime.'

Zoya is grinning but studying his reaction almost the way he has been studying the rhino. He looks up at the elevated walkway that circles the garden from the veranda and back. He understands now – but has so many questions.

He can see that the space leads to an open plain beyond the garden and that the rhino – Molly – can pass under the walkway and into the field. She rips some leaves off a branch and chews – but he can't hear it through the plate glass.

'How…? How have you got a rhinoceros for a pet?'

'I told you – Dad used to be a zookeeper.'

This doesn't seem like enough of an explanation – he's pretty sure zoo-keeping is one profession you literally can't take home with you – but it will have to do for now.

'Come on, let's go up,' Zoya says, leading him back through into the kitchen.

He notices a long ramp that rises up and around the room, cornering at little landings, until it disappears, high above them, through the ceiling.

'What's that for?' he asks, puzzled, then immediately remembers.

'To make life more fun!' Richard answers, entering the room as if on cue and illustrating his *joie de vivre* with a wheelie.

'My dad,' introduces Zoya. 'He loves to show off.'

'You must be Reed. Pleased to meet you.' Richard offers a strong handshake that Reed is quick to accept. 'She kept quiet about *you*,' he adds. 'How long have you been in town?'

'Just, a little while... It's great to meet you, Mr Carmichael.'

'Oh, "Richard", please.' He dismisses the formality with a wave of his hand. 'Come in, come in. Let's get acquainted,' he says, gesturing for them to follow.

***

In the parlour upstairs, they settle at a low table by conservatory windows. It overlooks the rhino habitat, as Reed must now think of it.

He takes a seat and looks out at the enclosure, still fascinated by the actual rhino grazing contentedly below. He looks at her saddleback curves, thick neck and tiny tail. Absolutely, definitely, not a horse. Molly flicks an ear and munches, slowly turning her head.

The table has been set for elevens.

'Beautiful, isn't she?' Richard says.

It feels like a trick question – what do you think of my rhino or what are your intentions with my daughter. Zoya notices Reed's uncertainty and interjects, keen to clarify and stop him feeling uncomfortable.

'Dad only has eyes for Molly now. We call her his second wife – and mum probably would have argued that Molly was his favourite.' She laughs lightly.

'She must have known we were having visitors today – spent most of the morning up by the house,' Richard adds.

'Another show-off,' Zoya quips.

They're both looking at the rhino like she's a member of the family. Molly is nosing through a quivering pile of leaves.

'She's magnificent,' Reed answers. 'I've never even had a cat...'

'Oh, we know what we're doing.' Richard looks over with a twinkle in his eye. 'I used to be her keeper at Geddle Zoo.'

'I'm sure you do, Richard. She looks very well cared for.'

'Well, I get a lot of help.'

Richard looks to his daughter and rubs her arm. Zoya looks cute when she's being modest, Reed thinks. Molly starts trotting around.

The doorbell rings, some system making the chime sound throughout the house.

'And there's my other deputy keeper now,' Richard says.

Zoya is already on her feet, her eyes glowing. 'That's Auntie Abigail,' she explains. She is getting up to go and answer the door. She seems excited. 'We've got time for a coffee with them before we set off, haven't we?' She is already disappearing down the ramp. 'She's amazing, I'm sure you'll love her!'

'I'm sure I will.'

***

Later, they are on the road; just the two of them. Zoya is driving her Suzuki. Sunny fields spread out beside them and the traffic isn't too bad. Her car is neat and nippy. A Wonder Woman air freshener dangles from the rear-view mirror and a bottle of water is sloshing around on the back seat.

'So, I had a normal dream last night,' she says, briefly looking across at Reed. 'I say *normal*... Some penguins were running a tropical beach bar – but you know what I mean.'

'Sounds good. I haven't been sleeping so well these past couple of nights. Wish I could have joined you.'

Salty air flows through the open window and ruffles his hair. Zoya's is tied up on top of her head. 'Yeah, well, I wasn't really there. This was just a normal dream.'

'I know, but dream-teleportation would make life a lot easier!'

'Lazy!' Zoya says, teasing. 'So, you haven't been up to much adventuring?'

'None.'

He hasn't told her about the attack.

'It's funny, isn't it,' she says, 'how people can set alarm clocks to wake up, but you can't set anything to get you *off* to sleep for a particular time – I suppose that's why we've been missing each other.'

'Yeah: out-of-sync dreams.'

'But I wanted to ask you about it – my penguin dream. I think I woke up to the *dreaming*, where we've been…' She shows him a crooked smile, thinking how to phrase the rest of the sentence.

'… hanging out?' he suggests.

'… *looking at the stars*,' she says, inventing an alternative euphemism. 'But then I just sort of stayed there – in bed – and drifted off into the penguin dream.'

'Because you've already had enough of me.' Reed affects a mock sullen expression.

'Yes, that's why I invited you to come away with me for the whole weekend,' Zoya replies, flashing him a warm smile.

Reed watches her as she drives silhouetted against the glinting blue sea. He thinks about the penguin thing. 'Yeah, that happens. We still get normal dreams. I *think* this "dreaming" thing is like a staging post and if you just relax and don't go… exploring or whatever… you fall into the normal sort of dream.'

Zoya turns off the coast road and switches the engine up a gear. 'A dream within a dream?' she asks, considering Reed's explanation.

'Something like that. *Who knows?*'

They are heading inland to an A road now, away from the coast for a while. Reed closes the passenger window, rests his head on the pane and watches clouds passing in the sky above.

After a pensive five minutes, Zoya comes out with some conclusions.

'You know, we probably *need* to – do normal dreaming. Aren't dreams important for our brains to mend themselves or consolidate learning or something? We can't be using our minds 24-7.'

'Maybe, yeah.'

'And there's the other thing.'

She waits until she has his attention.

'Do you think everyone can do it? Or *anyone* even? Like, we all pass through that staging post and people can *learn* to stop off there, like we do. I mean, you seem to have been doing it since you were a child – and maybe I have too – but maybe it's more recent for me, like maybe I'm just learning?' Then her face falls. 'It's not just something I can only do when *you're* there, is it?'

'No, I think you are probably a person in your own right.'

They laugh.

'But I never went out and about before you came,' she adds, serious again.

'Well… you never made it out the front door that time.' He remembers waiting in the garden, dejected.

'Maybe my powers are growing.' She laughs.

'Trust *you* to make it like a superhero thing,' he says.

'Me? What do you mean?'

'Well, you're all "action", aren't you?'

She raises an eyebrow at him. 'Hey, *you're* the one who chases people across fields…'

***

Later in their journey east, they are wearing novelty plastic sunglasses and singing along to the radio. The approach road gives them a wide view of the city.

'There it is – almost there! You've been here before, right?' she asks, visibly excited.

He removes the childish sunglasses. 'Looks bigger than I remember.'

As they drive towards the heart of the city, Reed looks at all the people going about their business. The rows of houses sliding by are replaced by shops and the flow of traffic becomes punctuated by quick-changing traffic lights. All sorts of people are ambling or striding around; some with children, some walking dogs, some trying to fit a sofa into a van.

He sees delivery vehicles illegally parked on pavements, people carrying stacks of precarious boxes, and couples meandering along, holding hands. Bike couriers nip in and out of the traffic, taking their life in their leather-gloved hands. A samba band is amassing in a side street – he sees the flash of colour as the Suzuki zooms past.

They seem to be following a main artery to the city centre. Zoya slows the car so she can read a road sign and then makes a strategic turn.

'You know, I haven't actually been to a city for... a long time,' Reed says.

'Really? But... you can go anywhere.'

'Yep. I've *been*... everywhere... But it's... *lonely* in a city all by yourself.'

'I thought you liked being on your own?'

'But it's different doing the dreaming thing in a city – where there's meant to be thousands of people, who just *aren't there*. You'll see.'

'Anyone can find cities lonely, though. Anyway, *I'm* here now, too.'

She pulls up at a junction and smiles her radiant smile. She seems excited about the festival. He hums an agreement that doesn't sound so convinced.

'Maybe you've got too used to living your life in the dreaming?' she suggests. 'But the world is full of people and places and we're part of all *that* too.'

'You think I should... integrate more.'

'But, why wouldn't you? I haven't stopped talking to my dad or seeing my friends, just because of this *thing* we can do.' She is peering at a road sign, trying to figure out the route.

'But you have people,' he eventually answers, flatly.

'So would you – if you didn't always keep yourself to yourself.'

Reed wants to protest but the words don't come – because she's right.

She turns down a side street that can only mean they are nearing the hotel. She looks out for the address while Reed slumps, thinking, her words churning around in his head. They arrive at a small car park that has been studded with neat little trees. The sunny leaves flash bright green rays.

The red stone hotel rises above them. Zoya leans forward in her seat to check it out, then looks back at Reed. She pushes the novelty sunglasses up on her head and her eyes seem bright with thrilling possibilities.

'Would we even be here together if you hadn't discovered me in a dream?' she ponders.

She seems enthused with the wild coincidence of the very strange thing that has brought them here together – to this point in time and space – but he still takes it as a gentle admonishment.

The unspoken answer has to be 'no'.

CHAPTER 30

I wake up, alone, in the hotel bed. The warm, contented feeling spreads from the follicles of my scalp to the tips of my toes – which sink into the thick pile carpet. A gold-green glow lights the room. Moonlight shines through the gauzy curtains, glances off the walls and glides over the sheets. The fine netting gently billows on the air.

I slip on the robe and walk to the open window. That's where he'll be, waiting.

I look outside to find Reed on the balcony. It isn't really a balcony but a patch of roof you can get to by climbing out of the window.

I climb out to join him. The air prickles my skin. The empty wall of soundless night is at odds with the vista of city lights sprinkled ahead of me. It feels like I have suddenly gone deaf. Then I hear Reed exhaling.

He is straddling the lichen-patterned stone parapet, one leg dangling over the side. A soft cloud of smoke is dissipating around him.

'Thought you said you didn't really smoke?' I ask.

'Define "really".' He smiles and then stubs out the cigarette butt on the wall, making an ashy smudge across the stone. 'I don't.'

I straighten up and take in the silent city. 'Spectacular view.'

He nods, looking around.

I walk nearer with a question playing on my mind. He looks at me.

'You prefer this to waking life, don't you?'

His brow furrows but not because he doesn't know the answer, I think.

'Don't you think it's better to have more of a balance?'

At that, he pretends to wobble like he might fall off the parapet, then jokes: 'I think my balance is pretty good!'

Then he gets up off the wall and stands behind me, his arms softly imprisoning me in an embrace.

'We could go anywhere,' he says.

We stand like that for a while and I think about Dad and Molly.

'I *will* leave, one day,' I say, with quiet determination.

And I will.

'Hey, let's get our exploring kit on, then,' I suggest, and we clamber back into the room.

***

Soon, I am tying the lace on my trainer while he is standing ready by the door.

'Not that way, though,' I say. 'We can wander the streets tomorrow. Tonight, I want to stay up high.'

'Just like a superhero,' he comments, following me out onto the roof.

'Well, aren't we?' I ask.

He aims a perplexed expression at me.

'One of the perks of this whole thing though, isn't it?' I say. 'If we fall off a roof, we wake up alive?'

I lead the way along the building, past some other bedroom windows to where the ledge corner forms a step to another roof. Reed looks less happy about this than I feel.

'I might not be as good at this as you,' he says nervously.

'You're fine!'

'Well, let's just stay a little bit safe,' he says. 'I don't want the night to be over yet.'

We climb onto the next building and the next. It's not too difficult because the roofs are basically the same height. At the end of the row, we corner towards the sea. The flat roofs make it easier. We can see the pier from here, stretching away into darkness.

Then, we have to stop because there is a gap – an alley running between the buildings, plunging below us like a ravine. I turn my face to him and flash a cheeky, hopeful expression.

'No. We are not leaping across that gap.'

I study the space between buildings while Reed sits down behind me. 'Yeah, I'm not sure *you'd* make it,' I tease.

'Hey,' he says gently.

I look at him sitting there, resting his arms on his knees.

'This is quite special, just this. Sit here with me?'

I do so, copying his pose, and we look out again at the seaside landscape – bigger and more eerie than the one I'm used to at home. The lights are more plentiful; strings of them bobbing on the breeze. He puts an arm around me.

'See, it's not so lonely in the city,' I say and then wonder: 'Which city did you mean?'

'Lots of cities.'

'Oh?'

He squeezes my shoulder. 'I've been to lots of places. Once borrowed a yacht, once stayed in a castle.'

I look at his face. He's not joking.

'We can go anywhere we want,' he reminds me, softly.

I rest my head on my hand, dizzy with the possibilities.

'You okay?' he asks.

'Just… thinking.'

'It *is* weird, though, isn't it – the city all asleep? Can't see anyone or *hear* anyone. Listen.' He pauses. 'Where are all the cars?'

'Yes, where *are* all the cars?' I ask, not rhetorically.

I can see parked vehicles here and there, as you would normally, but not *one* driving around. I already knew this, logically, but it is a lot more noticeable here than back home – where the streets are dead in the night-time, anyway.

'So, it's like how we don't see the awake people – or anything they are moving around – not while the things are moving anyway. I don't know, but that's my only explanation. And why I don't drive in… the dreaming. Remember, you asked me, and I said it was dangerous? I think it interferes too much with the… dimensions?'

He uses a rising inflection and waggles his head to show he's not convinced this is the right term. I don't think we're going to come up with anything better.

'Right, we move things and they stay moved,' I say.

'I've done it though. Had a little joyriding phase.'

'You rebel!'

'I've done a lot of things.'

'Not in real life, though?'

'Define "real"…' he says, quoting himself.

'So, did something bad happen?'

'Not really, but I scared myself thinking about it, because – where would the car go? What if I parked it somewhere something already was? Seems too big of a thing for reality to… reconcile.'

I cross my legs and look around. 'You know what I find the eeriest?' I say. 'No birds.'

We listen to nothing but the strange low moan of wind channelling through the city and the distant crash of a pebbled beach pounded by a shadowy sea.

'I like the seaside,' Reed says, 'because it just carries on the same, and stops things getting too silent. And I prefer small towns and villages now, because the contrast isn't so great. I mean, I don't want to live in the wilderness skinning rabbits, but I like the sleepy places now – they feel the same in the dreaming as they do in waking life. And I like living on the road.'

'But don't you want to…' – I'm not going to say 'settle down' – 'Don't you want people around who know you? You don't have to live your life all at night.'

'It's different for you; you've had someone to talk to in all this. I've been doing it all alone – before I found you. It's a barrier. Don't even try to explain it to them.'

He looks at me seriously when delivering this advice. I haven't yet, but I might.

'Listen…' I try not to sound patronising, but it has to be said. 'I know you like to play the loner, but I've seen you with other people – you perk right up.'

'I don't have a problem with other people, but there's only so close we can get.'

'Isn't that the same for everyone, though?'

'Look, I tried to explain once – back then I thought this happened to everybody – and it ended up losing me a friend, a brother, really. This is such a big part of my life and other people can't understand it. Except now, there's you.'

He takes my hand in his but keeps on looking out at the view, blinking like his eyes are moist.

'I've tried it; it never works out,' he says conclusively.

I know he's just trying to protect me, and to explain himself, but I can't help feeling that his way isn't the only way of looking at this. And I want him to feel better.

'But you still live in the same world as everyone else, only you just get extra dreams,' I point out.

'But it's *not* the same.' His voice gets louder. 'Because I can go *anywhere* I like, take – or borrow – *anything* I find, there's no one to stop me. And it changes your *whole* perspective on the *entire* world. "This is my house – this is your house. This is one country – this is another. These are my things – those are your things"… I'm like the only person living without boundaries, except the boundary between normal and… *this*.'

I nod and keep listening. He forces a brighter tone of voice.

'I've been looking for another... "dreamer", every single place I've been.'

He puts his palm on my face and I touch his hand.

'That's why I like to check out weird stuff, like the poltergeist thing. I'm always hoping it is someone pulling some prank.'

'Well, it has to be, right?'

'I mean someone like *us.*'

'I see – using this... ability... to do pranks? Have you done that?'

'Just a bit, when I was younger. But I'm not into freaking people out now – I'd rather they didn't notice me at all.'

'Is that what happened with your... brother?'

'Friend. No, I just tried to share it and... long story short... he called me a liar and said we couldn't be friends anymore. So that's when I realised that being different makes you alone.'

He tries to inject a comedy performance into this last bit, maybe to deflect from the utter bleakness of what he is saying: you've got to laugh, or you'll cry.

'We're *all* different,' I say.

'But some people are more different than others...'

He mouths this onto the wind like someone talking to themselves.

CHAPTER 31

The next day, they are standing in a colourful, characterful crowd. The festival is in full flow and Reed and Zoya are hanging out in the sunshine. The park is busy with live music and fairground rides. Street food scents the air and barefoot children play on the grass.

Zoya hands Reed an ice cream.

'There you go, sonny.'

They share a look.

The festival is taking place in a large city park, taken over for the weekend by stages, tents and fairground rides.

'So, that band I was telling you about are on soon,' Zoya says.

Reed licks the ice cream, nodding.

'Shall we head for the main stage, then?'

The day feels very relaxed despite the crowds and noise, though Reed could do without the random hippy drumming. They are standing near some stalls, within ear-shot of sizzling food and running beer taps. A strong, sweet scent emanates from the candy floss stall. He watches the sugary sculptures being spun from wispy strands.

Zoya touches his arm. 'I think we've got time for a ride…?' She nods towards the Waltzer.

'Yeah, okay,' he says, not entirely enthusiastically.

'Come on!'

She takes Reed's hand and leads him through the crowds.

***

Soon, they are squeezed into the plastic seats of a Waltzer carriage with a man and woman who they don't know. The fairground ride is coloured canary yellow, baby blue and mint green, and follows an undulating track. The carriages are attended by a teenager who doles out extra spins.

Zoya is instantly pally with the strangers, chatting with the woman next to her. Somehow, Reed has been stuck next to the man – apparently the brother: silent, so far, and dressed in a Teddy boy suit. He's a big man too and Reed feels squashed in at the edge, like an afterthought.

The safety bar jiggles as the carriage spins them over the rise. Zoya and her instant new best friend take it in turns to scream and squeal in mock excitement; a parody and not a parody at the same time.

The brother is now talking to him.

'Are you two…?' the man asks.

'Yes,' Reed replies, too quickly.

'… on holiday?'

'Yes, we're, er… having an adventure.'

The women are laughing so hard now that their eyes are moist with tears. Their ecstasy is catching. Everything becomes a blur of fun and colour and Reed feels wide open to it all.

The ride slows and the carriage swings, losing momentum. Reed can hear the woman inviting them to a party at an art gallery.

'Yeah,' begins Zoya, then stops herself to check with him. 'Want to?'

'Yes.'

The word springs out of him, taking him by surprise.

Then he adds, brightly: 'Yes, I *do*.'

***

It's night and we are standing outside the contemporary art gallery. The paving flags are washed with high, bright lights but the glass-walled gallery stands empty and dark. Zoya realises where we are.

'Hey, we're back at the party! But nobody else will be here...'

She's practically tap-dancing on the pavement as she says this, pointing a toe, hop-scotching the pattern of the flags. I catch her hand in mine and she smiles.

'I know,' I say. 'It just gave me an idea.'

'You want to pull an art heist?' she asks – more wild guess than suggestion.

'No, I just want to look at the art.'

The automatic doors won't ever slide open for us, so I pull open a side door and we go in. The entrance hall has a smooth, shiny floor and a marble wall that leads past the shop and café bar to a sharply cut set of stairs.

The chairs have been stacked in the bar and the floor mopped but there is some evidence of the party.

'Ah, the ghost of a party always makes me feel sad,' Zoya says.

We walk towards the end of the hall. Light spills in from the city outside.

'Did you enjoy it?' she asks.

She's right to assume that socialising is unusual for me these days.

'I really did,' I answer, truthfully. 'Now – time to art!'

The smooth floor is giving our footsteps a clipped 'foley' sound and we strut along to make the most of it, in a syncopated beat. The cavernous lobby also reveals an echo that follows us through the space.

She makes for the elevator while I turn towards the stairs.

'Oh, not the lift,' I explain: 'electronic.'

She nods and follows me, then runs on up the stairs. I scramble to catch up, taking two steps at a time.

On the upper floor, we enter the main gallery. I flip on all the lights.

Artworks are hung all around us – perfectly positioned throughout the clean, white space. I pause to read the introductory panel that explains the theme but Zoya immediately gravitates to a painting that catches her attention. I stop reading and walk further in.

We don't go round together but end up zigzagging one another, crossing paths now and then.

'My granddad was an artist,' Zoya says.

'Oh...?'

'I'll show you his paintings some time.'

Gradually, we begin to touch things. It feels like shouting in a library, but we are respectful, gentle; only stealing the odd caress. We probably shouldn't be doing this but are we really doing any harm?

I come upon Zoya, standing by a large nude. It's the type of painting where the woman doesn't get a head.

'If we slash things, they stay slashed?' she says.

It sounds like Zoya is just querying the rules of the dreaming, but I understand that she means something else. I watch her for a moment but then she just moves along.

It's not the suggestion of vandalism that unsettles me, but a shiver of realisation that she and I don't really swim in the same ocean, after all.

She has experiences and thoughts that have never occurred to me. We don't see everything the same way. A sense of disconnection opens beneath me like a dark, dangerous swell, but I just keep looking at the art and then my mood changes, as simply as a tide.

'Look, here's a good one.' I beckon her over to a collage with lines of colour radiating from a glued scene at the centre. I look at the label and laugh.

'*Bottomless Dream Vacation,*' I say, reading the title aloud.

We look at each other and move onto the next piece together, this time, my arm around her waist.

***

Later, I am sitting on a small visitor couch at one end of the largest room. Zoya is climbing on a sculpture – a sturdy-looking steel thing that nobody could wreck.

'I should have been a gymnast!' She steps elaborately along a beam. 'Are you impressed?'

A rush of endorphins makes me call out my answer. 'Yes, *amazing*! I *love* art!'

Monday brings a cooler wash of September sunshine. The rays settle as watercolours over Whale House and the sculpture on the rooftop gazes blankly over the bustling little town with its small, stone eye.

Zoya slows her Suzuki, confused about all the vehicles parked outside her home. She spots Dennis Teague's car – with its Tyrfell Wildlife Park decal emblazoned on the side – and her face falls. She pulls on the handbrake and dashes inside. Reed follows.

As he closes the front door behind them, he can hear her in the kitchen, calling for her dad.

'Dad? Dad? Is she okay? Why's Dennis here? What happened?'

'In here,' Richard calls, from the living room, sounding serious but not panicked.

She follows his voice to find her dad with Dennis and a few others engaged in some kind of meeting. A short, small-shouldered woman with folded arms looks at her with a sour expression on her face.

'She's fine, love,' Richard continues. 'It's just that Mrs Wood here has taken it upon herself to call in the authorities.'

Zoya glares at the woman then rushes to the window. She locates Molly with a couple of vets over by the yard. She looks perfectly healthy and happy. The vets are giving the rhino a once-over and Molly doesn't seem to mind a bit. Zoya lets herself relax.

'Hi, Zoya,' Dennis says, greeting her in his usual friendly way.

Richard notices her looking at the other, unknown faces.

'This is David Woodward from the Zoos Inspectorate, and he's brought a couple of colleagues – outside with Molly – Carolyn and Jim?'

David nods a quick confirmation.

'And this is Kelly Jones from the RSPCA.'

A smart young woman in a uniform flashes a calm smile in greeting. 'They're just checking her over, love. Everything's fine.'

'So, what's the problem? What's going on?' Zoya asks, relieved but still confused.

'There hasn't been a problem for fourteen years, has there, Dennis?' Aunt Abigail pipes up.

Zoya hadn't spotted her sitting in the corner but is glad that she's still here.

Reed loiters at the back of the room, not getting in the way.

A small sneeze draws his attention to a little pug padding around. It paces around the room, lead trailing, before settling down in a bored little pile in the corner. Reed perches on the arm of a chair.

The calm young woman with the RSPCA uniform and neatly tied hair takes control of the conversation.

'So, let me get this straight' – she looks at Richard – '*You* are a qualified zookeeper and used to work at Geddle Zoo, until you retired due to the onset of mobility problems?'

Richard nods but responds with an amendment. 'That's right, but don't judge my abilities because you see me here in this chair. I worked there for twenty years, even *after* they put me on wheels.'

He's right, of course. Zoya knows that by *that* time he was senior enough to direct a team of more hands-on colleagues. Dennis was one of them before he went with some of the animals to Tyrfell Wildlife Park in the next county. The RSPCA officer, Kelly, seems to know all this too.

'And *you*' – Kelly looks at Dennis – 'used to work with him at Geddle, until it closed and the animals were moved onto other establishments.'

'Best boss I ever had,' confirms Dennis in his usual jovial manner. 'Molly went on to a park up north with the other rhinos, but her health suffered. She became lonely and sad – seems she was missing her old buddy here.' Dennis lays a hand on Richard's shoulder.

'And I was missing her too,' Richard says softly. 'I'd been with her ever since she was born.'

'Do you know she even saved his life once?' Abigail asks, standing up.

David from the Zoos Inspectorate and Kelly from the RSPCA are furrowing their brows but Dennis, Richard and Zoya seem to know what she's referring to. Reed watches quietly from the sidelines, intrigued.

'Nonsense!' Mrs Wood refolds her arms. 'How could a jungle creature save a man's life? Crush him to death, more like.' She looks around at the assembled authority figures as if summing up a case for a jury. 'And that's what I'm worried about. How many times has it rampaged through the town before I moved here and did something? I would never have moved here if I'd known you were all keeping this... secret. We have laws in this country for a reason...'

'We aren't breaking the law!' Dennis replies, in a voice used to commanding elephants. 'This enclosure is regulated by Tyrfell – the operator' – he directs this terminology at David, the inspector, who already knows – 'as designated premises, and it's inspected regularly, like our other habitats... twenty-eight days' notice, the whole shebang.'

David nods, looking through a file of notes. They've been through this already.

'And welcome any time,' Richard adds.

'Are you calling me stupid?'

Dennis just sighs.

Mrs Wood moves on to the Zoo Inspector, hoping for more of a response. 'It's plain to see this is a dangerous situation' – she looks at Kelly from the RSPCA – 'Someone had to intervene!'

'And you thought *you* were the one?' Abigail retorts.

'Okay, so,' – Kelly raises her voice to resume the wrap up – 'Mrs Wood, we're glad you raised your concerns with us. All animals must be respected and treated with compassion, but everything is in order here.'

Carolyn and Jim appear in the room now, carrying their boots, their overalls slightly muddy.

'All okay?' David asks quietly.

'Good health, welfare excellent,' Carolyn replies.

'Medical facilities in perfect order, enclosure good, perimeter secure,' Jim adds.

They both look bemused at the call-out but happy to have had time with Molly. They check over their paperwork then hand it to David who adds it to the file.

'The only concern we may have,' Kelly continues, addressing Richard specifically, 'is how you manage the more demanding aspects of care, given your physical limitations.'

Zoya is quick to answer and Reed hears rising emotion in her voice. 'He has help. We all look after her. And Vanessa comes in every day.'

'Looks in on me, mucks out with her,' Richard quips.

'And I've been keeping her since I was ten!' Zoya says.

'Fifty kilograms of plant matter. That's what she eats. Every day. Saplings, twigs, ficus… mangoes are her favourite. Gas-pressured RCI dart system. Approved by the BSVAVA. We're compliant with the Firearms Act, 1968. We've got all the veterinary facilities required.'

Most of the people in the room know this information already, except Kelly, who seems impressed, and Mrs Wood, who looks annoyed, and Reed, whose eyes glisten with admiration.

Zoya addresses David directly. 'If you need me to take my diploma so I can take over formally from Dad, I'll do it.

I've got my three years already; I've studied all this stuff.' She looks at her father. 'I can do it.'

Richard beams with love and pride.

'My dad's known her from a calf, and she's lived here for fourteen years without any problems.'

'No reason why any of that should stop,' David says conclusively. He exchanges a look with his colleagues, and they start collecting their stuff.

Zoya kneels by her father. 'I'm not going anywhere. I can do it – be the keeper. I don't mind.'

Richard takes her hand. 'Thank you, love, but I think we're just fine as we are.'

He glances around the room at the assembled authorities and everyone seems happy with his assessment.

Kelly from the RSPCA steps forward to shake Richard's hand, and then Zoya's. 'Well, it looks like she's a picture of rhinocerine health, especially for thirty-two You're obviously doing a great job.' She shakes Abigail's hand too. 'All of you. It's such a privilege to see her; I normally just deal with malnourished dogs.'

She looks down at Grumbles, who has been sitting quietly in a corner looking confused, as if to give him a once-over. Mrs Wood glares back indignantly, standing stock-still while everyone starts to leave.

'I think that's it,' concludes Kelly.

'Are you staying for a cuppa, Dennis?' Richard asks.

Dennis smiles. 'Seeing as I'm here.'

Kelly from the RSPCA and the Zoos Inspectorate team are leaving by the front door.

Mrs Wood follows, remonstrating. 'That's it? You're going to let them get away with it? Oh, well, why don't I get myself a pet tiger then and join in all the fun?' She catches up with Kelly. 'You're really not going to stop them?'

They all flow out of the house and onto the path. Kelly goes to her van, David and his team to their cars. Mrs Wood stands, watching from the garden.

'A crime has been committed and justice must be done!'

Nobody responds.

Richard, Abigail, Dennis, Zoya and Reed are watching from the hallway. The visitors drive away. Kelly beeps and waves.

'Hey – you've forgotten something,' Richard calls from the threshold.

Mrs Wood turns back to the doorway, silent with exasperation.

Richard hands over the small dog.

'Please *don't* call again!' Aunt Abigail adds, closing the door.

Inside, they all celebrate. Then, as the others head outside to see Molly, Reed takes Zoya aside.

'You were amazing; I never knew you did all that.'

Zoya laughs, then replies, quite wisely. 'Sometimes there are good reasons to stick around in the same place.'

She notices a shadow fall over his face.

'Hey, are you okay?'

'Well... a crime *has* been committed...'

They look at one another gravely.

'And I should do what *I* can... to get justice for that woman. We don't even know who she was.'

Inside the police station, I make my way through the open-plan office. I suppose that there are officers here all night but maybe only staffing the duty desk. At least, I don't notice any telltale cups of tea on the desks.

I find a side room full of filing cabinets, which are probably locked – but not to me. They open with a creak and clang. Exploring the contents, I pull out various files marked with complicated-sounding titles but find nothing to do with actual crimes. I push the drawer closed, wincing at the rusty metal screech, and carry on looking around. What else can I see?

There are some desks with personal computers in one section of the room and some disks stored in special cabinets nearby. I can't even look at those. I'm an idiot. What did I expect to find?

So, I walk on around the corridors and offices, feeling just as useless as before.

I think there's a word for this eerie feeling – when a busy place is empty and filled with silence – but I can't remember what it is. There are small signs of life – a cardigan slung over a chair that may well live there permanently, a few pot plants, a framed photo on a desk – but the drab, unsettling nothingness bleeds through all the corridors, stores and offices, drowning them out.

I'm bored and not getting anywhere but I can't just leave.

I should have done something ages ago. Maybe she was even still alive when I found her clothes that night in the shed. Maybe I could even have saved her life. Maybe the killer was still around. The police say it happened before I even got to town, I remember that now, but what have I been doing to help? Partying and going to a festival? I should have done something before now, something useful, but I never do. What is the point of me? Sometimes I feel like Zoya is wondering the same thing about me too.

I go into a large office and find something interesting – a whiteboard with extra bits of paper pinned on it – the inquiry room, I'm happy to see. It looks a bit like in the movies but less aesthetically designed. There are more words and fewer images than the ones they have on TV, but, as I get closer, I do see one photograph – the victim looking back at me. She looks so passionate and strong that I start to interpret her expression as reproachful – but there I go again, making it all about me.

As I study the picture, I realise that it was taken at a music gig. The woman is on stage, fronting a band, and her defiant, punky attitude was all about the performance – not aimed, in any way, at *me*. She looks happy underneath the aggressive posturing, lost in the moment of playing her guitar but also connected to the audience. It's a photograph of someone who was really *there*.

That's what people are like when they have found their thing and are in the flow of it. I think back to our expressive dance-off. Zoya was in the flow of hers then.

I see another, more sedate, photograph of the woman; I think it might be from her place of work. She is less sweaty and more put together in this one, standing by an office wall somewhere – but she still wears her leather and metal jewellery, and her hair is sticking up. You can't see from the photograph, but I bet she was wearing DMs.

Donna Verity. I have her name now. I don't think they even told me what it was before. Perhaps a questioning tactic to see if I'd let it slip. They soon realised that I don't know anything, that I have no connection, that I'm a person of zero interest, and let me go.

I look at Donna again. There are probably tons of people grieving for her right now. Who would even miss me?

I read all the information, writing down her name and her Axworth address in my notebook. A question mark attracts my eye to a statement: 'Connection with Shilly-on-Sea unknown.' The detectives don't seem to have made much progress. Why would a murderer bring her all the way down here and put her in someone's shed when they could more easily have cast her body out to sea?

I wonder at my dark thoughts. Why am I thinking like the perpetrator? Maybe it is just my fear of drowning, being lost beneath the water, never surfacing...

I wonder about finding the evidence room but decide not to bother. I wouldn't know what any of it means. And it's not the physical facts of her death that I can help with, but perhaps the traces of her life.

I'm going to visit her home, I decide. Maybe there's something they have missed.

***

They are sitting on their bench overlooking the beach, sipping coffee in mugs from the café and holding hands. The bench stands where it always has, over the road from the beach café junction, just above the sand.

Zoya's hair, tied in a ponytail, is softly twisting in the breeze, tickling her neck. She looks at her watch. 'Best be getting back to work now.'

Reed nods and drains his mug. The pale grey sea reflects the bright but sunless sky and sand squalls chase along the beach.

'I'll be back tomorrow. I think,' he says, standing up and kicking sand off his trainers.

Zoya holds out a hand for his mug, stacking it on her own. She tucks a twirl of hair behind her ear. 'Well, you know my number,' she says, smiling. Then she pauses thoughtfully. 'Hope you find something useful.' It seems an appropriate thing to say.

Pale-peaked waves roll endlessly towards them. The water dissipates on the shore and is dragged back to sea with a hiss.

'Sure you can't come with me?' Reed puts an arm around her waist.

'Working.' She nods to the café.

The mood has grown serious because they have both been thinking of the dead woman. He aims to lighten the atmosphere with a joke. 'It's really because you don't want to sleep in my van!'

'Wrong! I'd love that.' She looks at it, parked on the road beside them, and then gazes offshore. 'I'd love to wake up by the sea.'

'Can be arranged.' He moves in for a small kiss.

'Promise?' she asks.

He nods gently as they look into each other's eyes for a moment and then start to disengage.

'I think it's good that you're going to try and help with all this,' she tells him. He is moving to the driver's cabin purposefully. Zoya has something she wants to make clear. 'But none of it is your fault in any way. You know that, don't you?'

He climbs in and leans out of the window. 'Okay, I better get going.'

She stands on tiptoes and they kiss goodbye. Then she moves to the pavement as he starts the engine and checks for traffic.

'We'll have a sleepover when I get back,' he offers, smiling, and begins the drive out of town.

Zoya likes the sound of that and waves him off before getting back to the café.

***

The landing is grey with peeling floor tiles and a few dead plants. As it happens, I don't need to read the apartment numbers because a small pile of flowers, candles, cards, little toys and keepsakes has been laid by Donna's door. I was right – she was loved.

I pick up a plastic doll with luminous green hair and an animal print dress and then gently put it back in place – next to a card that says 'Donna, you will always be Pizzazz to me. I will miss you forever, princess. Love always, Robin'. I straighten up.

I pause for a second with my gloved hand on her apartment door and then I go in.

Inside, I find the modest flat to be a warm, happy space. She has painted the rooms brightly and there are gig posters, bits of art and colourful clothes. In the living room, I look at the comfy sofa and imagine two friends – Donna and Robin – settling in for gossip and TV.

You can tell she was into her music. Amps, guitars, pedals and so on are lined up carefully behind the sofa. It all seems a little bit plundered now – her personal effects put back by the police, but perhaps a bit out of place.

There is a calendar hanging on a nail showing appointments, gigs and meetups that she never got to go to. I remember that she had some serious-sounding job she probably worked hard at and cared about and was useful to the world.

Her shelves feature novels, political biographies and comic books, no fashion magazines, some copies of *NME*. Over in the corner is a small desk piled with papers, a fold-er marked 'family tree' and a stack of notebooks. I pick one up. Random squiggled notes, thoughts and doodles are scattered over some of the pages, together with song lyrics and sections of musical notation.

A lot of it seems not to make much sense to me – because it was never written for *me* to read: these are Donna's scribblings for *Donna*. If Zoya were here, she'd be questioning me about respecting privacy and 'Is this okay just because the writer is now dead?' – and I don't know that it *is* okay, but I can't stop looking. I flick through the notes, like a picture book, but nothing grabs my eye.

I pick up the next book from the pile and stumble upon a page where the writing seems denser. I read on, keen to see more of her personality.

I turn the pages and my attention is caught by an accusatory passage: the word 'you' written repeatedly in heavier strokes of the pen.

YOU don't get to decide anything for me anymore. YOU stole a big piece of my youth. YOU made me feel scared for years. YOU made me think it was normal. YOU told me it was love. YOU made me lose friends. YOU made me doubt myself. YOU made me blame myself. YOU changed me forever. YOU stopped me holding hands with men I've loved. YOU took my physical freedom away. YOU gave me nightmares and robbed me of sleep. YOU left me with images I can't get out of my head. YOU made me feel dirty. YOU made me feel sick. YOU had no right. YOU stole my confidence.

YOU buried me under a terrible secret. YOU gave me invisible wounds. YOU made me get stuck in the past. YOU stopped me trusting people. YOU made me frightened for all girls. YOU made me feel I had no rights. YOU made my mother lose her daughter. YOU made me disconnect from my body. YOU shut me down. YOU silenced me. YOU maimed my spirit. YOU put a simple life out of my reach. YOU made me angry. YOU made me live despite all this crushing me. YOU made me feel alone. And what did I do? I SURVIVED.

I sink onto the sofa, feeling weak.

CHAPTER 34

I walk out of the front door. Tonight is mine and mine alone.

The night opens up before me: the town, the bay, the world. Where to go first? I like knowing all the shortcuts, but I *will* leave, one day.

I jog down the hill to the park. The swell of sweeping midnight lawn ruffles like velvet. I make my entrance rolling down the slope, just like I did as a child. I come to rest where it flattens, the springy grass welcoming me like a blanket. I lie there looking up at the stars for a minute, listening to the bubbling of the brook. Shadows dance in the trees.

I take off my trainers and socks to paddle in the stream. The cool, crystal water swirls between my toes. I remember doing this with mum.

I walk across the bowling green. By the time I reach the local history museum, my feet are dry. I lean on the weather-battered panel to put my shoes back on. The moon falls brightly over the text, so I read it. I knew this place was something to do with old Ephraim Alderney, the local philanthropist, but I've never paid much attention before. Now I look, I can see his name still carved on the wall: The Alderney Educational Institute.

The panel tells me that it occupies the site of an earlier building that was used as a Ragged School – a sort of evening school for the poor. Apparently, old Ephraim built them a new building but only admitted men. Fucking Victorians. This information sign doesn't seem to be making enough of that small fact. I feel like the phrase *'where they could direct their attentions in respectable education, undisturbed...'* deserves to have been challenged a bit more.

I remember that the museum has some of Great Aunt Jolien's papers: letters detailing her adventures travelling the world; the ones mum based her novel on. I briefly consider going inside for a look, but don't.

***

I'm sitting in the small church where my parents got married. The ancient wooden pew creaks as I move. It's orangey dark in here. The light filters through the stained-glass windows in a soft, pleasant way.

My eyes are adjusting to the cosy gloom. The kneeling cushions and fraying hymn books are as fusty as anything in the museum. The floor is covered in stone slabs, visibly worn away by generations of feet.

I never come here and neither did my parents, not really, except for the wedding, because everyone got married in church back then. I like to imagine it in 1958, full of all the bouffant hats and skinny ties. I wonder if it felt rebellious at the time – if it felt like the town's first mixed-race marriage or just a happy occasion. Certainly, the wedding album is full of smiles.

I think of something and charge off through a small doorway. I want to have a go at ringing the bells.

***

Later, I am in the fire station, having thought of something else I've always wanted to do. I'm at the top of the fire pole, pulling my sleeves down to protect my palms. Then I wrap my knees and ankles around the pole and slide down. It's not as exhilarating as a zip wire, but still fun.

I see the fire engine – ready and waiting – and hop up to peer inside. I don't get in or touch anything, though. I don't want to mess anything up in case there is actually a fire.

***

Then I'm in the pool hall, a basement room that has been collecting its own particular smell for years.

I flip the switch. Rows of green baize tables are illuminated by the march of light. A long bar stretches along one side of the room, cue racks mounted on the opposite wall. The tables are scattered with balls, triangles and cubes of blue chalk.

I would never normally come here on my own, even though I know how to play pool. I rack up at a table with spots and stripes.

Then I find a cue and have myself a little game. I have to play myself, of course, because tonight I am the only player in town. I impress myself, playing some pretty good shots. Perhaps it is the dreaming, making it come freer and easier, or perhaps it is just better *not* being watched by a room full of beery blokes.

Inevitably, I beat myself and celebrate my win. One game is enough. The stench of lager and cleaning product and ash is making me want to leave.

***

Back on the street, I follow my nose to the town hall; no traffic, no pigeons, no packed lunches in the square.

I walk past the flower beds and benches to the statue. There he is: Ephraim Alderney in a prim Victorian pose. I examine the face to see if it has any kind of personality, but it just looks the way they all do. I can't decide if all the Victorian philanthropists had the same face or if that's just the way the sculptures came out. Probably both.

I leave Ephraim and go into the town hall. I wander up the ornate staircase and discover a warren of wood-panelled rooms. In one, I see the mayoral chain locked away on a stand.

I notice that the corridor is lined with very boring portraits of old, white men. They run in sequence from long dead to recently retired. I imagine the last couple of Lord Mayors enjoying a round of golf before getting home to eat dinner with their loyal wives.

***

Back outside in the little square, I find myself annoyed. This must be what old Ephraim wanted all along: no women in his education institute, a line of white-haired men wearing the big necklace in the town hall.

I take all my clothes off and throw my knickers at the statue. They snag and hang around his blank stone face. I couldn't have got a better shot if I'd tried. *Distracting enough for you?* The pants aren't falling off. I throw my head back, laughing. I'm just going to leave them there.

When we throw things, they stay thrown.

***

Now I am running, naked and barefoot, down the high street, along the mossy verge and towards the sea. I remember running with Reed that night, but then I push him out of my head again – because tonight is all mine.

***

The sky is brightening now. I find myself at the old lido and decide to have a swim. All the chairs have been stored away for the season, but it won't feel cold to me.

I look at the pool, dancing with silvery starlight.

I slice through the surface. I feel the water rippling over my skin and through my hair. I float on my back looking at the sky. It feels like gliding through the galaxy. The constellations make me think of him.

Of course, this is the fun bit – nothing but oxytocin and adventures – but I barely know him yet. Maybe soon he'll start telling me what he wants me to look like, what words he doesn't want me to say. Maybe he'll start talking over me, making decisions for me, feeling entitled to things. We'll see.

For now, he is someone who still makes me smile. I let myself think about him until I reach the end of the pool and then I put him away.

I step out of the lido and watch the first rays of dawn shimmering over the sea. The breeze is lifting droplets from my skin, but I still feel dream-warm and open and free. I stretch out my arms to bathe, naked, in the new day.

***

Next, I walk inland to the fancy streets where we ate eclairs and looked at diamonds. I see the formal-dress-hire shop and open the heavy door.

Macaron-coloured tulle and satin dresses clamour for attention from the rails. They snatch at my legs as I pass. I push through the forest of prickly ballgowns and into the men's section at the back; dark jackets, crisp white shirts and well-pressed trousers.

I indulge in a spot of dressing up; kitting myself out in a swanky suit fit for the opera. I even find a top hat to go with my tails.

Feeling a wonderful combination of dapper and comfortable, I strut along the paved street. There's only one place I can think of going dressed like this – the ornate hotel by the sea.

***

I push open the double doors to the lobby, then ascend the grand staircase to go and explore.

After a nose around the suites, I work my way down to the kitchen, where I fill the top hat with fancy-looking nibbles and help myself to a bottle of champagne.

I find my way to the breakfast room on the first floor. A long balcony runs above the promenade. I weave my way through the frilly tables to go outside. The sunrise is already glowing over the bay. Glinting, sun-pricked waves fill my field of vision. I drink it all in.

I pull a chair into position, pop the cork and cross my feet on the rail. Everything in this moment is just, perfect-ly, as it *is*.

CHAPTER 35

Reed is driving back into Shilly-on-Sea, despondent about the lack of any shiny new clue, burdened by what he has read. The stream of traffic approaching the town has slowed to a crawl.

An irritating song plays on the radio. He turns it off. Maybe Zoya can make him feel better.

The van rolls along, braking and moving, moving and braking.

At least he had seen something of Donna Verity as she was in life – the connected, creative, bold young woman who played gigs and formed lifelong friendships. *Lifelong.* Her life hadn't been that long, in the end.

The traffic has come to a standstill and he winds down the window for some air. There is a heavy smell on the breeze. Nobody is moving. Engines are being turned off.

Reed leans out of the window for a closer look and happens to make eye contact with a passer-by.

'Doesn't look like you'll be getting through any time soon.'

'What's happened?' asks Reed.

'A fire, I think.'

Reed opens the door and cranes to see the route ahead. He smells the carbon but doesn't see any smoke. He can see the arched roof of the old theatre, but it isn't engulfed in flames.

He hops down to the tarmac and closes the door, deciding to take a walk along the road. Up ahead, the street has been closed and a fireman is warning the gathering group to stay back. Beyond the barrier, he can see sweaty-faced fire fighters standing about, emergency over.

The engines *are* by the old theatre. Reed remembers Quentin Tosca's flat. He pictures the magic tricks and the photographs and the embers dying in the grate.

He slips the barrier, scanning the square, looking for the old gent he has never actually met. A fireman blocks his path.

'Keep your distance, folks,' he tells the crowd, placing a gentle hand on Reed's chest. 'Behind the barrier, please, sir. We've got it all under control now. There's really nothing to see.'

Reed allows himself to be corralled back behind the barrier but keeps searching the scene.

There he is: a white-haired man of about seventy, swathed in a blanket and clutching a large, white rabbit to his chest. He still resembles the 'Amazing Marvello' posters that Reed has seen. He is chatting to some medics and looks fine.

Reed exhales.

Time to return to his vehicle. He wonders how long the roadblock will take to clear.

A fireman in full gear walks out onto the street and removes his helmet. A jolt of recognition.

A big tall man with no hair.

The face is more than familiar. Reed can still see him – staring at Matthew with menacing fear.

Reed ducks involuntarily. He tries to hide in the crowd, but they all seem shorter than him. He shuffles backwards and hopes it isn't too late.

He knows that the fireman doesn't know him and has no reason to be looking but he feels the strongest urgency not to be seen.

Reed retreats, making for his van. He jogs then runs along the white lines back to where he left it. He jumps in and turns the key. He executes a clumsy many-point turn before speeding off in the other direction, looking for a different route into town.

He has some information for the police.

***

Reed sits at a table spread with photographs. Through the window, he saw Matty, Sarah and Dan arriving and being ushered into another room. The door to that office remains closed.

Reed looks at the photograph again. He recognised him immediately but takes his time to be absolutely certain.

'Yeah, that's *him*.'

'Are you sure?' Sergeant Brooks asks.

'Yes, that's definitely the man I saw.'

'But you only witnessed him staring at the child, not actually committing any crimes?'

'Yes, I saw him in the street and I also saw that it scared Matthew Stevens out of his skin. I just thought you would find that information useful. It was definitely the same man.'

Reed taps the selected photograph again. They are using staff photos provided by the fire service. The police sergeant stands across the room with his arms folded.

'He also fits the physical profile of the man who attacked my camper van a few nights ago.'

'And did you report this vehicle crime?'

'No, but I saw it happen, and Dan Mather in there could testify about the broken door handle because he fixed it for me the next day.'

Constable Walker is sitting on a chair in the corner. 'Okay, thanks. That's really helpful,' she tells Reed.

She shows him out of the office and to a row of chairs where he can wait for the Stevens family to emerge. First, he sees the detectives having a word with the chief inspector, then a string of officers dashing past.

Reed discovers that Dan, Sarah and Matty are also watching the commotion, standing in the doorway next to his chair.

Reed looks to Dan. 'What's happening?'

'Looks like you both picked the same guy.'

***

From his Rover 800 series, Frank Barrow surveys a wide scene. Beyond the shrubbery, he can see the officers taking pains not to dislodge pebbles as they creep along the path. There are more, covering the door at the back.

The property seems quiet except for the ever-changing lightshow of a television that flashes at the living-room window. No other movement can be detected inside.

He looks around the cul-de-sac. He sees the ghostly flash of a face at a neighbour's window before the net curtain is quickly dropped. Time for action.

Through a well-rehearsed sequence of radio messages and hand signals, the team sync up and await instruction. Frank radios the go-ahead to the coordinator who silently signals the advance officers to proceed.

They approach the front door, shout to announce their presence and immediately go in.

Frank watches the doorway. Nothing happens for a long five minutes.

Then the team troop out of the property, returning to their vehicles. Frank sighs. Sergeant Brooks reappears outside the bungalow, looks in Frank's direction and reaches for his radio. His voice crackles over the airwaves.

'Looks like he knew we were coming, boss.'

***

A blue Volkswagen and a russet Cavalier pull up at the house. Their engines sigh simultaneously as the convoy comes to a rest.

Reed walks up the moss-threaded driveway to join the family as Dan, Sarah and Matthew emerge from the car.

Sarah has a protective arm around her son's shoulders as she ushers him from the back seat and into the house. Reed hears his scratchy footsteps and her praise.

'You did so well today, Matthew. It's all going to be alright now. You were really brave and it's all over now. I think someone deserves extra sausages for tea.'

Dan has waited more deliberately for Reed to join them and is smiling. He looks relieved but also perplexed.

'Hey.'

'Hey.'

'But why didn't you say anything before? I mean, I get it, you didn't actually see this fireman committing a crime... but you never even *mentioned* him, even to *me*.'

Dan is acting friendly but seems quite hurt beneath his questions. Reed wishes he had a good answer. The day is now too cool for short sleeves. He folds his arms for warmth.

'I didn't know...'

'No, you *always* seem to *know*,' Dan says, interrupting sharply, 'but you never explain *how*.'

'Pushing an innocent man's face into the mud for no reason, I guess...'

'Okay,' Dan replies. Dan doesn't sound convinced. He moves the conversation back to dinner. 'So, is it sausages all round?'

Apparently, Reed is still invited for tea.

Sarah is jiggling her keys in the front door. She looks up to say something then notices that her son has stopped dead in the driveway. 'Come on, Matthew, it's all going to be alright now. The police will get the bad man and we don't need to think about it ever again.'

She gestures for her son to come inside. Matthew hesitates.

'What is it?' Dan asks.

'But, Mummy,' Matthew says, and then, as if it is self-explanatory, 'there was another man there too.'

***

The next morning, Reed is standing on the pavement outside the police station, watching Sarah leading Matthew to the Cavalier by a tightly held hand.

'Mum, can we get a hamster?'

'No.'

'Are you coming with us, Uncle Reed?'

'No. Uncle Reed's going to stay here and look after the house for us.'

She shoots Reed a hard, admonishing stare. Matthew stops walking and looks at him, but she moves the child on; no opportunity for a hug goodbye.

'Come on, Matthew, time to get in.'

She deposits the boy in the back and firmly closes the car door. Then she gets into the passenger seat and becomes a shadow.

Reed notices Dan standing beside the driver's door. He is holding the car keys and leaning on the roof, watching him.

'So...' Reed says, searchingly.

'So,' echoes Dan, with more finality in his tone. Then Dan begins a terse summary of the situation. 'So, now we know there were two of them and the police don't have either one. They *do* know the identity of *one* of them but have no idea of his current whereabouts. And they can't connect him to the victim anyway. "At large", I think they say.'

Reed moistens his lips and swallows. A candy-striped paper bag is being blown along the street. 'How long do you think you'll be away for?'

'As long as it takes,' Dan answers, spreading his hands out. 'They'll be safer at my place. I'll call the house later with my number.'

'Yes, of course.'

Dan starts to pull the car-door handle and then lets it rest because he has something to say. He looks to the sky, shaking his head slightly, before making eye contact with Reed again. He has some questions.

'You know… I just don't get it. Why do you keep things to yourself like that? You knew the victim was there,' he recounts, pointing the car keys like a finger. 'You knew the perpetrator!' His voice rises with emotion. He seems like a man betrayed.

'No, I… It was just a… hunch.'

Dan nods, rapidly. 'So you say.' Then he opens the car door. 'You know, if you don't start being honest, I don't think we can be friends anymore.'

He gets in and slams the door.

Reed stands where he is, a lone figure on the street. The car ticks over and pulls out into the road. It moves away slowly.

Reed notices Matthew looking out of the back window, his little hand doing the special 'wave' goodbye.

CHAPTER 36

At the end of the promenade, Reed puts his foot down and the van begins to motor uphill.

'Where are we off to?' Zoya asks.

'Well, a special beach date requires a special beach...' Reed answers, with stagey comic charm.

'Am I a special lady?' Zoya says, raising an eyebrow and joining in.

'A very special lady.'

Zoya laughs. 'You're so smooth... Anyway, I know where we're going. I *love* that beach!'

The van chugs along as the coast road swerves inland and begins to climb a long hill. It's Zoya's first time in the camper van and she's taking it all in: the blocky seats, the spindly steering wheel, the rattling windows.

'You *don't* know. It might be some place you've never been before.' Reed changes gear and looks at her.

'I've been everywhere around here,' she says.

He pulls a sulky face.

'But not with you,' she adds.

It makes him replace the fake scowl with a genuine, luminous smile.

They are driving west. The road curling before them is lined with bristling banks of grass. The sun is casting a pink glow across the sky. Even the gulls are hushed.

As the rise levels, they pass a scrubby drive leading off to the right. Reed sees a cluster of run-down buildings and some kind of pitch. The fencing gaps and sags.

'What's that place?' Reed asks.

'Old sports ground.'

Zoya doesn't seem interested. She is casting her gaze out to sea. 'So, what's for dinner?'

'Only the finest beach feast you'll have ever experienced, little lady.'

'I'll be the judge of that,' she replies. She affects a cynical tone, but her eyes are twinkling.

***

After dinner, Reed refills their glasses with wine. Around the blankets, pale heaps of sand are softening in the sunset, sparkling like sugar.

They are picnicking on a small, secluded beach that only locals would know. The hillocks frame a strip of blue sea. Long-beaked shore birds feed at the water's edge, their twiggy legs strutting through the waves.

Zoya pushes her bare feet into the sand. The sun has slumped towards the horizon, painting the tide with crimson flecks. In the shelter of the horseshoe bay, the waves sound muted, like a seashell cupped to an ear. They have the beach to themselves.

Zoya breathes in the salty evening air, closing her eyes to listen. She hears the water, rhythmic and calming, the faint calls of lofty birds, and reedy grasses tussling in the breeze.

'You know, I've never slept at the beach before.'

'Really?'

'Yeah, never.'

'You've lived at the seaside all your life, but never slept out?'

'Always wanted to.'

He looks puzzled.

'It's different when you're a woman,' she explains. 'Personal safety issues.'

'I never thought of that.'

She doesn't say anything.

Reed looks at the acre of chequered rug between them. 'Permission to board your blanket?'

Zoya laughs. 'Is that a euphemism?'

'No, I...' His hopeful little expression cracks into a fluttering, bashful smile.

She shuffles across to *his* blanket and into the warm space under his arm. The sky is turning from blue to peach to red.

***

Later, in the back of the camper van, Zoya is having a good poke around. 'There's more room than I thought.'

Reed leans against the cupboard, watching her, casually folding his arms. He shrugs. 'Roomy enough for one. Or for two people who are very much in... *like*.'

After a moment, Zoya breaks eye contact and continues her nosing around. She finds the child-sized cowboy hat and picks it up. 'Bit small for you, isn't it?'

She gently puts it back. When she opens the cupboard with the poltergeist clippings, Reed waits for her comment, but she just smiles and closes it again.

She has almost come to the end of the 'tour'.

'Check this out,' he says, filling the pause.

She watches him converting the seat into the bed, demonstrating the feature as if she is a potential buyer. But then, there it is – the made-up bed. And there they are – two people very much in *like*.

***

Much later, when the sky is inky and moonlight beams through the windows, they are lying naked together, listening to the soft shush of the sea. A candle flame dances gently in its glass lantern. The dishevelled bed is flesh-warm and smells of their wine-scented breath.

Tangled in sheets, they are holding hands on the pillows above their heads. Zoya adjusts her position and sees Reed staring at the ceiling, looking sad.

'Hey, what's wrong?'

'It's nothing. It's not about us, this, tonight. I don't want to spoil anything.' He looks at her with a fleeting smile and softly strokes her hair.

'You're thinking about the...' She tails off before having to choose between the words 'body', 'murder' or 'dead'.

She watches his angular face in the soft darkness, waiting for him to say more.

'I just feel... I should have been able to do something... that first night... or now.'

'But you tried.'

He sighs. 'Yeah,' he replies, almost sarcastically. 'But what's the point of me? Of being able to do what I can do?'

He sits up, rustling the bedding, and rests his arms on his knees.

'You know...' she starts gently, 'maybe you shouldn't let this dreaming thing define you.' She rests her head on her arm and rearranges the covers. '*I* haven't,' she adds softly, by way of example.

He turns to face her, nodding ever so slightly. 'But you do a lot of things for other people. I'm just...' He flops back down onto the bed.

'You know a great phrase I heard?' Zoya continues. 'Don't let the past define the future.' She lays a hand on his chest. 'You can be or do or achieve anything you want to.' And then she giggles. 'And if you want to book onto my motivational course it's only nine ninety-nine ninety-nine ninety-nine.'

Her joke doesn't make him laugh out loud, but he squeezes her hand.

'But I could have done *something* that very first night, when I found her, but I didn't. All I did – all I *ever* do – is watch.'

Zoya pulls her body closer and wraps her arm over his chest. He holds her against him and caresses the back of her neck. Waves slide over the shore.

'You know when we fall asleep tonight?' her muffled voice says at his collar bone.

He can feel her warm breath on his skin.

'Let's *not* go exploring. We've got everything we need right here.'

'Deal.'

***

I wake up but don't see her beside me. The candle has died, and I am left with the sudden, grey bleakness of night. The moon has slipped across the sky.

The waves sound closer and choppier and are pungent with seaweed.

I lie here, waiting. The bedsheets are lumpy and awkwardly tucked.

I think of the woman called Donna who played guitar and liked purple. I think of the words I read in her notebook. You, you, you... I wonder if she ever told that 'you'.

I think about her clothes in that shed. I remember that I thought it odd enough to sit and watch and wait, but that's it. Zoya would say that I couldn't have known – but it's not true; I could have figured it out.

I lie here, remembering and obsessing, waiting for Zoya to appear. I wait, studying the texture of the ceiling. I wait, looking at the shadowy curtains. I wait, listening to the chilling rasp of the waves. I wait, as if alone.

Eventually, I slip the tangle of bedsheets and pull open the camper door. I drop down and my feet sink straight into the cool sand. I don't see her. The night beach seems like a totally different place.

Snaking patterns are picked out by hard-shone moonlight at the shore. I can hear the rocks moaning with wind, but the grassy slopes shelter me from the blast. I can't feel it against my skin.

I cast about for a glimpse of her. Nothing. She is nowhere on the empty beach or the tufted hills. I wade out across the sand, away from the van, calling her name. I plough into the grey gloaming and the beach becomes scratchy underfoot. I stay away from the dark, encroaching waves.

I wheel around, looking for her, hoping she will emerge from the van, but she doesn't appear. It looks exposed and vulnerable again, like the night someone came for me. I shout Zoya's name as loud as I can, but the sound is snatched away. Waves roar and crash onto invisible rocks and I feel smothered and small.

'There's nobody here, is there?' I ask, shouting, but I know it. No answer, no echo.

The smell of something rotting drifts towards me. I jog up the steep, grassy bank. Sharp shoots pierce the ground where beach becomes dune becomes hill. I don't see her anywhere.

The swell splashes and drags, splashes and drags, splashes and drags. It annoys me.

I stand here, waiting. Nothing. Then, I go for it. I throw myself down the slope towards the shadowy beach.

***

Reed wakes up. Zoya is sleeping beside him and doesn't stir. He looks at her peaceful, beautiful face on the pillow and places a hand, softly, on her back. She doesn't move. Eventually, he lies back down, waiting to drop off again, or for her to wake or for morning to come. Something.

***

Later, the dawn grows steadily in the east, clearing the hill and lighting the sheltered beach. Reed is still awake. He picks up his clothes scattered randomly in the throes of passion, gets dressed and clambers into the driving seat.

He starts the engine and slowly pulls away from the beach. Back on the coast road, he drives over the long hill and towards the town. His eyes water as he squints in the morning sun.

***

At Whale House, he pulls the hand brake on and turns to look at Zoya asleep. She begins to stir, rustling the sheets and running a hand over the empty half of the bed. It looks like she was expecting to find him within cuddling distance and to wake up in a warm embrace.

'Morning,' he says, twisting round from the driver's seat.

She rubs her eyes. 'Morning,' she chimes, enjoying the soft hug of the bed.

Then she sits up.

'I can't hear any waves! What happened? Why aren't we at the beach?'

She can see that he has brought her home. He watches a frown settle on her face.

'I just started thinking...' he explains, 'maybe it isn't safe to be there. Seems like there's at least two murderers on the loose...'

'Okay.' She sounds disappointed. She sighs and rubs her scalp, fingers twisting in her curls. She looks at him again, more alert now.

'I think we missed each other last night...?'

'You never appeared,' he replies.

'I did. I waited for you for ages. Then I took a swim in the sea.' She runs a hand over her arm, triggering a thought. 'Hey, pretty good solution! Get totally wet – wake up dry!'

'You went swimming?'

'Yes, it was lovely. Don't you...?'

'No, I... I'd hate to drown because there's nobody to save me. And I honestly don't know what happens if you die in the dreaming... seems like–' He interrupts himself. 'You went without me?'

Zoya is pulling on her clothes, under the sheets. 'I waited.'

She gets her things together.

'Anyway,' she adds forcing a breezy tone, 'we don't have to spend *all* of our dream time together, do we?'

She hops out onto the pavement and continues the conversation through his window.

'Well, we're here now,' he says, 'sorry about that. I suppose I'll see you later...?'

Zoya opens the driver's door. 'Don't you want to come in for breakfast? I smell pancakes...'

CHAPTER 37

'We're back!' Zoya calls cheerfully as they go into the house.

The delicious smell emanating from the kitchen gives Reed a pang of hunger that he didn't know he had.

'You're back!' Aunt Abigail greets her niece with a cuddle. 'Did you have a good time, honey?'

They link arms and wheel around the corner. Reed follows.

'Just in time for pancakes,' Richard says, chirpily, from the hob. He pours batter into the sizzling pan.

'I love pancakes!' Zoya says, leaning over to kiss her dad's cheek.

Abigail collects the stacked plate by Richard's pan and serves it on the table next to the chocolate spread, sugar and lemon juice. Zoya takes a stool and Reed follows suit.

She takes a pancake and starts sprinkling a fine veil of sugar over it. She looks up when a man walks in and returns to his seat.

'Hi, how are you?' Zoya says. 'Reed, this is Carl, an old family friend.'

'And backgammon adversary,' Abigail adds.

'Less of the "old", thank you.'

Before Reed can mention that they have already met, the conversation takes a different direction, but the two of them nod in greeting.

'So, who's winning the infinite tournament at the moment?' Zoya asks.

'Carl's been on a lucky streak recently, has to be said,' Richard answers, flipping a pancake on the stove.

'Not *that* lucky,' Carl says, giving Abigail a flirty wink that makes her laugh musically.

He puts an arm around her to emphasise his meaning and she rolls her eyes and gently pushes him away.

Zoya offers a pancake to Reed who takes it and considers the toppings on offer. The chocolate spread looks good.

'But how can an infinite tournament ever be won?' he asks. 'I mean, how can it ever end?'

'Well,' begins Carl, 'we'll see how things stand when one of us dies…' He chuckles.

Richard looks at Reed as if he has some wisdom to impart. 'No, no, with life, it's not the final score that counts, it's enjoying the game along the way.'

'Mmm, philosophy and pancakes – my favourite!' Zoya jokes, springing from her seat. 'Anyone want coffee?'

Carl grins at Richard. 'Just as long as it's *my* headstone that has "backgammon champion" engraved on it for everyone to see…'

'These are really good Mr… er, Richard,' Reed says, appreciatively.

Richard's eyes are dark and twinkling. 'Top tip: if you want to keep her interested, learn to make 'em.'

Zoya laughs but adds, very seriously: 'He's right, though.'

'Okay.'

'Oh, Zoya,' Richard says. 'Do you remember those photographs of the writing workshops your mother used to do?'

'At the youth clubs? The ones on the wall upstairs?'

'Guess who's in one. Abigail spotted him' – he nods towards Carl – 'only Mr Ridgeway, here.'

'I don't...?'

'This is before we knew him – over in Axworth, used to run sports clubs over there. Didn't you live around there then?'

Carl shakes his head. 'Closer to Vereshot.'

'Yeah, anyway, before he moved back to Shilly, before we got to know him properly, something like '67, wasn't it?'

'Yeah, after my father died.'

'It's a small world.'

'Ah, you two were destined to become best friends,' Abigail comments, nodding sagely. 'I think it's cute.'

'Anyway, let's not bore the youngsters,' Carl says, depositing a pancake onto Aunt Abigail's plate.

'Hey, Richard,' Abigail calls, 'come get your own breakfast.'

'Yes, Dad, come sit yourself down.'

'Child,' Richard says, with a twinkle – she knows what's coming – 'I'm already sitting down.'

***

After breakfast, Zoya leads Reed up to the decking. The Carmichaels seem to call it 'the veranda' but he still thinks of it as the Ewok village.

They are standing at the corner of the elevated walkway that looks out on the expansive field. Zoya hands him the binoculars. He leans on the railing to steady the lenses and take a look.

'Look, she's there in the far corner.'

Reed points the binoculars at Molly the rhino and watches her tearing up the grass. It almost seems normal to him, now.

'You have a lot of land,' he says.

'Just as well.'

He can hear the smile in her voice.

From their vantage point, he can see the full swathe of land and a low building to the left surrounded by a concrete yard with metal barriers. The gate stands open now.

'Is that her house?'

'Yep,' Zoya answers, glowing.

'It's all so impressive,' – Reed removes the binoculars from his eyes – 'what you've done here.' He hands them back and looks around at everything. 'And this house. I can see why you wouldn't want to leave.'

Zoya puts the binoculars up to her own eyes. 'I *will* leave, one day.'

Then she stays quiet. Reed begins to feel like he's in the way. He can tell Zoya is keen to get into the muddy field and see her rhino. Maybe he has outstayed his welcome.

'So, do you need any help looking after her today?'

'Don't you have to get back to Sarah's house? Weren't they going to phone you today?'

Reed looks at his feet, mulling things over, nodding. 'I suppose I should.' It feels like his cue to leave.

Zoya hasn't taken her binoculars off the distant corner of the field, but now drops her arms and looks at him. 'You can come visit her another day.'

His crestfallen expression surprises her.

'Cheer up, you're having a lucky escape.'

'Lucky escape?'

'Today, I've got to collect up all her droppings for the garden centre. They love it. Actually, we've got a good arrangement with that nursery – shit for saplings.'

Reed thinks the scenario through, then, after a beat of comic timing, leans in to kiss her cheek. 'You are such a good person,' he says, meaning 'rather you than me'.

She laughs.

'Want to meet up later?'

'I don't think I can, actually,' Zoya replies. 'We're going to visit my uncle down the coast.'

It doesn't feel like a specific enough answer, but Reed realises he should get going. He *is* supposed to be looking after the Stevens house.

'Okay, well, I should get started,' Zoya announces, making to go back inside.

'Okay, well, I'll be at the house, then,' Reed says, following her. 'Call me when you are free?'

Reed is in the Stevens house. He is sitting on the sofa. He is staring at the wall.

The afternoon sun slices the room with light and shade. The darkness angles across the carpet with the slip of time, like a sun dial. A vase of wilted flowers litters the window-sill with crumbling, papery petals. The day wears on.

Reed's gaze has settled lazily on the small picture frame hanging on the opposite wall – a Bible quotation.

The ticking clock is growing irritating. He might need to hide it away.

He has showered and tidied and eaten and washed up. He doesn't want a beer. There is nothing on the television, the radio, nothing interesting to read. There has been no phone call, no message. Maybe they've forgotten that he is here.

He sits, thinking.

There's no real reason for him to be here but nowhere else he needs to go.

The Bible quotation is too small to read from the sofa. He gets up and walks across the room.

'Then I saw a new heaven and a new earth, for the first heaven and the first earth had passed away, and the sea was no more. Revelations 21:1'

Sometimes, he reads poetry and it makes more sense than this.

What would Jesus do? he thinks wryly. It must be comforting to have a ready-made role model like that. Slowly, the meaning drifts towards him. The quotation is probably inspirational for someone adjusting to a new life, like Sarah.

He plants himself at the bay window. Out there is the edge of the rest of the world.

A red Ford pulls up across the street. He sees the driver looking – looking straight at the house and looking for too long. He ducks behind the curtain and tries to peer out without being seen.

He shakes his head and mouths something to himself: 'All I ever do is watch.'

He resumes his position at the window in full view of the man in the red car. He's still there, looking, but Reed can't make out his face.

What would Dan do?

In a flash, Reed makes for the front door and strides down the garden path to the street. He bounds across the tarmac towards the red car.

'What do you want?'

He hears the engine revving. He gets a hand to the driver's door but the car lurches into motion and speeds away down the street. Reed sprints to chase it, but the car soon disappears.

Panting, he doubles over with stitch. He rests his hands on his thighs.

Eventually, he straightens up and hobbles back to the house. He feels pointless and powerless and weak.

***

Later, Reed finds himself by the sea. He is sitting on the beachfront bench – *their* bench as he used to think of it – staring out at the same old waves. The camper van is by the kerb.

The low wind picks at the sand with blustery, changeable eddies; tiny tornadoes dancing along the beach. Grasses are tugged in one direction, then another, drooping as the breeze dies.

Reed has been lighting matches and watching the flame flicker back and forth, blowing each out before it burns his fingers.

He is thinking and not thinking, in a world of his own. There are people around – couples walking past and a group of young men on the sand – but he doesn't notice. Gradually, he becomes aware of something – a shadow and a noise.

He looks up to see Carl approaching the bench. The noise resolves itself into his name. He gets the impression that Carl might have been talking to him for a while. The group he is with are sticking posts into the sand for a football match.

'Reed, hey Reed, join us for a game?'

'Oh, I'm not really a sportsman,' he says dismissively. 'Remember?' Reed summons a smile to show no ill feeling.

'But maybe it's team sports that you need?' Carl suggests, using a friendly tone and raising his eyebrows hopefully.

Reed's gaze drifts back out to the blue-grey water. 'Thanks, but I'm okay.'

The men are warming up now. One of them boots a football over to Carl who catches it with a thud and a flick of sand. The man shouts something that Reed can't make out but that probably ends with 'ref'.

'Why do you play on the beach?' Reed wonders aloud, although he's not that interested.

Carl laughs. 'Why *not* play on the beach?' he counters, nodding to the group of men.

Reed doesn't have anything to say. He wants Carl to go away. He stands and dusts stray sand off his jeans. Time to make a move.

'Well, I'm just off to…' He leaves the sentence trailing. 'Have a good game.'

He walks past the van and into the beach café. It is quiet today. Lee sees him by the door.

'Cheese toastie, is it?'

Reed finds himself nodding and almost takes a seat, but then pauses where he stands. 'Actually, can you wrap it up for me to take away?'

When the order is ready, Reed pays at the counter and glances towards his van.

'Going somewhere nice?'

'Oh, just for a drive.'

'Oh?' Lee says, angling for conversation.

Reed drifts away without responding, wrapped up in his thoughts.

'See you again!'

Reed doesn't answer.

He gets into his van and drives away.

***

West along the coast road, Reed happens upon the lane that leads to the old sports ground. He taps a finger on the steering wheel then makes the right turn. The driveway is threadbare with gravel, overrun with weeds and gaping with potholes. It comes to an end at a collection of squat, derelict buildings.

He stands on the wasteland, taking it in: rusty fencing, graffitied concrete, rotten panels and plywood that bangs in the wind. There's not much to see. He makes out the changing block by the pitch and an equipment store ahead.

Rubbish swirls around in the stuttering, intermittent breeze. Reed looks at his feet and sighs. It feels like a no man's land. He can't even see the shore from here.

Reed circles the store, dusty gravel dislodging and dragging underfoot. He finds it locked with a metal shutter. He could get inside in the dreaming, but there's no reason to and he's not going to waste his time coming back. *Nothing for me here.*

A crow rustles the leaves of a nearby tree and caws.

Reed completes his ambling circuit and heads back to his van. He trips over a latch in the ground. There is a met-

294 • JENNY CUTTS

al panel set into the concrete, perhaps somewhere to store balls. He gets up, dusting himself off and rubbing his knee.

A hard crack to the back of his skull makes him crumple. He falls to the concrete, unconscious.

***

I come to, lying on the ground. It is dark. The night sky floats above me. The back of my head aches and I remember the blow. What happened?

I sit up. No one seems to be around. Time has twisted on without me.

I stand up and stretch. I feel the warmth of the dreaming, but something's different. The hairs on my forearm are standing up. I can feel a ball of anxiety revolving in my gut.

I examine the back of my skull with my fingers. My hair isn't sticky with blood. Why would it be? I remind myself of the facts: I'm here but also not here.

And then I worry. How injured am I in the waking world? Am I dying but not dead?

The decayed buildings loom before me. I jerk my gaze. The black emptiness of the deserted pitch seems menacing, as if the shadows are hiding something.

I stagger to the nearest building. Where is the boundless dream energy, now? I can still open locks, though. The metal shutter slides open with a shriek.

I see only darkness. I feel around for a light switch, but I don't know if I should be turning them on. I lean on the doorway, trying to work things out. What are the 'rules' again? Could somebody be here? My attacker is only back there in waking life, where my unconscious body lies. That's not reassuring. I turn the light switch on.

The strip blinks with brilliant light and feels harsh on my eyes. It takes a minute for my vision to adjust. I can't decide whether the glare is making my head hurt more or if I only feel like it should.

I look around the store.

There is nothing but boxes, but they seem recently placed and neatly stacked. It feels like stolen goods. I look inside one of the boxes – CD Walkmans – but that doesn't tell me anything much.

Why did I even come here again? What was the point?

I turn to leave but feel hesitant about going back outside. I don't know why. There can't be anyone lurking in the darkness – can there? Is anyone out there?

Light from the doorway spills over the scratchy concrete and I see the trapdoor. That's where my sleeping body is, unless I have been moved. I must be alright or else I wouldn't be *here*. That's right, isn't it?

My head swims and my thoughts won't stay still. I have the strongest urge to get back to waking reality before I slip away.

Is this it? Am I dying now? What would happen if I did? Would I stay here in my lonely in-between world or blink out of existence and disappear? I don't know any of the answers and I feel like I can't breathe. Would Zoya ever find me – when she goes to sleep?

I look at the latched opening. There is a fuzzy space where I can't see myself, no matter how hard I stare.

What is the state of my body – back there in the real world? Am I in need of medical attention? I feel so vulnerable and so blind.

A fall. I just need to fall and wake myself up.

I don't want to plunge back into the pain of my injury, but I'm in danger if I don't.

Just a little fall should do it. If I fall, I wake.

My first attempt is too feeble. I'm too scared and just fold to my hands and knees. I see a dark patch by my hand and wonder if it is my blood. I feel weak.

Get up, do it properly, do it now.

The padlocked bolt is shining in the moonlight. I should be looking inside. I won't be able to unlock it on the other side of the dreaming, but I can't waste any time. I have to save myself by waking. I have to do it now.

But what is behind that lock – too new and shiny-looking for the grimy store? If there is another dead woman hidden down there, I have to help her to be found.

My lids are heavy. Wake or open the lock.

I wrench the bolt back. It moves too smoothly, and I shiver. I don't want to be right about this. I fling open the metal doors and my strength fades and it's done.

I breathe.

Shakily, I stand. I look into the pit.

It is empty except for a pile of clothes that shouldn't be there. I understand it as only I can.

I back away involuntarily, imagining what can be seen in the waking world.

I have already seen a corpse. I know what it looks like: drained pale, shadowed with congealed blood. The smell.

I find myself running across the grass, thinking of Donna Verity.

I don't know who this other person is. I don't want to know. I don't want to wake up beside it and see.

I keep running and cross the coast road and keep going to the cliff and the sea. I need to breathe real air in my real lungs – or *not* to. I need to be *more* here or *less* here, but not *this*. I need to break out of this stifling in-between world where I'm all alone but crowded by corpses. I need to wake up from this worst of bad dreams.

I am running over cool mosses towards the dark shore. I pick my way through the wild growth and feel the sharp smack of a cold, hard gust blowing up from the spiky sea. The night air slaps my skin. I see the moon-cut, glassy jags of waves peaking below the drop, their crash suddenly deafening.

I throw myself off the edge.

CHAPTER 39

That's the sound of floorboards creaking. Someone is creeping around the house. Waking with adrenaline pumping through her bloodstream, Zoya sits up in bed. No, this isn't the dreaming. No, that isn't Reed visiting in the night.

Her eyes are wide in the darkness, focussing on the sounds. No, definitely not Aunt Abigail's footsteps. Her skin prickles. Someone is there.

She eases herself silently out of the bed, listening. She thinks of her dad sound asleep across the hall, her Aunt in the guest room. She creeps to the door and evens out her breathing. *Zoya, this is down to you.*

There is a narrow crack at the door jamb, not big enough to see much at all. She watches and listens. Did the shadowy darkness move out there? Was it a trick of the mind?

A sharp sliver of light slices through the crack and a flicker of movement suggests a dark presence in the hall. She feels around for some kind of weapon. All she can come up with is a candle holder.

There is a noise; someone shifting their weight on the other side of the door. Her heartbeat quickens. She attempts to control her breathing and move her feet without a sound. She listens, hard.

Come on, come on, you're braver than this, she psyches herself up. Then she opens the door.

The dark figure whirls around at the sudden commotion, a hand still gripping the handle of her father's room. The face stares at her.

'Oh... what are *you* doing here?'

***

Reed wakes up, dry as a bone. He sits up and feels the back of his head, finding a little scabby area that hurts. He can smell something metallic, perhaps blood – maybe his? He's at the old sports ground and the sky is dark. He looks at the cluster of buildings and the dark pitch.

He remembers the gaping hatch behind him, and still dare not look. He scrabbles away on hands and knees and rushes to his van. Everything else blurs. He's got to report the body.

His hand is shaky on the handle, but he finds his way in and turns the keys. The engine doesn't start. *Not now!* The cold night air wicks perspiration from his body and he feels a deathly chill prickle his skin.

He tries again – nothing – and again, again – nothing, still. He is desperate to get away from it – far away – as soon as he can.

He gets out of the van and starts running down the patchy lane, back to the road. Casting about, he sees the coast road running away into greyness – no sign of a phone box in either direction.

He starts to jog back towards Shilly. This is going to take a while.

His trainers slap against the tarmac. He tries to pace himself. He jogs past half-remembered scenery, the incessant waves a soundtrack, relentlessly attacking the shore. He keeps his feet in rhythm, pushing onwards. No passing cars, no houses, no phones. At first, the road feels soft under his feet but, once his legs tire, it pushes back, hard. Sweat begins to collect at the small of his back and the sound of the swishing sea merges with the rush of blood roaring in his ears.

A small house appears out of the gloom, crouching behind a garden wall. He runs up to it, wades over crunchy pebbles and bangs on the door.

He catches his breath and waits – but the waiting stretches on too long. The small cottage stays silent. He shouts for help. The windows remain dark and the door unopened. There's no car in the drive. He sees a bicycle propped against the wall and takes it, stumbling at the pedals, before cycling off down the hill towards town.

He reaches a small hamlet and sees a phone box up ahead. He dismounts, letting the bike fall onto the grass verge. He picks up the receiver and smiles with relief to hear the tone. He dials carefully, steadying his breath.

'I'd like to report a body…'

***

'You caught me.' Carl smiles at her.

Zoya puts the candle holder down and breathes out. Carl is standing by her father's bedroom door.

'I didn't expect to see you,' she says, explaining her reaction.

Moonlight falls through the veranda doors, framing him in rectangles of thin shadow.

'Oh, this isn't the bathroom, is it? I rarely come up to this floor.'

Carl's voice is croaky but warms up as his sentence rolls on. It is so normal for her to see him in the house, but this feels odd.

'Oh, no, it's that way.' Zoya points out the bathroom to him, her own voice a whisper of relief.

A confused frown finds its way onto her face and she begins to shake her head. She is trying on different scenarios but none of them quite make sense. Carl doesn't stay over and it's the middle of the night.

'Couldn't sleep either, eh?' he is asking her. 'Join me in a hot chocolate? I know where everything in the kitchen is, at least.'

It sounds like a nice way to calm down and get back to sleep. Maybe she'll be treated to one of his stories – maybe one she's never heard before.

Carl is shuffling off to the bathroom now, but she has to ask. 'Are you… staying over?' She says it in a low voice, not wanting to wake everyone up.

He pauses, turns and whispers his reply. 'Ah, well, I, er, *we,*' he glances over to Abigail's room, 'weren't going to make a big deal of it, you know.'

'Oh!' The word is breathy and her eyes round.

'Well, we're not dead yet.' Carl displays a cheeky grin then puts a finger to his lips. 'Shh, she's sound asleep.'

Zoya isn't happy with her reaction and composes her expression into a more accepting one. She supposes they make quite a sweet couple.

'Very charming woman, your auntie, always thought so.'

Zoya nods too many times and realises that she's still acting weird about it.

'No! Yes!' she exclaims, finding words again.

'Doesn't matter how old people get,' he says, 'we still like looking at the stars.'

***

The police cars overtake Reed as he cycles back to the scene. With heavy legs, he turns the bike into the drive. It wobbles over the aggregate.

The police have already installed bright lights by the ball pit. Car headlights pool as more officers arrive.

Reed is surprised to see an ambulance there too.

He edges towards the body but doesn't really want to see. Some officers are looking at his van, which he left with the door hanging open.

'That's mine,' he explains.

He creeps towards the hole, wanting to know what's happening but keeping his distance so as not to see too much. *I am such a fucking coward,* he thinks. At least he did the right thing, at least, he helped. The authorities can take it from here.

He spots Chief Inspector Barrow by the trapdoor, leaning over the stretcher.

'He's still alive,' Frank announces, summoning the medics. 'Weak but alive.'

Reed pulls closer.

He sees a man with a shaved head: Dom Henderson, the missing fireman.

Frank leans closer. It looks like he is listening, not to breath but to *words*. Reed can see Dom's face. He is whispering with effort. Reed watches his lips. It looks like he is saying a name – a name he knows.

There is a burst of activity. Paramedics rush one way, police the other. Reed recognises some of the officers running past him to their cars.

He stands watching, feeling like a shadow.

The chief inspector comes up behind him and says, firmly: 'This doesn't concern you, Reed.'

Then, he is gone.

Reed stands, watching the cars disappear. The borrowed bike is lying dumped somewhere on the dark grass.

***

Zoya pushes open the small door at the top of the stairs.

'Come on in. My favourite room in the house.'

Carl is carrying the two mugs of hot chocolate and she holds the door open for him. She turns on the cosy lamp by her mother's old desk so they can find their way through the jumble of furniture and keepsakes to the telescope.

Carl's eyes widen, and he looks suitably impressed.

'I never knew... this was here.'

Zoya beckons him to the telescope, gesturing where to set down the mugs.

'Let me show you how it works,' invites Zoya, excited to share.

'Such a privilege, thanks.'

'Here, put this blanket round you,' – she pulls open the sash window – 'we'll get a better view without the glass.'

'Careful...' Carl worries.

She ties the cord in place and moves back to the telescope.

Carl relaxes and looks around the room, taking in the eclectic contents, recognising a picture of Calliope on the wall.

Zoya removes the lens cap and adjusts some knobs. A cosy, chocolatey smell is curling its way to the far reaches of the room.

'There, I promised you stars.'

She indicates that the telescope is all set up for him and Carl tries it out. When he moves back from the eyepiece, he sees her grinning and sipping the hot chocolate. He returns her smile with an even bigger one of his own.

'Wonderful, this is wonderful. I bet you can see the whole town from here.'

'You can!'

Carl gestures for Zoya to take a turn. She moves in and refocuses the view.

'There's Sunnyview Lodge' – he swaps in for a look – 'see, beyond the tops of those trees, that's the Glebe down there.'

He comes up smiling and she moves the telescope round again.

'And that's the beach café, all the way down there; you get a good unobstructed view because of the high street.'

He takes a look there too. Her turn. She finds the town hall for him. He looks and laughs.

'That reminds me, they found someone's underwear hanging round old Ephraim's face, did you see it?'

'No,' she replies innocently, and smiles a small smile.

She retrains the telescope on the next landmark, but something catches her eye. She focuses on the flurry of movement and identifies a police convoy speeding along the street. They disappear behind buildings, weaving through the town, but she manages to pick them up again by Victoria Park.

'Something's happening.'

'What do you see?'

'Lots of police cars. Looks like a raid.'

'Where are they?' Carl stiffens behind her, interested. He closes in, ready to take a look. 'Where are they?' he repeats.

'They're stopping; they must be going in.'

She reports the live scene unfolding before her eyes. She senses him tensing up behind her.

'But they're at…'

'Where?' he demands, fists clenching.

Zoya lifts her head from the telescope to look at him. She swallows.

Carl seems suddenly angry and fierce. She backs away.

'… *your* house,' she says, in a hoarse voice.

She expects an explanation, some further information, some insight that he can share – but he pushes her, pushes her backwards, pushes her again.

She puts an arm out behind her to steady herself on the wall – but it isn't there.

Falling backwards through the open window, she manages to grab hold of the sill. Still, Carl advances, shocking rage on his face.

This isn't someone rushing to get her to safety. No regret, no compassion, no help. It doesn't make sense. Her knuckles are white now with the strain of hanging on. Her feet are scrabbling for a foothold, searching for something in the architecture that can support her weight.

Carl is staring at her blankly. It doesn't make sense.

He looks around the room and picks up an old cricket bat. He moves in.

'What are you doing? Help! Help me!' she shouts in horrified surprise.

'Shut up, shut up, shut up.'

Carl raises the bat, ready to smash onto her fingers.

The door bursts open, flung by a tall figure in the doorway. Carl wheels round in shock. Something is being pointed at him. He sees the shining muzzle of a gun.

'Don't you touch my daughter!' Richard shouts, and pulls the trigger.

A shot fires and Carl goes down, knocking furniture as he tumbles.

Zoya has found a ledge for her feet and manages to re-adjust her grip. She hears a second slump; her dad, whose legs have buckled, sinking onto the cushions piled by the door.

'Dad?' she calls, urgently.

'Are you okay?' Richard replies. 'I can see your fingers. Hold on, I'm coming.' She hears him grunting with effort. 'I'm coming, love. It's just my legs have gone…'

'I'm okay, I'm okay, I can climb back in.'

Zoya summons all her strength and climbing skills, pushing up and pulling herself onto the window frame. From there, she uses gravity to help her tumble back into the room. She thuds onto the floor, happy to be alive, then scrambles to her knees, looking around.

There is Carl, lying slumped on the rug. There is her dad, sitting on the cushion pile.

'Is he dead?' she whispers.

'Just tranquilised.'

She recognises the tranquiliser gun in Richard's hand. Carl stays down but covers his face.

Her dad catches his breath and leans his head back on the wall, closing his eyes. 'I think he'll live.'

Then he thinks of something and his eyes shoot open.

'Check on Abigail!' he implores.

Zoya rushes out of the room.

CHAPTER 40

'You shot me,' murmurs Carl, breathing shallow little breaths on the floor.

'*You* pushed my daughter out of the window!' Richard responds, his voice getting louder with every syllable. 'I just put *you* to sleep.'

'I'm still awake,' Carl says, moving slightly. It seems to take great effort.

Richard is sitting upright on a heap of cushions. Carl is splayed on the floor, like an ungainly carcass, his dribbling mouth squashed against the rug.

Richard listens for Zoya and Abigail before turning his attention back to Carl. He looks at his friend and his face hardens in disgust. *Friend...?*

'How did you... stairs?' Carl mumbles wetly.

Richard rolls his eyes. 'Just because I use a chair doesn't mean I can't *ever* use my legs. You should know that. My legs get weak but I'm not *totally* useless.'

Richard leans his head back against the wall.

'So, tell me why you did it.'

'... didn't want her to know.' Carl's eyes don't seem to be focussing.

'You killed that woman from Axworth,' Richard says. It doesn't seem any more believable, even when he says it out loud.

Spilt hot chocolate drips thickly from the small table, congealing in messy splats on the floor.

'... *my* daughter... I didn't know...'

Richard stares.

'Why would you... How could...?'

He has difficulty finding the words. Carl seems barely conscious. The animal tranquiliser is taking effect.

'I never knew you had a daughter...' Richard says.

'Neither did I... Then, what she told me... Had to shut her up... Needed her... stop talk... ing.'

Carl's speech is so slurred that Richard can hardly make out the words.

Richard is enraged but his legs have no strength. He leans forward to sharply prod Carl awake with the tranquiliser gun. 'Why?!'

Carl makes a noise that fades like a dying balloon. 'Shh...'

'Why? Why wouldn't you want to know she was your daughter? Why?!'

Carl's tongue spills over his lips.

Richard thinks of the youth club photograph and a shiver prickles his skin.

The door swings open and Zoya bursts in.

'Is he...?'

'He's out.'

'He tried to strangle Aunt Abigail! The ambulance is on its way.'

Richard finds a boost of adrenaline and raises his hand. 'Help me get to my chair.'

They leave the room together, as the sound of an approaching siren pierces the dawn outside.

***

A short time later, two stretchers are being carried out of the front door and through the rose garden. Calmer weather spreads over the bay this morning and the town is now lit by the welcome light of day. Birds are filling the sky with song.

A pair of medics are taking Abigail to one of the ambulances. The other is for Carl. Richard, Zoya and Frank Barrow fall into silence as the second stretcher passes them at the porch. Richard looks away. Zoya offers her dad a drink of water from her glass. He shakes his head.

'Medics say she's going to be alright,' Frank says. 'You don't need to visit her until tomorrow. Better to stay home now and get *your* rest.' He watches as a constable gets into the second ambulance, accompanying Carl. 'Sounds like the end of it too, now we have witness testimonies. We can wait until tomorrow for yours.'

Richard nods his understanding, still shaken by the night's revelations. Zoya has a hand on his shoulder and he holds it tightly.

'Are you sure?' Richard asks.

'Absolutely, they're just taking Abigail in for observation. You've all had quite a night.'

The paramedics and police officers drive away, leaving only Frank.

'Dad was amazing,' Zoya says. 'I don't know how he even knew…'

'The phone call. Woke me up. Didn't you hear it? Said the police had found the fireman, that they had rushed off to arrest… someone.'

He means Carl but cannot say the name.

'*What* phone call? *Who* said that?'

A youngish man cycles slowly up the hill, panting loudly. He parks the bike in a bush that quivers on impact and rolls his tired body onto the thickly grassed lawn.

'Your gentleman caller,' – Richard gestures with a nod of the head – 'Reed.'

Reed looks exhausted and rolls onto his back, drenched in sweat.

'Reed!' Zoya rushes over to him. 'Are you okay?'

'I'm…' – he pants, looking up at her – 'I'm fine… can't feel my thighs… how are you?'

Reed's expression seems delirious. He picks up a rock from the soil.

'I'll fight them!' he gasps, trying to fill his lungs with air.

'We're okay! We're okay!' Zoya assures him.

She gently pours some of the water over his red, sweaty face. He raises himself onto his elbows to accept the glass to drink. She sees dried blood in the back of his hair.

'Looks like you already have.'

'I've come to save you,' he goes on, his voice half gasp, half whisper.

He lies back on the grass.

She pushes the wet hair from his brow. He smiles and closes his eyes, holding her hand in his, clasped to his chest.

CHAPTER 41

'Thanks for the lift.'

Reed gets out of the police car and makes his way up the path. No cars in the driveway, nobody home. He works the key in the lock.

The familiarity of the quiet little house makes him glad to be back. He is tired and grubby and could really do with a bath. He looks forward to the caress of a soft towel afterwards, which always reminds him of being a child.

The phone in the hallway starts ringing.

'Hello, 893 8621? Dan! Hey, good to hear from you.'

'Hey. So, the police called – they've got the murderer *and* the accomplice, and I hear we've all got *you* to thank.'

'Oh, no,' Reed replies defensively, 'I missed all the action.'

'But you found the bad guy! I'm guessing using your special "psychic-not-psychic" powers that you're never going to explain.'

Dan's joke makes Reed smile. It feels good to hear his chuckles again. He sits on the telephone bench, his limbs aching all over.

'I was just bored and poking around. It was a…'

'Hunch.'

They say it at the same time.

'So, you're okay? And everyone's okay?' Dan asks eagerly.

'Zoya and her dad were amazing. Couple of action heroes. They shot him with a tranquiliser dart!'

'Don't mess with zookeepers, I suppose. So... we've been having a bit of drama of our own.'

'Is Matthew alright? And Sarah?'

'Everyone's fine. Physically at least. But Paul turned up – you know, Matty's dad – yesterday, as we were picking him up from school – made a big scene with Sarah about her moving on too soon. Wants her to give him a second chance.'

'I thought it was Paul who had moved on...?'

'Yes, well, he was really angry, thinking she had moved a new man into the house.'

Reed shifts in the seat, thinking it over.

'I reckon he must have seen you there and jumped to conclusions,' Dan says.

Reed stands up and touches the back of his head. 'He knocked me out!' he announces, jumping to a conclusion of his own.

It all fits though – the red car driving off, the blow to the back of his head.

'What?' Dan asks, more than a note of alarm in his voice.

'Probably. Someone followed me and gave me a whack on the head.'

'Really?'

'Laid me out cold.'

'And you think it was Paul?'

'I never saw anyone… but I did see him outside the house earlier. Tried to catch him but he drove away. Could have followed me.'

Saying it out loud sounds like conjecture, but Reed grows more and more convinced.

'Anyway, I'm fine now. No compression. They checked me out. I just have this feeling it was him.'

'Right. And it seems like Matthew *has* been talking to him…' Dan continues.

'Sarah's friend was right about what she'd seen?'

'Looks like. You know what car he drives now?'

'A red Ford Orion,' they say, in unison.

They both smile into their telephone receivers for a beat or two.

Then Reed asks: 'So, when are you coming back to town?'

We are sitting on the bench together. The evening is blustery and warm. It's not even dark yet but we both needed to give our bodies an early night. We see the sand, hear the sea and feel the breeze on our skin; here and not here again. The water seems calm tonight and a large pale moon hangs in the sky.

'A child's moon,' Reed says, pointing it out.

'Aw,' – I put a hand to my chest – 'that's adorable.' Then I remember something and start to laugh. 'So, you were going to save me with that rock?'

He laughs along too. I think he knows that I'm also touched by what he did last night. We look each other in the eye.

'Your knight on rusty bicycle.'

I take hold of his hand. 'I'm not so into the chivalry, but thanks for trying to help.'

'So, you won't be wanting huge bunches of flowers, then?'

'No, I'm okay for crazy big gestures, thanks.'

'Hey, I climbed up the fence for *you*.'

'And I climbed *down* it for *you*.'

Reed puffs his cheeks, then blows out the air and shakes his head.

'Good job you got your climbing practice in...' He looks at me, seriously.

I breathe in deeply, remembering what it was like. It feels scarier now to remember it; now that the moment – and the adrenaline – has passed. I flex and rub my hands. 'Yep.'

He takes me under his arm and squeezes me against him.

'Yeah, I'm okay for climbing adventures for a while, thanks,' I say.

The soothing splash of waves fills the silence.

'So, what made him do it?'

The jokes we've made drift away on the evening. It's hard to feel relieved and happy, knowing what we know now.

'He killed his own daughter,' Reed recaps slowly, incredulously, 'and hid her body in a garden shed?'

I nod soberly and add: 'According to that other guy.'

'The fireman,' Reed notes.

'According to Frank, Dom Henderson was just passing by that night… something to do with the stolen goods ring. It was Dom's padlock on the shed.'

'Good of him to tell the police,' Reed says, sarcastically, adding pointedly: 'in the end.'

'Yeah – after Carl tried to kill him off too… I've been hearing about those raids on the news. Said he saw Carl on that path, having some kind of disagreement, and when he reached them, Donna was dead.'

We are repeating what the police have told us, trying to understand it for ourselves.

'Carl had already suffocated Donna and roped in Dom to hide the body? And he did?! Doesn't seem like a normal response. Why would he do that? If it wasn't even his crime?'

Reed is very animated as he asks the questions that everyone has already asked.

'Carl,' I say, simply, giving the answer. 'I can see it now. He's got this power over people. I think it starts out when he coaches them as kids and... never goes away.'

'You know, I read some of her journal, or whatever. At her flat. She was writing about child abuse. That never seemed to have gone away, either.'

We sit together in glum silence.

'It looks like he was after that photograph – the one of the youth club – because Donna was in it. Both of them: Donna and him.'

'To destroy it or to look at it, do you think?' Reed asks.

I shrug.

'I keep seeing him there – with his hand on the door to my dad's room.' I can't help but shiver as I'm saying it, and my voice sounds thin and frail.

We sit there, watching the tide.

'His own fucking daughter!' Reed exclaims.

I stand up and start kicking at the sand.

'What's the matter? Did he ever...?'

'No.' I cut off the question. I'm so angry.

'Then what is it?' Reed asks, imploringly, concerned about me.

I calm myself and perch on the bench, clutching the edge. I try to explain.

'It's just that' – I take a deep breath – 'people keep saying that. "His own daughter." And it makes me feel sick. Would it have been okay to kill her, if they weren't related?'

'I didn't mean...' he says, but I continue: I have some things to say.

'Or would it have been okay to have the "relationship" with her when she was underage if they weren't biologi- cally related? Or was it okay because he didn't know they were?'

I actually want to punch something, and Reed looks worried it might be him.

'I thought,' Reed begins, gently, trying hard not to say the wrong thing, 'that he kept saying he only wanted to shut her up, because he was shocked when she came to him and reminded him who she was and told him that they were related, that he didn't mean to kill her, that...'

'Yes! *That's* what happened! And he *did* kill her!' I shout. 'Carl's intentions and feelings are *not* more impor- tant than Donna's life! I wish we'd shot him with a real gun.'

I look down at the sand, steadying my breath. Our eyes find each other's again.

'No,' Reed says, '*none* of it was okay.'

I'm calmer now and settle back into his embrace. Up close, he is warm and strong. We hold each other.

'Do you want to get away from here?' he asks, his face in my hair.

I look up at him.

'With me?' he continues.

I nod, ever so slightly, almost involuntarily. 'You know what I would like?' I ask.

'To wake up by the sea?' he suggests.

I smile and gently kiss his lips. 'Yes, and we could go travelling…' I say.

'I'd love that.' He squeezes me tighter. 'Let's do that forever!'

I laugh and raise an eyebrow. 'Hold on… *forever*, in a camper van – with *you* – is a big commitment. Let's just see how it goes.'

'When can we go? My van isn't back from the garage yet but…'

He seems eager to formulate an actual plan and I pull back a little.

'Well,' – I start to strategise – 'Aunt Abigail's still in hospital…' and things feel less rosy before I even finish my list.

CHAPTER 43

Reed wakes up on the sofa; the telephone is ringing in the hall. He wriggles his feet from the tangled bedding and manages to pick up before it rings out.

'Hello 893 86…'

'She's dead.'

Zoya is sobbing on the other end of the line.

'I'll be right there.'

***

Soon, he arrives at Whale House. His shirt is on inside out and there are tangles in his hair. He leans the bike against the battered bush, noticing all the parked cars. A cloud dulls the garden. People are filing into the house. Reed follows them, confused.

Once inside the kitchen, he scans the groups, looking for Zoya. He spots her just as she sees him. She rushes over and he holds her. She looks up and dries her eyes.

'It happened last night.' She seems smaller today. Even her hair is hanging flat. 'When I woke up this morning, Dad was already outside.'

They move into the back room but when they reach the picture windows, she turns away from the sight. There are vets in the garden again but this time Molly is lying immobile on the grass.

'He must have known,' Zoya says.

Richard is sitting on the ground and touching Molly's face. The tiny rhino eyes are closed, as if asleep. The vet talking to him places a comforting hand on his arm.

In the background, someone is righting Richard's wheelchair, which lies abandoned in the mud.

Abigail slips an arm around Zoya. 'Has he moved yet?' Abigail brushes a stray hair from Zoya's wet cheek. 'He's alright, honey. She didn't die alone.'

Zoya nods. 'I'm glad about that.' She sighs. 'It's Dad, I'm most sad for.'

She looks at Reed.

'You know she once saved his life?'

'That really happened?'

'Back when he was her keeper at the zoo,' Abigail explains, 'when his legs buckled, and he collapsed in the enclosure.'

'With *all* the rhinos,' adds Zoya.

'Could have been dangerous' – Abigail is nodding – 'but Molly stood by him protectively.'

'Calling for help, until somebody came.'

'Calling for help?' Reed knows that it's not the time for being cynical but can't help being confused.

'They sound a bit like squeaky balloons – honestly – or whales or something, Molly hardly ever does it – except for that one time.'

'Except for that one time,' Abigail agrees, a faint smile lighting her eyes.

'They obviously shared a close bond,' Reed says. 'I'm glad I got to meet her.'

He looks at the busy hall. He recognises some of the faces.

'What are all these people doing here?'

'They've come to say goodbye,' Abigail says.

'Come on, let's go outside,' Zoya suggests, leading the way down the corridor.

'Good to see you've recovered, Abigail,' Reed says, as they emerge into the garden.

'Thanks, honey.' She smiles.

There are people ringing the decking, looking down on the garden below. The vets have covered Molly with a sheet now, and Dennis Teague is helping Richard into a chair. Reed sees Frank with his arm around Vanessa. She is dabbing her eyes with a tissue.

He whispers to Zoya. 'The whole town is here! I never knew so many people cared so much about her.' He looks at the lifeless animal and sees the soles of her flat, dusty feet.

'They're also here for Dad. Shh, he's going to say something.'

Richard is now seated by Molly. He has laid a hand on her shoulder. The assembled well-wishers look down on the leafy stage, hushed.

Richard begins, projecting a strong, clear voice. 'You all know how much I loved Molly, but this sad passing isn't the end of that love.' His words rise to the trees. 'Our love for Molly will go on in our gratitude – the gratitude we feel in our hearts for having had so many wonderful years with her, and for the special bond we shared.'

Reed is finding the rhino eulogy surreal, but he seems to be the only one.

Richard is speaking again. 'When we lose *any* of our friends, family members or partners, we don't have to be only sad for what we have lost, but happy that we had them in our lives at all.'

Zoya is watching her dad intently, her eyes glowing with admiration. Reed forgot that Richard was a widower. Now, it all makes more sense.

'I know why you are all here today,' Richard continues, 'and it means a great deal to me. Thank you.'

Everybody remains respectfully silent but many offer Richard touching smiles. Abigail rubs her brother's shoulder reassuringly and steps forward to speak.

'We're having coffee and muffins in the kitchen. Please, all of you, stay and help us celebrate her life.' Her tone of voice signals a mood change and people begin making their way back inside, chatting happily to one another.

Zoya turns to Reed. 'You go ahead and save me a muffin, will you? I'm going to stay here with Dad until they take her away.'

'Okay,' – Reed kisses her on the forehead – 'but come and find me if you need me.'

He moves towards Richard. 'That was a beautiful speech.'

Reed heads inside with Abigail and the vets, and Dennis moves off to beckon the truck.

Zoya squeezes her dad's shoulder, then he takes her hand in his clasp. His eyes flit from her face to Reed's back.

'You know, he seems like a good one. You should go get some adventures with him.'

He looks at her with his big brown eyes, as wise and mischievous as ever.

'I won't leave you, Dad. Not after this.'

'You know... there were a lot of reasons your mother and I shouldn't have got together...'

She wonders where this is coming from.

'... the age difference... what people thought about the colour of our skin... But I'm so glad we did.' He looks around at the strange enclosure surrounding them and at the people milling about inside. 'Lots of reasons why I should have moved into more suitable accommodation and left this house.'

She wonders what he is getting at.

'Lots of reasons not to take *this* one in' – he strokes Molly's shoulder through the sheet – 'but it's all been wonderful because we *did.*'

She smiles the big smile he says is beautiful.

'I'll be fine, love. Don't miss *your* chances in life.'

On the day of the fair, the Glebe has been transformed. Stalls have appeared around the edge of the park and bunting has been strung between the old sycamore trees. Wood pigeons peer out at the jigsaw of canvas tents.

The park is zigzagged with lattice paths and a small helter-skelter is being erected on the grass. The Audobon brothers are walking around, looking hopeful and pleased.

An elegant magician with snow-white hair pedals his trike around the corner. He waves to Zoya as she waits to cross the road.

'Hello, my dear!'

'Hi, Quentin! Good to see you!'

The fluffy rabbit in the basket wiggles her pink nose, sniffing the world passing by.

'You too, Mrs Miggles!'

Quentin cycles into the fair.

Zoya walks across the park, carrying a box of muffins. Ropes are being hammered into the ground. Above the whirr of a generator, she detects growing chatter and children laughing.

She makes for the beach café stall. There are lots of people to say hello to on the way: Cara is setting up a tombola and arranging the prizes; Kelly and Dennis are talking by the guinea pig village; Doris is settling in at the lost children point, unscrewing a flask.

Zoya arrives at the stall and sets down the baked goods. Reed hands her an apron. He is already wearing his, over jeans and a short-sleeved shirt. He lifts an urn into place on the counter, causing the teacups to rattle on their saucers. Zoya is arranging the muffins in a basket but pauses to watch him move. She allows her gaze to linger on the curve of his bicep then flashes him a small, appreciative look. He folds his arms to pose for her, but a chuckle breaks his cool. The freshly baked smell of the muffins drifts across the green.

Finishing touches are being made to the helter-skelter. Reed is watching the group of men working on it together. The banging of nails stops.

'That's the guy we mud-wrestled,' Reed says, pointing out Brian Eaves up a ladder, tightening some screws.

Other residents from Sunnyview Lodge are piling up mats for the children to use. Some of the men are setting up a 'beat the goalie' net nearby.

An enormous bush of flowers and foliage is walking across the park. Reed and Zoya exchange perplexed looks. As it passes, they can see that Dale from the nursery is carrying it. He greets them and makes for the show tent.

Felix Audobon dodges out of his way and walks towards the stall.

'Tea or coffee?' Reed offers, smoothing his apron.

'Two teas please,' Felix responds, 'and a couple of cherry muffins too, I should think.'

'Turnout seems promising,' observes Reed conversationally, getting to work on the hot drinks.

Felix reaches into his pocket for some money.

'No, no, it's on the house,' insists Zoya, 'as a thank you for organising all this.'

'Thank you, my dear. Yes, it seems to be going to plan so far.' He turns and scans the field. 'Though I seem to have lost Caspar...'

'Is that him over there?' Reed suggests, pointing towards a bit of drama by the helter-skelter.

Caspar is busy removing bits of paper that a sallow-faced man in an old jumper is pinning into the wood. Felix rushes across the Glebe towards them, and Zoya follows in his wake. She joins the small crowd growing around them.

'No, you can't put them up.'

Caspar and Vince Derby are tussling over a pile of printed posters.

'Why are you trying to ruin a lovely day?'

Vince drops the papers and grabs a loudhailer. He starts gabbling something unintelligible through the device and runs out of Caspar's reach. He swerves into a police officer who takes hold of his arm.

Zoya realises that she is standing next to Frank Barrow.

'He obviously has... problems – you don't have to arrest him, do you?' she asks, looking up at Frank.

'Don't worry, we'll get him some help.'

She watches Constable Walker talking to Vince. She is saying something that makes him laugh.

Zoya walks back, past the other stalls. She sees Tom and Rhoda Sorrel picking out a tiny Babygro at a clothing stall and can't help but smile.

The next tent has been set out like a small theatre and she pokes her head inside. Quentin Tosca is setting up for his magic show and is busy backstage. She lingers long enough to hear his footsteps, the clicking of metal rings and the munch of raw carrot.

She returns to the café stall, passing a couple of bars. Each is being set up by a man in a Dr Who T-shirt. They notice one another.

'Favourite episode?' they ask, together.

They offer handshakes.

'Kev.'

'Dave.'

Zoya reaches the café stall and kisses Reed on the lips.

'I don't think that is a very hygienic thing to do around food preparation,' snaps a woman's voice. 'Where's the manager?'

They look up to see Mrs Wood with the pug in her arms and a sour expression on her face. Zoya rolls her eyes and sighs. 'You again. You might be interested to know that our rhino has recently passed away – from old age.'

Mrs Wood seems temporarily flustered and then sad. She gives Grumbles a gentle scratch between the ears. 'Oh, I'm sorry…'

Zoya's frostiness evaporates. She smiles. 'Thanks.'

***

Later that afternoon, Reed spots another commotion. Dale is standing at the mouth of the show tent, shouting. 'Hey, you can't do that!'

A wild-eyed man is weaving through the fair having snatched up all the flowers he can carry. He blunders through the crowds, shedding petals. Water is leaking onto his trousers.

He catches up with Sarah and Matthew, rounds on them and falls dramatically to his knees. He holds out the ridiculous armful of flowers and launches into a breathy speech.

'Sarah, please, I love you. I made a mistake, a huge mistake. I miss you and I need you and,' – he looks at Matthew who is clutching her hand – 'I love our son. I love you, Matthew.'

The boy smiles widely but Sarah glances around, embarrassed by the scene. A number of people have stopped to watch. Some are considering whether to intervene.

'Are you okay?' Dale asks. Then he addresses Paul, curtly. 'People have spent months creating those displays.'

Paul keeps talking. 'Don't you want your daddy back? I can get you that bike.'

'How dare you?' Sarah hisses.

'I'll change, I'll be better, Sarah, please – won't you take me back?'

She hesitates. 'No,' she says, quietly.

The pile of foliage droops in his arms.

'No, I will not be taking you back.' She is resolute. The flowers fall to the ground. 'But you must be a better father to your son – he misses you.'

Friends in the crowd seem pleased. She rises above the embarrassment with an air of dignity and pulls her shoulders back. 'We'll talk over arrangements another day.'

She walks off, holding Matthew by the hand, leaving Paul on his knees on the muddy grass.

Matthew looks back at his dad, smiling, but soon remembers the magic show and skips ahead.

They reach the tent in time for the performance. Sarah drops some coins into the theatre restoration fund and then finds a seat. An array of cushions has been laid for the children with chairs for the adults behind.

Sarah sits down. Her heart is still thumping, and her mind races with access arrangements and plans to get a divorce.

An elderly man with waved hair and a dapper suit has stepped onto the stage with a flourish. He announces himself as 'The Amazing Marvello'. The audience hushes.

Matthew has disappeared. Sarah scans the room urgently, telling herself not to panic.

'Looks like I've got myself a magician's assistant.'

Quentin steps aside and Sarah sees her son at the back of the stage. He is busy stacking a deck of cards in a pyramid. Sarah exhales with relief.

Quentin doesn't seem to mind at all and begins improvising. 'Allow me to introduce my fellow magician.' He whispers to Matthew, finding out his name. 'Matthew the Mystical!' Quentin announces theatrically.

The crowd applaud and Matthew steps forward to the magician's side. Sarah joins in, clapping and smiling at her son.

'And now for my first trick…'

Quentin shows an empty top hat to the audience, before tapping it with the wand and saying some magic words. Then he reaches inside and pulls out Mrs Miggles, to the delight of the children, some of whom gasp. The fluffy, white rabbit dangles nonchalantly, used to the old routine.

Then, Quentin hands her to Matthew to hold. He takes her carefully and confidently. A delighted smile spreads on his face.

CHAPTER 45

Reed and Dan are sitting at the booth by the window, mirroring one another, silhouetted against the pale beach.

Dan leans forward to cradle his steaming mug of tea.

'So, I didn't tell Sarah that Paul attacked you.' He looks up apologetically.

'We don't know for definite it was him,' Reed replies.

'Looked shit-scared when I mentioned it to *him* though,' Dan says, straightening his back.

Reed understands the meaningful look in his eye: he has delivered some kind of warning.

Dan shakes away the expression. 'The thing is, I *know* Paul; that's not really him. If I thought, for one second, that he would, ever, *ever… hurt* Matty or Sarah I'd…'

Reed nods. 'A one-off. Look, really, I don't want to report it, anyway. I'm fine,' – he runs a hand through the back of his hair, absentmindedly – 'we don't know, anyway.'

Dan's mouth twitches at the corner, developing a funny sort of smile. His shining eyes saccade from Reed's left eye to his right.

'Are they getting back together again?' Reed asks.

'Nope.' Dan grins broadly. 'That's the best thing. Matthew gets his dad back. Sarah gets her independence and… spirit back too.' He breathes a short nasal laugh. 'Even dusted off her old guitar. It's for the best all round.'

Dan takes a swig of coffee.

'And *you* won't have to see so much of Paul, every time you want to hang out with Matthew,' Reed adds perceptively.

'Going to be seeing a lot more of the boy – they're both moving in with me!' Dan's grin blooms and he resembles an excited little boy. 'Truth be told, I've been rattling around in that house… and they've settled in already, and it's not far from his school and his friends.'

Reed watches, quietly smiling, as his friend explains the situation.

'You know,' Dan pauses, 'you'd be welcome to stop by – any time you like.' He gives Reed a long, unblinking look to convey the seriousness of his offer.

'Then I shall,' Reed responds, resolutely.

They sit back in their chairs and look out on the sunny day, contentedly. A couple of children are racing each other along the promenade. In the distance, someone is flying a fluttery little kite. A dog plunges through the waves.

'So…' Dan says.

'So…' Reed responds.

Tom Sorrel offers them more coffee. They accept the top-up with nods and smiles.

'So, you're going to stick around for a girl?' Dan asks.

'Nope. The girl's coming away with me.'

Dan raises his thick brows. For how long?'

Reed flexes his shoulders in a happy little shrug. 'We'll just see how it goes.'

'Good to hear it.'

'So… have you got much sceptic investigating on?'

'I'll find something.'

'I'm sure you will.'

'Is that a psychic prediction?' Dan quips.

Reed laughs. 'There's no such thing.'

Dan gives a wink. 'Just a hunch?'

Reed laughs, louder and more freely. 'Not exactly.'

They look across the table at one another, thinking.

'You know,' Dan begins, 'even though there's something about you that I'll never understand... I'm okay with that.'

Reed holds his gaze, smiling. 'I'm glad I met you too.'

Dan clicks his fingers as an idea comes to him. 'You know,' – he opens his palm as if making an offer – 'we should team up! Your hunches, my investigation skills...'

'Which one of us is Scooby Doo?'

'Well, you've got the right vehicle for it...'

'That reminds me.' Reed reaches under the table and places a small, tan cowboy hat on top. 'I want Matthew to have this.'

'No, no, no... No, that's yours... No. Look he doesn't even have a "horse".'

Reed smiles – the widest, brightest smile that Dan has ever seen appear on his slim face – and nods towards the wall. A BMX bike has been propped up there all along. His bright, green eyes bore into Dan's blue ones, insistent that he accept the gift.

'That's so kind.' Dan cocks his head. 'He'll be so happy. He thinks you are really cool. But I can't accept *this*.'

He moves the cowboy hat back to Reed's side of the table. 'You've been carrying it around for years.'

Reed moves it back towards Dan. 'Take it. I really don't need it anymore.'

'In that case' – Dan takes a deep breath and sits very straight in his chair – 'Only if we swap.' He flops his own fedora onto the table, like a poker move.

'But you wear it every day.'

'You know… Maybe it's time for a change.'

'But it's your–'

'No. It's *your* hat.' Dan cuts him off with strong conviction, leans over and places the fedora directly on Reed's head. 'And it already looks better on you, dammit!'

Reed sits still, allowing this to happen, but questioning Dan with his expression.

'Look, I really don't mind if you don't want to wear it,' continues Dan, with quiet honesty, 'I just want you to have it. Carry *that* one around for the next twenty years. Or until you forget all about me.'

He sits back in his chair; debate over, as far as he is concerned.

Reed shakes his head gently. 'Okay.'

***

Outside on the street, Reed stands clutching the fedora like a prize. The sky is becoming very blue overhead as the dots and dashes of cloud drift out to sea. He watches Dan wrangling the child's bike into the boot of his car. A mixed flock of birds flit between bushes before disappearing over the rooftops in pursuit of a new adventure.

Dan closes the boot and straightens up. 'Well... I better get going. You've got my number?'

Reed nods.

'And address?'

He nods some more.

The two men stand in the street, regarding each other, mirroring the same pose. Reed starts to speak. 'So, thanks for–'

'Come here, man.' Dan cuts him off and charges up to him, taking his friend in a bear cuddle that almost knocks Reed off balance. He puts him down and hurries away swiftly, his eyes brimming and his voice wobbly.

'You take care,' Dan manages to utter, no longer looking Reed in the eye.

'And you,' Reed answers.

Dan pulls the car door open, offering a soft smile for 'goodbye'.

The russet Cavalier moves away down the street and Reed watches it go. He follows, walking in its wake along the middle of the road, waving with the wide-brimmed hat in his hand.

CHAPTER 46

Zoya wakes, feeling glorious in the soft sheets of their bed. The sunshine filters through the small high windows. She stretches her body and runs her fingers through her curls, splaying them out on the cotton pillow.

She notices the curtains moving in the gentlest sway, not from driving but from the fresh air flowing into the cabin and tickling her toes. Sitting up, she sees warm light falling through the open door. She hears the gentle breath of sea breezes and the percussive splash of waves. The air is scented with salt and seaweed, and pancakes cooking on a stove.

She wriggles out of the bed and swaps the softness of the sheets for the woollen embrace of his jumper. The beach is waiting for her outside.

At the van door, she pauses to take in the wonderful, new view. Clear, rippling waters curl over pebbly sand, reaching for the bright wood beyond the shore. The wind is making tendrils of her hair.

He is there, on the blankets, a stack of pancakes by his side. He sits contemplating the ocean, wearing a wide-brimmed hat.

She drops softly onto the cool, morning sand. Waves plash at the shallow shore, echoed by fluttering trees. The long beach stretches away, peppered with colourful shells.

Reed looks at her, offering a mug of coffee and a smile.

She snuggles in behind him, wrapping her arms around his chest and kissing his cheek.

The camper van's white roof gleams under the bright cottonwool sky. Glinting sunlight counts the string of ornate streetlamps curving up the hill. The village sleeps on. The sun's rays sweep like a searchlight from one pane of glass to the next, mapping the lanes and alleyways of the hamlet in soft shadow. Two bicycles advance through an alleyway; children pedalling together, matching their front wheels for pace.

THE END

If you enjoyed this book, please leave a review.
You will help other readers to find books they love and
make the author very happy.

Follow Jenny Cutts on
Goodreads, Bookbub and Patreon.
www.jennycutts.com

Titles in this series
The Invisible Body
The Long Lost Sunset
The Never Ending Fall

Read on for an excerpt from *The Long Lost Sunset*…

THE LONG LOST SUNSET
CHAPTER 1

I open my eyes and scan the blocky Dublin rooftops ahead of me, the muffled blue-grey dawn at my back. I'm standing on top of the dome of the Museum of Archaeology and I'm feeling very alone.

The silent city spreads before me, oblivious. Everywhere, a bland backdrop of a morning, pungent with black brewery scents, unspools across the sky.

The normal sounds of city life seem sponged away by the muffling winds unfurling around me, but I know they just aren't there. I'm used to this, but still. Breezes catch at my hair with tingling twists and cool my skin with gentle moisture; a soft, impish tickle at my neck, a grazing kiss at my cheek. The slow rumble of the river floods my ears with its distant, rolling churn.

I see the city stretching out before me, shaded with precipitous crevices; perfectly pointed brickwork folding in origami angles, hidden ravines that plunge to the streets below. I wish I had the binoculars – but I let Zoya take them with her.

I pivot slowly as I scour the view, careful not to smash through the oculus or slip off the dome. I wonder, for a moment, if the low, whispered rumble is the sound of the distant river or the pumping of my blood. It's surprising how quiet a city can be when all the people have disappeared.

I make my way to the corner, where the round part of the building meets the square. Grappling with the Palladian wedding-cake cornicing, I clamber down to the storey below.

Here, I inch along the curving ledge, clinging to each marble column as I pass. I reach a position above the main entrance and stop. I'm about fifteen metres above the ground still, but I feel a bit more relaxed, tucked in here. I sit in the space under a window and let my legs dangle over the edge.

I look across at the mirror-image National Library, the same colonnade, balcony, columns and dome. I want to describe it as looking like a long-lost twin – but these buildings have been staring at one another for a century. Long, maybe, but not lost.

I let my gaze rise above the rooftops to the blank patch of sky. I think about the library and the museum and the all-sorts-of-everything that must be trapped inside: the shelves of books containing all those immortal thoughts of dead men; the discarded objects used by ancestors; the bones.

All those lives, preserved and packaged and catalogued, lingering long after death. And me, sitting among them, and nobody even knows that I'm here.

I laugh out loud at my own patheticness, suddenly splitting the silence. The sound echoes through the square.

A speck of movement behind the library catches my eye. I think I see someone darting along the far edge of its dome, mostly obscured from my view. It can *only* be her, can't it? I move position and crane to spot the disappearing figure and then I'm falling – the hard, thick stone of the balustrade hurtling, suddenly, toward my head.

***

The next moment, Reed wakes with a jolt, in a narrow single bed. He has been churning the sheets over and over in his sleep. The thin, grey morning tells him that it is still really early, and the small room reminds him where he is – the tatty bed and breakfast on the other side of the river. He decides to get out of there and go for a walk.

Hastily dressed in his clothes from the day before, he strides along the pavement with no particular plan. Gulls tug at fast-food wrappers. He walks along, lost in his thoughts.

Even now, as the city starts to shake itself for a new day, he is trying to outpace a loneliness he thought that meeting Zoya would have killed. If it *was* her that he had seen in the dreaming, why was she running away? She had said she wanted to travel solo for a while so why was she still in Dublin? And if it wasn't Zoya, then who else could it possibly have been? His thoughts loop while he walks. The soles of his Converse slap sonorously on the paving stones.

Crossing the O'Connell bridge, the wide green ribbon of the river interrupts his puzzling, strobed with the fall of daylight and churning its water against old algae-greened stone. He realises he must be heading to Kildare Street – drawn back there for no reason that makes any sense.

He notices the gradual swell of the waking city: delivery vans reversing; the whirr of street sweepers at kerbs; the hiss and growl of engines marking the incursion of bus timetables into the dissipating night.

Rounding a corner at a junction on the south side, he is stopped by a wall of air.

A dark blur has appeared at his feet. Now it is forming into a chillingly recognisable shape. A man lies spreadeagled on the paving slabs. A man who seemed to materialise out of thin air. A man whose crumpled frame looks like it fell from the sky, narrowly missing Reed's head.

Reed looks up and sees a scaffold-clad building. He looks down and sees the man on the pavement still, straggly, sandy hair flung across the face.

Reed makes the mental adjustment from the word 'man' to 'body'. His feet haven't moved an inch.

He remembers his own sense of falling and the impossibility of bracing for the impact of stone smashing into skull. It feels as though the dark-clad figure could be his own shadow self – but it just lies there, bleeding and becoming more real with every passing second. More real and more surreal at the same time.

Reed makes an effort to flip realities in his mind – the one where he idles on rooftops isn't real and the one where a dead man lies by his feet, *is*. A small crowd is gathering in the street.

He stares at the man, feeling thankful that he cannot see the face. This is Reed's second dead body and, apparently, they don't get any easier to see. He finds himself in a ring of people – early risers who have rushed over to help. He hears cars being left in the middle of the road and shouting and emergency calls being made.

Reed has no idea how much time has passed but sirens can be heard. A sergeant arrives and starts taking control. The group are encouraged away from the accident and Reed's feet finally unstick from the spot. The body is obscured by a tent.

'We'll be wanting to find out what any of you saw soon enough, but we need to move you back now. Are you alright, madam? It's a terrible thing, yes. Please move back now. Give the man some respect.'

Reed allows himself to be moved on with the crowd, but, in the jostling, slips away. He walks around a corner, turns up a dark alley and leans his forehead against the wall. Maybe he had had a premonition of this happening – a dream about a fall.

Reed catches himself before his thoughts stray into supernatural territory. He doesn't believe in any of that. For him, physical reality is weird enough as it is.

He gently bangs his brow against the wall. He's aware that a man has plunged to a messy death on the pavement and that he's still somehow making it all about *him*. The man landed close though, almost close enough to kill *him* too. He leans over and vomits against the bricks.

The Long Lost Sunset

A haunted hotel. A mysterious plot. But who is running out of time?

Scotland, 1991. Dan is too busy working to have a relationship. So, when a paranormal investigation takes him to Edinburgh, at least he can catch up with old friends. But when he overhears a mysterious plot, he discovers another reason to stay.

Dan enlists the help of a friend with strange abilities but doesn't like what he finds. Soon, the hotel fills with secrets and he doesn't know who to trust.

When a ticking clock points to danger, Dan must decide whether to leave the only person he has ever loved.

Is it a matter of time before Dan's heart is broken or is the situation deadlier than that?

The Never Ending Fall

A risky habit. A dangerous drop. But will a murderer make her watch her step?

England, 1992. Zoya is a free spirit with a risky habit trying to find her place in the world. When she lands a place at an isolated dance school, it seems like the perfect fit. But, following a mysterious death, the countryside doesn't seem so idyllic anymore.

When the police aren't making progress, she starts asking questions of her own. By refusing to accept it was an accident, she finds herself walking a lonely, dangerous path.

Can Zoya bring the murderer to justice or should she tread more carefully?